To Anne
Nice to meet you!
Peggy

Lily in Bloom

Margaret P. Cunningham

Lily in Bloom

Margaret P. Cunningham

Black Lyon Publishing, LLC

LILY IN BLOOM
Copyright © 2008 by Margaret P. Cunningham

Our books may be ordered through your local bookstore or by visiting the publisher:

www.BlackLyonPublishing.com

Black Lyon Publishing, LLC
PO Box 567
Baker City, OR 97814

This is a work of fiction. All of the characters, names, events, organizations and conversations in this novel are either the products of the author's vivid imagination or are used in a fictitious way for the purposes of this story.

ISBN-10:   1-934912-02-6
ISBN-13:   978-1-934912-02-7
Library of Congress Control Number: 2008921585

Published and printed in
the United States of America.

Black Lyon Contemporary Romance

To my husband, Tom Cunningham,
who agrees that it's never too late to bloom.

1.

Eau de Mother-in-law

Lily McVay sat on the wooden steps of Howard's mother's back porch and thought about her dead mother-in-law. It was a year ago today that old Mrs. McVay died, and eleven months since Lily and Howard had moved into her mausoleum of a house.

Four months later Howard ended their marriage of twenty-five years and moved into one of the new Camellia Courtyard condominiums with Heather, his twenty-something-year-old executive assistant. A recent graduate of the local junior college, Heather had learned, among few other things, that she should be referred to as an executive assistant instead of office help, and that an ambitious girl can marry more money in five minutes than she can make in a lifetime as an executive assistant.

In his final round of divorce negotiations, Howard had astonished everyone (whose mouths were still hanging open from the whole Heather thing) by offering the house that had been the birthplace of four generations of McVays to his soon-to-be ex-wife with the following stipulation: Lily was to restore the back garden (which had not been touched since before Mrs. McVay's death) and host the annual garden club soiree.

His mother, Rosemary McVay would be honored at this prestigious event for her lifelong dedication to the beautification of the city. After much consideration, Lily had concluded that in Howard's convoluted thinking, this would restore his Heather-induced loss of reputation in the town and atone, although posthumously, to Mrs. McVay for the loss of the ancestral home. Howard's behavior during these past months was so out of character that it was the best she could come up with.

Her lawyer instructed her to stop trying to figure out the motives of a man well past his prime who was thinking with an organ other than his brain and to jump on the deal, which she did. In an especially cruel twist of fate, however, Lily signed her divorce papers and the deed to Howard's largest asset on the same day—her fiftieth birthday. It had been quite a year for Lily McVay.

So the place was Lily's now, but in her mind (and everyone else's) it remained Howard's mother's house. Once Howard had vacated the premises, she'd defiantly remodeled the primitive kitchen, redone the drapes and upholstery to her own taste, and repainted every rose-hued wall. Yet Rosemary McVay, who happened to be buried in the cemetery across the street—well, you might say she lingered. This was especially noticeable in the former parlor/now den where Mrs. M. had spent most of her time.

Plantation shutters replaced heavy drapes and cornices that had been the most peculiar shade of pink. Torture devices in the guise of Victorian settees were banished to the attic along with an enormous mahogany étagère and its various figurines and knickknacks.

Comfortable sofas and a lovely little pine desk took their place. Where a threadbare dark oriental carpet used to lie in wait to trip up visitors, a sisal rug and a large potted palm freshened things up. But it was here that the shadow of Mrs. McVay's peculiar scent, the fragrance of Chanel No. 5 fouled by the reek of fresh perm, wafted through the corners on a sharp, cool breeze, raising the hairs on Lily's arms and neck, and driving her, as it had on this particular afternoon, out into breathable air.

What with her mother-in-law's disturbing aura and uncomfortably close physical proximity, Lily had been experiencing an excruciating bout of approach-avoidance regarding the aforementioned garden. Due to its prior beauty and prominence in the town, it was an awesome responsibility. Knowing that her mother-in-law had invested heart, soul and most waking hours in its creation and maintenance had sapped Lily's last drop of horticultural confidence.

On top of that, Lily was convinced that the very idea of her as proprietress of McVay House, not to mention the McVay garden, had the old lady spinning like a wind chime in a cyclone over in the McVay mausoleum. Whenever this visual crept into her psyche, which was every time she tried to get started on the yard, it intimidated her to the point of total inactivity.

Mrs. McVay had been maniacally possessive of every bulb and bloom, placing their exclusive trust in the hands of a sainted man named Jake Johnson, who had worked for the McVays as long as Lily could remember.

Shortly after Jake's death, Howard's mother had gotten sick herself, and though the garden's decline was her greater disappointment, she would not allow anyone else to take over its care. Instead, she sat at her bedroom window watching it mirror her own deterioration. By the time she died, both she and her beloved garden bore little resemblance to their former selves.

It had long been a secret dream of Lily's to make the garden her own. She had felt as much comfort in that garden as she'd felt discomfort in her mother-in-law's, presence. In spite of her feelings for it, memories of its understated perfection and the knowledge of how disappointed her mother-in-law would feel about the recent turn of events made the challenge so overwhelming that she hadn't gotten further than a little weeding.

And below this fertile layer of insecurity concerning old Mrs. McVay and her delightful garden, there lay deeper feelings — the roots of the problem, as it were. These were the bitterness and bewilderment that come when a woman realizes she's been tossed onto the compost heap of life for a younger, fresher flower.

When Rosemary McVay passed away, Lily expected to feel nothing but relief. After all, she'd been swallowing her mother-in-law's cold domination (along with a boatload of antacids) for years. As Lily's friend, Helen sarcastically put it, upon hearing of Rosemary McVay's demise, "Eighty-two years of southern charm and hospitality — gone."

But to her surprise, feelings of remorse reared their ugly little heads. The two McVay women with their shared love of Howard and of Lily's twin daughters, Elizabeth and Virginia, not to mention their mutual passion for gardening, should have connected. Now there would never be that chance. It was such a waste and another entry on what Lily perceived as her growing list of failures.

At the top of that list was her marriage, of course. Sadly, she hadn't even known it was a failure until she found the letter. To Howard. From Heather. Full of "I love you's" and references to romantic dinners. "Mistakenly" sent by Heather to McVay (no Mr. or Ms. Or first names) at their home address.

Howard chose to believe it was an innocent accident on Heather's part and predictably, blamed Lily. She had opened his mail, hadn't she?

"The best defense is a solid offense" was a principle he adhered to on every playing field, whether it be football, business, or personal issues.

"Unlike you, Heather appreciates my guidance. Heather understands me." He cleared his throat. "And I'm sorry, Lily, but I find myself in—uh, in love with her," he said.

Lily's knees were giving way, so she slumped onto the arm of Howard's leather chair, the one that had been his father's. Her throat was closing up, but she managed to croak, "Heather? That girl in your office? The executive assistant?" The blood was rushing around in her ears, and she thought she might faint. Instead she heard herself say, "She appreciates your guidance? What does that mean?"

Lily was aware she was being tiresomely repetitive, but it just would not sink in. Howard and Heather? Her brain simply would not accept it.

Howard had sighed, but had the decency to tear up at the sight of what he was doing to his lovely, devoted wife of twenty-five years.

"It means I'm moving in with Heather. I want a divorce. I'm very sorry, Lily. The embarrassment and everything—"

"A divorce? The embarrassment?" She was repeating again, sounding like a broken iPod or some other confounding electronic gadget.

She watched numbly while Howard packed a suitcase as routinely as if he were headed off on a business trip, back in a few days, etc. But he would not be back. Ever.

Lily had never been run over by a truck or hit in the gut by a professional boxer, but she now knew how both felt. She sat there on the arm of Howard's chair for the good part of an hour, trying to cry, trying to think, and finally settling for just catching her breath.

Then the big scaries began to swirl around the perimeter of this category-five domestic disaster. What about her girls? How would she tell them? What about the house? Howard (with Heather?) would surely want to move into the McVay House. Her old home had been sold. Where would she go? How would she support herself? Who would hire a fifty-year-old emotional wreck with no marketable skills? She was sure she was entitled to alimony or something, but she had no idea.

Plus, Howard had a slew of lawyers. She was bound to come out on the losing end financially as well. The more she thought about it, the worse it got. But at least she had moved on from the repetitive stage. Acceptance of the reality was beginning to sink in. Soon anger would take its rightful place as Lily began the agonizing dance through the hierarchy of human emotions required for survival.

Lily worked at staying in shape and looking good. She was pleasant—most of the time—and if pressed, would have described herself as very adept in the kitchen. And she was not half-bad in the bedroom. Probably not as good as Heather …

She shook the visual of Heather and Howard having sex out of her head, trying to keep her thoughts organized. Weren't these the things all husbands desired—making a good home, providing love and nourishment, staying in shape? According to her mother, they were the basic ingredients for a fool-proof marriage.

An outdated recipe from another era, Lily reminded herself, and though her friends would constantly reassure her with the old, "It's not you, it's him" line, and she knew in her head it was true, in her broken heart, she wondered. And the proverbial icing on this cake of humiliation was that she'd turned fifty. Fifty!

Time had marched across her fair skin, laying deep creases around her eyes, a web of spider veins on her thighs. The gray in her lovely auburn hair necessitated more frequent trips to her magician of a hairdresser. Indigestion matured into acid reflux. Daily jogs took more effort and produced more aches. Her body was still in pretty good shape from the regular exercise, but it had softened. *The force of gravity is not with us.*

Her brain was an overloaded computer, its memory compromised. She was up to a #2 level reading glasses. A hormone patch quieted hot flashes and sleeplessness, but it was obvious things were headed downhill physically and mentally.

Turning "the big five-O" on top of everything else had her feeling as if someone (Howard? Heather? Mrs. McVay? Mother Nature?) had come like a banshee in the night and stolen her spirit, her very self. There wasn't much left of Lily McVay, it seemed.

It was in this mud puddle of self-pity and despair that our heroine found herself when Howard walked out that day, and she had wallowed in it. But before we throw the towel of hope into the rag bin, let's not forget that good women like Lily always have something left, a little glimmer in the temporary gloom enveloping their souls.

2.

A friend in Need ...

It was while contemplating (for the millionth time) the cause and effect of everything that had occurred during the past year that she had felt it (an improbable occurrence on a warm, slightly humid gulf coast afternoon.)

It was an icy draft from nowhere carrying just a hint of Chanel and setting solution. And so she'd found herself on the steps of the spacious back porch, elbows on knees, staring out at Howard's mother's garden.

"Lily!"

It was Howard. She could hear him carefully closing the front door she'd left open to catch the breeze.

"Out here," she yelled and picked up her pencil and pad, trying to look industrious.

"Lily, why are the doors open?"

He was still paying the utility bills.

"It's such a pleasant afternoon."

"You know how it heats up the house."

He sat down beside her, the gleaming winged tip of his oxford next to her dirty clogs, and slapped the tops of his thighs.

"So how's it going?" he said, forced enthusiasm saturating his voice.

Lily looked out over the lush nightmare so full of potential—and weeds. It was going nowhere, was how it was going.

"Howard, I just don't see how I can get it in shape in time for the party. I'm still committed to all those ridiculous boards you talked me into joining, so my time is limited—"

Howard raised his hand, palm up. "Wait a minute. Which

board do you consider ridiculous?"

"The DOFDs? Just to name one. That's not a colossal waste of time?"

Howard sighed his exasperation. "The Daughters of Former Debutantes is one of the most prestigious groups in town."

The futility of arguing this point was obvious, but she pressed on in a slightly different direction. "As I was saying, Howard, my time is limited, and with the budget you've got me on, I can't hire anyone."

She knew she was whining, but Howard had a way of inducing childlike behavior in her during their discussions.

"Howard, I'm thinking of getting some help from the master gardener program. Helen said—"

He held his hand palm up again, like a crossing guard, pausing exactly three seconds to heighten the effect of his impending words.

"We've been all through this, Lily. McVays are benefactors. We don't take charity. We give it. Besides," he said with a humorless chuckle, "You're spending your garden money air-conditioning the neighborhood."

Hilarious, thought Lily, *and so original*. To Howard she said, "The air's not on. I was just trying to freshen things up. I don't know why it's still so musty in there."

The mention of the pervasive funkiness always agitated him, yet he denied its existence. Standing, he said, "Old houses are musty, Lily." He sighed wearily. "Well, it's back to work for me." Pause. "Remember." Longer pause. "An elegant soiree will be happening in this yard in less than three short months. I don't want you to be embarrassed."

"It's a big, fat shame you didn't worry about my embarrassment when you started up with Miss Junior achievement," she growled, but the back door closed firmly on her sarcasm.

Three months. No money. No time. And her back and hands were already sore from the small amount of weeding she'd done. As soon as she heard the front door slam, she picked up the phone. Dare she go against Howard's wishes and get gardening charity from Helen?

The tomboyish Helen and the elegant Lily had been friends

—the *I'll help you bury the body, no questions asked* kind of friends—
since childhood, and they shared more secrets and adventures
than sisters.

Helen and her husband, Sandy, didn't have children, so she
was the closest thing to an aunt that Lily's twin daughters had.
But as delighted as Helen had been to have her old partner
in crime back in the same town, she'd tried to talk Lily out of
marrying Howard.

When Lily forged ahead with the wedding, Helen put her
opinions in the closet and tried to be a friend to Howard as
well, biting her tongue until it bled when Lily naively defended
the McVay deficiencies. In Helen's opinion, these included a
complete lack of warmth and even a modicum of personality.

Helen had known about Heather even before Lily, and
she'd taken off from her job at the botanical gardens like a one-
woman rescue squad, bringing food, drink and support, and
even procuring her cousin's house in Seaside so that Lily could
escape the gossip frenzy that ensued.

When the marriage was finally put to rest, settling the
emotional dust a bit, Helen counseled her friend in practical
matters. For example, what was Lily going to do with the rest of
her life? She was a homemaker and volunteer. A very proficient
homemaker and volunteer, but still … A decline in income and
a long-empty nest necessitated an interesting, rewarding career
that actually paid a salary.

Then there was the even higher priority of Lily's social life.
With a husband who constantly traveled on business, Helen
filled her evenings with a variety of card groups, book clubs,
supper clubs, etc. and Lily became her "date" to many of these
outings. Helen was off-the-chart in knowing what was needed
when. Until it came to match making, that is. After all Helen
had done for Lily, this produced an acute feeling of obligation,
which resulted in poor Lily going out with an array of blind
dates, each one worse than his predecessor.

"Gotta kiss a few frogs before you find that prince," Helen
would admonish with a peculiar gleam in those crystal blue
eyes of hers.

Lily blamed this obsessive interest in her lackluster (non-
existent was more like it) love life on her friend's infatuation with

romance novels. Helen devoured one paperback after another, mystifying and amusing everyone who knew her. It simply didn't compute with the rest of her no-nonsense personality.

Lily braced herself for the inevitable fix-up whenever she happened upon Helen lost in one of these tomes, such as *Rapture in the Rotunda, Passion under the Palms*, or some such title.

The first hair-raising rendezvous had been with Dwayne Bond, the town's newly divorced "car wash king." He spent part of the year in an enormous birthday cake of a house he'd built on the river, and was reputed to be the catch of the state (in Lily's age bracket, anyway). He usually introduced himself by saying, "The name's Bond." With one eyebrow raised, he would level a steely gaze at the introducee while striking an exaggerated 007 pose. "Dwayne Bond." Okay, so that was mildly amusing. The first couple of times she heard it.

But then Dwayne, who could have been a Tom Selleck clone (in his younger days) and who owned car washes in three states, took her to a party that was miles out in the country. Unfortunately, Lily decided after fifteen minutes in the king's company, that there was more to a decent date than good looks and a willingness to throw cash around.

On the long ride out, the king drove as if he were trying out for the NASCAR circuit and talked nonstop, mostly about the various scents used in automobiles as they exited his car washes. The best seller by far, and his personal favorite, was piña colada. "Babes love it."

When not expounding on this and other high points of car wash lore, he was peppering his conversation with what Lily would describe to Helen as offensive car-isms. For example, he complimented Lily's legs by referring to them as outstanding "wheels." Breasts were "headlights." He didn't try to hide the fact that he was into extremely large headlights. When he withheld any opinion of her hers, Lily couldn't decide whether to be relieved or insulted.

It was not until they screeched into the driveway of party central that Dwayne broke the news that it also happened to be his ex-wife's house. Stacey Bond had an anorexic-thin body and a 60s big hair-do that made her look as if she might topple over at any minute. Her frighteningly long violet fingernails clutched a sweating tumbler of what appeared to be very strong iced tea, but was actually bourbon.

Before Lily could introduce herself, the woman (swaying dangerously beneath her over-sized coif) yelled, "Dwayne, I need to talk to you." At which point, Dwayne left Lily standing alone with a bunch of strangers and disappeared into the bedroom with his former wife, the ex-car wash queen. Lily was forced to beg a ride home with her absent hostess's very angry, very scary date.

According to Helen, Dwayne's compulsive womanizing and Stacey's obsessive jealousy had resulted in one of those tumultuous can't live with 'em, can't live without 'em relationships. In the obsessive-compulsive stand-off that was their marriage, Dwayne blinked first and filed for divorce.

The next day Dwayne had the nerve to call Lily with, "Hey, where'd you go last night?" and the even bigger nerve to ask her out again. Lily declined his gracious offer to "set things right with a big, ol' steak dinner."

Then there was the older fellow who seemed promising at first. He was recently widowed, interesting, smart and not bad looking in a mature sort of way. Halfway through dinner, however, he'd opened his wallet with a mischievous smirk and accidentally-on-purpose shown her a decaying condom he'd probably had since high school. Next to this artifact was a crumbling Viagra pill wrapped in a bit of plastic wrap.

Torn between laughter and tears, Lily faked a migraine, effecting a hasty departure from the restaurant. Like the car wash king, Viagra guy also had the nerve to call the following day, ostensibly concerned about Lily's health, but in actuality to ask her to go with him "on a little overnighter down the coast."

Lily also said no to this invitation.

When Lily shared these details, Helen was skeptical, sure her frog-weary friend was exaggerating.

"I ran out on my crème brulee. That's how bad it was," Lily said.

"You have to admire the old toad's perseverance, though," Helen argued halfheartedly, but did eventually admit to some guilt about this latest match making fiasco.

"Really, I appreciate all you've done," laughed Lily, "But I'm beginning to think it's just not worth it. When you're sitting in a bar at ten o'clock dreaming of your bathrobe and slippers … well, that tells you something."

"Your phone should be ringing off the hook," said Helen. "You're beautiful. You're tall. You're a size 8, for God's sake!" She shook her head. "I'd kill to see a size 12 again, but I'm getting off the subject. The point is you can't give up!"

"I'm sorry, but let's face it. I'm just not up to the challenges of today's dating scene."

Helen promised that the Viagra toad was her final foray into the establishment of a love life for Lily. For some reason, Lily did not believe it.

A few weeks later when Lily caught Helen with the newest Catherine Smyth novel, *The Shop Girl and the CEO*, she knew she was in trouble. Catherine Smyth was Helen's favorite author, and never failed to stimulate Helen's vicarious interest in anything of a romantic nature, especially when it concerned Lily's dating potential.

"Lily, if a mousy little shop girl like Jenny Swartz can find true love with the CEO of a major hotel chain, then there's got to be somebody out there for you!"

"Helen, you have to get a grip on this match making frenzy you've whipped yourself into. Jenny Swartz is a fictitious character as is the CEO she found true love with."

"Oh, right." Helen had the decency to look embarrassed for all of thirty seconds, before the glazed look of the incurable romantic settled in her eyes. "But, Lily, I wish you would read just one of Catherine Smyth's books. They are so optimistic and fun. They will give you a whole new outlook on the singles scene."

"Singles scene? Helen, there is no singles scene at my age." But she had to laugh. "I promise to read the Catherine Smyth novel of your choice as soon as I get through the Garden Club soiree."

"Great, because I do have one more very eligible possibility for you."

Lily groaned.

"Just hear me out. His name is Melrose McSwain."

"Sounds like a character out of one of your romances," Lily

grumbled.

Helen ignored this and pressed on. "He is an important politician in Covington County. I mean they call him Landslide McSwain. That's how popular he is. He's about your age and has never been married. And I've heard he's extremely nice-looking.

"You've heard?"

"Well, I've never met him personally, but he's a friend of a friend, you might say."

Lily knew there were more armadillos than people in Covington County, so Landslide couldn't be too important politically, and the fact that Melrose (what kind of people would name their son Melrose, anyway?) had never married caused a tiny warning flag to start waving in Lily's head. Wait a minute. *I know Melrose!*

It was coming back to her now. She had met the man several years ago at the Bi-annual Crow Shoot and Wine Tasting Festival up in Covington County. Melrose was five feet five inches of skirt-chasing, whiskey-guzzling country boy. According to the locals, he'd earned the nickname Landslide when winning the election by the smallest margin allowed. A lack of opposition in subsequent elections was the sole reason for Melrose's continued employment by the state.

My singlehood has turned Helen into a match making monster, she thought. For a second or two, she told herself she was being ungrateful and should try to make the best of what was destined to be another disastrous evening. Thankfully, sanity reared her lovely head just in time.

Lily sat her friend down and said as kindly as possible, "Helen, with the possible exception of Melrose, aka Landslide McSwain, I've gone out with every frog in the county. I've even kissed a few. I'm telling you, the princes are all taken. I'm sorry, but I'm done."

Helen took it pretty well and promised to hereafter confine her match making to fictional characters only. I know what you're thinking. Lily didn't believe it either.

The other bone of contention between Lily and Helen was Lily's decision to remain at "that mausoleum of bad memories, McVay House while restoring the garden of a woman (who, had she ever met one, would have treated a boll weevil with more respect than her own daughter-in-law) so that she could be revered by the entire town and be the all-time winner of the "keeping up appearances" game.

"And the worst of it all," said Helen, "is that you put yourself in a position of taking orders from that insufferable windbag, Howard."

When Helen was forced to take a breath, Lily tried to explain motives she didn't fully comprehend herself.

"First of all, it makes financial sense. As you pointed out, I have very few marketable skills, and I have to think about my future. At the rate time is flying by, I'll be at retirement age before I find a job."

Helen had to admit to the logic in this.

"Secondly, Howard's Mother was a witch to me, but she was good to my girls. They loved her. She tried to make me feel second-rate—and succeeded, most of the time—because she was jealous."

"I think you're proving my point, Lily."

Lily ignored this. "There was something between her and Howard that I could never figure out. I don't know why, but I think the answer is in that garden. If I leave the house now, the demons will simply follow me. I don't know exactly how I know it, but I know it. I've got to find out what it was that poisoned that family."

"It's called self-absorption, snobbery and dysfunction. They're textbook," argued Helen.

"You're probably right about that, but then there's the garden itself. Seeing it in its prime and the sad shape it's in today would break any gardener's heart. Believe it or not, I—and my girls —have a lot of happy memories of that place. Remember all the birthday parties and Easter egg hunts we held there? Besides, I'm dying to get my hands on that garden. I know I can bring it back."

"Even if it means dealing with Howard?"

"Yes. But you know something? That's not even the hardest part. It's his mother. It's like she's still there. I mean the place even smells like her."

"You must mean that beauty parlor smell! I had forgotten

about that. My God, the woman must have gotten a perm every other week. Her hair was like steel springs. An outward sign of her inner self, I'd say."

"But she wasn't always like that. For one thing, she loved music. I found all of her old Frank Sinatra albums in a closet in the parlor, I mean, *den*. And I've seen pictures of her when she was young. She looked happy, carefree, even. The pre-perm days."

"Well, something turned her into an old spook, and she's still making you miserable. Lily, you've got to get out of there as soon as possible. Your sanity is not worth the money or the garden. You've got to get yourself away from the McVays."

"Helen, I'm doing that garden."

"Okay." Helen raised her hands in submission. "If you're serious about taking on this—this huge restoration job, you're going to need help. Even Mrs. McVay had an experienced, full-time gardener, remember."

"But, Howard …"

"Screw Howard, Lily. It can't be done without help. And I have someone in mind—from the Master Gardener Program at the botanical gardens. Just say the word."

"Thanks, Helen. You're right. And I am thinking of taking you up on your offer even if Howard will have a fit. Taking charity and all that, you know. But I'm not finished telling you why I've gone along with Howard's insane idea of restoring his mother's yard. There's something else. And you're going to like it."

Helen leaned forward. She knew by the tone of her friend's voice that it was important.

"Revenge."

"All right! Now we're getting somewhere," said Helen.

"The only way for me to get even with Howard and Heather and Mrs. McVay is through that garden. I'll make McVay House the envy of this town. Everyone will see it at the soiree. Then I'll sell it for such a profit that Howard and Heather, who is obviously in this for the goods, will never get over it. Mrs. McVay never believed I could do anything right. Well, if there's a God, wherever Howard's mother is, she'll know not only can I restore her precious garden, I can make it better than ever. It will always be remembered not only as McVay Garden, but as Lily's Garden. Success is the best revenge, Helen. I learned that in junior high."

3.

A Girl's Gotta Do ...

Sitting there on the steps, thinking about her conversations with Helen and Howard, Lily made a decision that would have far-reaching results.

"Helen's right. To hell with Howard," she said aloud and punched in her friend's number.

Helen answered on the second ring.

"Helen, this is Lily. Listen. I've decided to take you up on your offer. I know Howard won't like it, but you were right. It's the only way I'll get it done ... Yeah, the guy you were telling me about ... He works for Maisy Downey? As in Crazy Maisy? No, of course I haven't been over there. What's the name of this super gardener? Will? Okay, I'll see if I can catch him."

Before she could put the phone down, it rang.

"Hello?"

Nothing.

"Hello?"

She knew someone was there, but whoever it was wouldn't answer. This had been happening on a regular basis lately and was starting to get on her nerves. After each of these calls, the word "Private" showed up on her caller ID. Probably just some bored kids, she told herself. But kids would be in school this time of day. Lily sighed. Something else to deal with—but later, she thought.

Putting the phone down, she hurried toward the back of the yard. There a nest of confederate jasmine held the sad remains of a gate to hinges embedded in a wall of hand-made bricks.

This wall, which encased the entire garden, was just beyond

a live oak that was older than any McVay could remember. Spanish moss caught at the coppery strands of Lily's hair as she ducked under a long, low limb, then pushed past the gate.

The last time Lily had been through this gate she'd just become engaged, and it was the first time she'd met the infamous Maisy Downey. Based on her in-laws' litany of complaints about their flamboyant neighbor, Lily had formed a decidedly negative preconception about the woman despite the fact that most people seemed quite fond of her.

Finally curiosity got the best of Lily, and she had volunteered to return Peewee, Maisy's enormous, trespassing Tom cat to his owner. Lily introduced herself to Maisy as Howard's fiancee.

Instead of congratulating her, Maisy's comment was, "You know, sweetie, death by boredom is a very painful way to go."

The unkind words turned out to be prophetic, indeed, but Lily had never forgiven Maisy for the hurtful words—or for being right. It was most unsettling to have a stranger peg one's entire marital future in one sentence, and this was the primary reason Lily hadn't made any of the usual overtures to her back-fence neighbor.

She told herself there just wasn't enough time to become involved with the likes of Crazy Maisy, which was Howard's condescending appellation for his life-long neighbor.

Lily had sent her regrets to the one invitation Maisy had extended—a costume party with music provided by Boy Cotton, a group of teenaged rockers Maisy had befriended. (The friendship included allowing the young rockers to hold their interminable practice sessions on Maisy's patio.) According to the local grapevine, while Boy Cotton deafened the guests, the tiny, wiry old lady dressed up in a weird, hippie approximation of a Gypsy (complete with a black wig that almost covered her own shoulder-length, platinum hair) and told fortunes.

Most people knew the fortune-telling business had been Maisy's custom for years. Oddly enough, this sideshow was always a hit because the fortune seekers seemed to benefit from their encounters with "Madam Maisy."

After that first meeting with Maisy, Lily soon realized that the old lady not only couldn't stand Howard, but Howard's parents as well. The feeling being entirely mutual, Mrs. McVay accused the Downeys of that social horror: nouveau riche-ness.

To lend emphasis to this proclamation, Mrs. McVay gave a small shudder when she said it, as though she were discussing a particularly odious contagious disease.

Social responsibility required the McVays to issue the Downeys an invitation to Lily's and Howard's wedding reception, since it was held in the now weed-infested McVay garden. And Maisy, never one to miss a party, had accepted. At the festivities, in true nouveau riche fashion, she had cemented the McVay impression of her when she interrupted Howard's father mid-way through his well-worn diatribe against women in the workplace.

"I'd love to continue talking with you, hon," she said, "But I'm tryin' to stay awake long enough to see them cut the cake."

This was the final straw in a veritable haystack of faux pas, according to the McVays. The garden gate was firmly shut, not to be opened again until today when Lily ventured through it in search of a landscaping miracle.

As she stepped through a break in a tall hedge of ligustrum that had been clipped to a shining, green rectangle, she found herself in another botanical dimension. In contrast to the untended jungle she'd just left, a small ornamental arrangement of beds interlaced with brick paths and rose beds lay basking in the slanting rays of the sun.

The darker green of a waist-high boxwood hedge bordered its far side. Beyond this was a large slate patio then French doors that lazed open invitingly. Above them hung a profusion of clematis, its tendrils and white blossoms in perfect disarray against the saffron stucco of the house.

A tall, young man in a faded green T-shirt lounged in one of Maisy Downey's delicate bistro chairs, his long legs and big boots stretched out over the slate. His head was back, eyes closed to the sun, black curls escaping from beneath a fraying yellow baseball cap.

"Assistant to the great Will, I suppose," Lily muttered, then stopped, took in the neat rows of tender, new plants, the perimeter of hard-angled hedges, the handsome young man sleeping on the job. *This isn't what I want*, she thought. She'd envisioned a garden free of straight lines, filled with unstructured, native shrubs that would compliment Howard's mother's house.

Oddly enough, Howard didn't agree. She'd had to battle him over every change in redoing the interior of the house, but where the garden was concerned, change became his mantra. He'd even gotten into the annoying habit of leaving pages torn from the executive assistant's cheap decorating magazines in Lily's mailbox. They were pictures of herbaceous borders in a Baltimore suburb, tropical pool sides in Boca Raton, even a San Francisco rock garden. They'd updated the plumbing, he'd said. Why not modernize the yard?

Looking at the parterre of perfection and its surrounding hedges miraculously sculpted into the historic, deep-south neighborhood of townhouses and cottages, Lily figured she and old Will wouldn't see eye to eye on anything. He and Howard would take sides against her and … well, it had horticultural disaster written all over it.

Completely dejected, she shook her head and started back toward the wild tangle she was in charge of taming.

"Uh, can I help you?" Assistant-to-Will called to her.

"No, I—no, thanks," she yelled back.

But he was coming toward her, striding through the hybrid roses.

"I was looking for Will, but I'll just catch him later," she called.

He was standing in front of her now, grinning perfect rows of white teeth at her.

"You can catch him now," he said. "I'm Will." He held out a hand.

"Oh. I'm Lily McVay, from next door," she said. Her hand disappeared in his, which was even rougher than her own.

"You're the one with the garden emergency."

"You talked to Helen."

"Yeah. You still need someone? I've got plenty of community service hours to fill in between my regular jobs."

"Community service" according to Helen was actually a time requirement of the master gardener program offered through the city's botanical gardens. In order to earn the title of Master Gardener, participants had to volunteer a certain number of hours beautifying the community.

Helen, as administrator of the program had decided that the McVay garden qualified as an historic landmark so was eligible for free semi-professional assistance, and according to her, Will was the man for the job. He was a natural at landscape design — an artist with more raw talent than she'd seen in all of her years at the botanical gardens.

Will was still smiling down at her, patiently waiting for an answer. He had enthusiasm, good humor, and most of all, a young, strong back. Lily looked over his broad shoulder to the lovely jumble of clematis above the open patio doors and allowed herself to hope.

"Follow me, Will," she said.

He followed her through the gate and ducked under the oak limb swatting at Spanish moss before stopping and taking in the yard. He stood looking for so long, Lily was sure he was trying to think of a way to get out of the job. Finally he turned to her.

"This is great!"

"Really?"

"Yeah. There's so much to work with already. The oak, all these camellias. A lot of shade, but that's okay, too. There's a lot of potential here. Someone did a heck of a job laying it out."

"Really?"

"Yeah." He smiled again. "Really."

Will had some very appealing dimples, she noticed.

"I see you've gotten started." He nodded toward the partially weeded beds. "So … Helen said you're working on plans. Mind if I take a look?"

"Yes, well, I sketched out a few ideas, very rudimentary, though."

He sat beside her as Howard had on the steps, and looked over her drawings, plant list and supply list. When he got to the budget, he shook his head.

"I know," said Lily. "It's impossible."

"Not impossible, but definitely a challenge." He looked out at the oak, thinking, and said, "I can get these supplies wholesale, and we'll make use of what you already have."

"Like what? I don't have anything."

"I could see the tops of some pines in your front yard over your roof. You must have plenty of pine straw this time of year.

Do you have a yard service?"

"Yes, but they just mow and edge the front. They'll be here tomorrow."

"Get them to save the pine straw, haul it back here. We'll use it for mulch."

Lily was embarrassed she hadn't thought of this herself, it was so obvious.

"I know a tree guy who owes me a favor. He can remove some of the limbs in that magnolia, let more sun in. Most of this job is labor," he continued. "But if you can put in a couple of hours a day and I can put in a few afternoons a week ..."

"Sure." *What choice do I have?* she thought.

"We'll have to get creative, use all of the plants that are already here. There's no telling what we'll find under all these weeds and vines."

He looked at her as if really seeing her and her problem for the first time. "It'll be fun."

Lily laughed, not sure if it was because of his ridiculous optimism or the delicious feeling of relief that was beginning to settle over her.

"I don't know about that, but I have to admit I'm starting to feel better about this project. My mother-in-law, who was an amazing gardener, died last year, and we inherited the house, which is now my house and well ... The garden is the only thing she and I ever agreed on, the only place we ever really got along." Lily looked around her, and went on. "Do you know all of the bulbs and several plants—like that Lady Banksias rose over there—came from Mrs. McVay's mother's yard? It was all very special to her. She was too sick the last few years to do anything, and it just went to ruin without her."

"She must've had help. I mean she didn't take care of all this by herself, did she?"

"No, she had the same man helping her for years. Unfortunately, he died just before she became ill. She wouldn't let me help—didn't trust me, I guess." Lily shook her head at the memory. "But we could always talk out here about the plants. We had that in common. It's important to me to get it as close to the way she had it as I can."

The more Lily heard herself articulate it, the more she

understood how important it was to do a good job. She knew it was more than the landscaping challenge and the litany of excuses she'd paraded out before Helen.

Lily did have something to prove to Howard, to the women in the garden club (who would be expecting her to fail), and crazy as it was, in order to put things to rest between them, to the spirit of her dead mother-in-law. But more than anything, she had something to prove to Lily McVay. Getting on with her life had become top priority, and the restoration of the garden was the only way she knew to accomplish it.

It suddenly occurred to Lily that her lengthy explanation was wasting valuable time (not to mention, it was probably boring this guy out of his mind.)

"The point is," she said, "I'm relieved but surprised you like my ideas. They're so different from Maisy's yard, which is very un-Maisy-like, by the way. All that order and symmetry really doesn't seem her style."

"I think that was the point. She likes being unpredictable, said she needed a change. A formal garden with lots of structure is how she put it. Not really what I like, but it was good experience, and it turned out pretty well."

He took off his hat, ran his fingers through his hair and grinned at Lily. "You can't believe what I went through to convince her to leave the clematis vines on the patio."

"That's my favorite part."

"Mine, too," he said, and stood up, towering over her. "Do you have any pictures of the garden the way it used to be?"

"There are bound to be some around. I'll look. And Will, I can't thank you enough."

"Like I said, it'll be fun." He smiled again. "Especially if you try not to think of it as a project." He offered his hand and helped her up. "Do you want to start tomorrow? I have a class on plant nutrition in the morning but I can be here, say … three o'clock?"

"See you at three."

She watched him amble through the weeds, stopping now and again to examine a plant then finally duck under the oak limb and disappear through the gate. She felt light-headed with relief, gratitude and even a tiny surge of confidence that it was going to be as she envisioned, as Howard's mother would have wanted it. And it was going to be fun!

She picked up the phone and touched the redial button.

"Hello, Helen? It's all set. Thanks so much for recommending him ... Yes, we're starting tomorrow. Yes, he is ... Well, you can't help but notice ..." Lily rolled her eyes. "Think about it, Helen. I have children close to his age." She started to laugh. "I have *bathrobes* close to his age. What? I am not exaggerating. He must be what, twenty-five? Oh, thirty-four next month. I think that still qualifies him as being in a generation different than mine. Besides, one pedophile in the family is enough, don't you think? Take my advice. Put down the romance novels. Get a good gardening book. You have not read them all ... Good-bye."

Lily was still laughing when she hung up. She crossed the porch and opened the door. Cold, damp wisps of air caressed her with traces of stale perfume.

"Oh, no," she said aloud, the smile fading from her pretty features. "You're not going to ruin my perfectly good mood."

But anyone who could ruin the lovely fragrance of Chanel No. 5 could ruin anything, Lily reminded herself. Now she was frowning. Why couldn't she rid the house of that blasted odor?

She left the door open, went into the former parlor/now den and threw up the windows. As soon as the front door was opened, fresh, soft air swirled down the hall, chasing the staleness out into the yard. Lily stood breathing in the freshness, then returned to the parlor. Howard's mother looked on disapprovingly from her portrait above the mantle, her hair permed into those tight, steel-gray springs, her eyes dark and condescending. Lily had taken the portrait down and then guiltily replaced it. Just until after the garden club soiree, she'd told herself, then it was Heather's.

Mrs. McVay hadn't wanted Howard to marry the beautiful, young widow, Lily Ross. It seemed like a lifetime ago she'd moved back to town with Elizabeth and Virginia, the tiny identical twins who were now grown and on their own. Howard was an only child, a thirty-six-year-old bachelor. He was too old to take on a "high-spirited" wife and two toddling girls, his mother had said.

Lily sighed. Howard's mother had been right. Helen had

been right. Even Crazy Maisy had been right. Lily, it seemed, was the only one who had been wrong about Howard. He loved Lily and her girls in his own way, she guessed, but as the years sped by, Howard became less involved in their world, more consumed by his own.

Business trips took precedence over family vacations, board meetings over school plays. Weekends were for unwinding at the club instead of the backyard. Yet Howard had the knack of smothering from a distance, of aloof control. After all, he'd learned from the master. Like a benevolent but domineering patriarch to them all, he was always on the outside of things, and just ended up making them nervous and sad.

It wasn't until after her mother-in-law's death that she'd managed to shrug off the cloak of Howard's oppression. It was as if she hadn't quite had the strength to fight the two of them, but just enough to stand up to one. The remaining tie that held Howard and Lily together—his domination of her—had finally been severed.

Howard's real family, the people he connected with, was his fellow club and board members, the town social and civic leaders. They were the ones who really knew him. They had been disappointed but not shocked as Lily had been, when he'd asked for a divorce and moved in with Heather.

With the divorce had come long overdue counseling for Lily and her daughters. (Howard refused to attend, of course.) And for the first time they had really talked about it all. Finally loosening the remaining shackles of duty and gratitude, they'd freed long-held words bound by confusion and resentment and guilt.

In six weeks of counseling, decades of stifled truths were revealed, she'd told Helen a bit dramatically. Emotionally, Howard was repressed to the point of non-existence. All those years she and the girls had lived under alternating layers of guilt and antipathy, trying to get close to him, to make him a part of their lives, and he didn't really exist. Not for them, anyway.

"What will Howard say when he finds out he's the recipient of gardening charity?" Lily said to the portrait. She could have sworn Mrs. McVay twitched at her. Taking her supper onto the back porch, she looked over her notes, and replayed the conversation she'd had with Will several times in her head. Soon it was as if he was actually there, reassuring her.

"It'll be fun." Lily heard him say, and she laughed out loud before she got up to shut the windows and doors for the night.

4.

Cultivating a Friendship

It was seven o'clock the next morning, and Lily felt positively giddy. She knew that Howard and Heather were on a plane for Chicago and would be gone the rest of the week. On business. You know how indispensable these executive assistants are.

"I can put off the come-to-Jesus meeting for a while longer," Lily told Howard's mother's portrait as she opened the shutters and raised the windows in the parlor/den. Sunlight tumbled into the room, chasing shadows away. She stretched as delicious morning air danced over her skin, awakening her.

Up in her bedroom, she started to struggle into a pair of pantyhose. As they crept up the length of her legs, it felt as if she were closing the windows again, one by one. By the time the hose had her rear end compressed and her tummy controlled, she was feeling downright claustrophobic.

"What sadist invented these things?" she asked her reflection in the mirror.

"Had to be some female-hating man," the reflection answered.

Lily peeled the dreaded things off, held them over her head and in her best Scarlett O'Hara imitation said to Lily-of-the-mirror, "As God as my witness, I will never wear pantyhose again!"

She tossed them into the trash can, made a few calls, got out of her GRITS (Gourmets for the Return of Ice Water Teas Society) and Boll Weevil Ball (don't ask) committee meetings, and put on her oldest, most comfortable pair of shorts. The garden was waiting.

"Downward facing dog."

The deep, male voice rose sonorously above the lilting melody of a flute.

What on earth?

Lily realized it was just Maisy's yoga group who met on the old lady's patio twice a week. She'd heard from Helen that the women, all of whom were over seventy, had been meeting with the same instructor for years. They had only recently changed their locale to Maisy's.

"Now, ladies, relax into child's pose."

Just my luck, thought Lily, but had to admit the music and the man's voice were strangely soothing.

On the porch, she watered the voluminous Boston ferns bursting from their wooden planters. They flourished against Mrs. McVay's antique wicker, which Lily had repainted dark green. Newly upholstered cushions in retro-stripe canvas of cool blue and yellow made the old sofas and chairs inviting. Lily was tempted to indulge in another cup of coffee and the morning crossword, but she started in on her list of gardening chores.

She spent the morning weeding the daylily beds beneath the porch, going slowly, savoring the delight of a new spring and the promise of summer that the unfolding day brought. She stopped to chat on the phone and enjoyed a glass of iced tea, adding a sprig of the fresh mint that spilled out of a clay pot by the steps.

In spite of the leisurely pace and her determination to follow Will's instructions to not think of this as a project, she had accomplished quite a bit by lunchtime. She realized, in amazement, that her back and hands were tired but didn't ache as they had before. However, the morning's labors had given her quite an appetite.

She put on some music, sautéed a few chicken tenders with fresh basil in olive oil, found some romaine, some walnuts and grapes, a sweet Vidalia onion and a perfectly ripe avocado, and threw a salad together. She spread real butter (she deserved it, by God) on hot French bread and headed back to the porch.

The salad and bread quickly disappeared, leaving her full and sleepily enjoying the seductive ambience of Howard's mother's creation. The place had a unique personality (as all the best gardens do) and the way to bring it out was coming to her in bits and pieces.

Lily's and Maisy's streets formed a V and intersected at the far end. The McVay property was situated on a lovely, tree-shaded corner at the widest part of the V. This resulted in a deep, narrow lot that was atypical for the old, urban neighborhood. In addition, the yard felt even more spacious than it actually was due to a small park and well-tended cemetery, which sat across the narrow side street. It was here Mrs. McVay and generations of old families were buried.

Lily's house had been built so that the front yard was just a small patch of lawn and beds, leaving most of the unusually deep lot for the back garden. The entire area had been sectioned by artful plantings so that there seemed to be several small gardens. These were laced through with interconnecting paths. The clever design made the space seem as if it went on forever with a surprise around every corner. These floral spaces were still in evidence, and though the "bones" of the garden were obvious, there were some major problems.

A magnolia near the porch kept the ground bare and full of roots beneath the wide circle of its limbs. It put out too much shade, and gardenias that once enjoyed full sun were shadowed, their leaves covered in black, sooty fungus from untreated white fly infestation. Clematis and jasmine vines fought to envelop the garden shed whose paint had faded to the wood.

The gate was falling apart, and more vines and weeds choked the hydrangeas and shaggy Formosa azaleas that took over an entire corner of the yard. The biggest dilemma was a large patch of dead shrubs, dirt and weeds. A walkway of old brick that started at the back steps and was the connecting point for the other pathways continued around the unsightly area that had once been the focal point of the garden.

A small but deep fish pond against the wall on the cemetery side of the yard was stagnant and clogged with debris. At one time it was home to flashing coy and gold fish—another unexpected delight in this once-magical place.

But by May, the magnolia would be full of spectacular blossoms the size of pie plates, their perfume scenting the entire neighborhood. The hot pink of the azalea buds poked encouragingly through the tendrils of honeysuckle, and the lines of the gate and shed held some promise, too. The towering gardenias didn't look too damaged by the white flies, which could be gotten rid of with a couple of sprayings of summer oil. In the beds beneath the porch, the soil looked rich, and the clumps of daylilies suddenly appeared healthier now that they had been freed of weeds and plant debris.

Though there were bare areas where many of them had died, Lily was pretty sure she could put her hands on the same variety to use as replacements. If not, she would divide some of the bigger clumps to fill in the gaps. Trays of annuals (that Will would hopefully be able to get wholesale) would finish the beds out nicely and put on quite a show for the soiree.

The fresh green of new leaves finally able to take in the noonday sun was a lovely reward for the morning's labors. By late May the daylilies should be blooming, their soft yellow faces and new buds dazzling against the gray wood and white trim of the porch. They would continue their show throughout the summer. The old pond could at least be cleaned out and filled with fresh water and some lilies and hyacinth for the party. Maybe some floating candles in the hyacinths …

Lily was still jotting notes when she heard the unmistakable trill of Maisy Downey's voice. "Thank you, sweetheart. See you tomorrow?"

"Yes, ma'am," she heard Will answer. He came through the gate pushing a wheelbarrow loaded with bags. His dirty clothes, sunburned face and arms, and tired eyes told her he'd been working all day. But he grinned at her as he strode through the yard, and she was filled with gratitude that he was there.

"Did you do all this?" he asked.

"I decided to cancel my meetings. I'm taking your advice and enjoying gardening for a change. Believe it or not, this is the nicest day I've had in a long time."

He looked at her for a few seconds, a quizzical smile playing in his blue eyes.

"What?" said Lily.

"Nothing. It's just that, well, that's what it's all about, isn't it?"

Before she could answer, he'd pulled on a pair of gloves, grabbed a spade and started in on the honeysuckle in the azaleas. Lily found her own gloves and went to work beside him.

She began tugging at a handful of vines. They refused to budge. She changed position and tried again as Will watched her out of the corner of his eye. Suddenly, the honeysuckle lost the battle, sending roots, dirt and Lily flying into Will. He threw an arm around her waist to keep her from falling, and for a second or two held her against him until she caught her balance.

Lily was surprised at how comfortable she was in the arms of this relative stranger. But he didn't feel strange at all. As a matter of fact, he felt great. And to her surprise, pressed against Will's warm, muscular body, Lily felt completely comfortable. Comfortable, yet excited—as if some forgotten switch had suddenly been flipped on.

She was amazed at how pleasurable the simple brush of his breath on her face was when he laughed and said, "Hey, a little less muscle over there. Let's try some teamwork. Let me loosen it up for you first."

I've been celibate entirely too long, she thought, trying to catch her breath and get her mind back on weeds.

They soon developed a rhythm with him digging and her pulling, careful not to take the new azalea buds off with the vines. The pile of uprooted honeysuckle increased until the azaleas were finally free. Will fetched a bag from his wheelbarrow and began sprinkling granules around the newly cleared soil. He worked it in a bit with the shovel, and Lily realized that she was staring at him, enjoying the sight of his strong arms and back beneath the thin T-shirt. She felt her face go red and hoped he would think it was just sun or exertion. If he'd noticed, he didn't let on, but went on talking.

"This is a good azalea food with an iron supplement," he explained. "Probably should've been done a couple of weeks ago, but I think it'll be okay. Do this again around the first of June."

"If these azaleas get any bigger, they'll take over the whole yard," said Lily. They're so beautiful for the few weeks they're in bloom, but …"

"I'll show you how to prune them after the flowers are gone. They won't be small, just shaped better."

The simple statement made her very happy. Not because it meant he'd still be around after the azaleas finished their show, she told herself, but because it meant she would have the benefit of his horticultural expertise. She had to admit it, though. He wasn't bad company. And oh, okay, he was downright great to look at. So what? She was middle-aged, not dead, right?

"There aren't that many of these native azaleas left," he was saying. "This town used to be full of them."

"Oh, I remember," said Lily. "My parents would drive my friends and me all over town to see them when they were at their peak. The most spectacular ones were down on the old Pearson property by the river. They were huge—the biggest ones in town and varieties I'd never seen before."

"They're still there."

He put the rest of the plant food back in the wheelbarrow. "Okay if I store this stuff in there?" He nodded toward the shed.

"Sure."

She was placing a soaker hose beneath the azaleas to give the fertilizer a good watering when Will finally emerged from the shed carrying a large, clay planter in the shape of a frog.

"Look what I found," he said.

"I'd forgotten about him. He was a present to my mother-in-law from me. I gave it to her years ago. I can't believe she kept it."

She looked at the silly face, now green with time and algae, and had to smile.

"He's aged well, don't you think?"

"Yeah," agreed Will. "You ought to be able to use him somewhere."

"Put him there by the steps for now. He'll be our finishing touch."

Will set him down with a flourish. "Every garden needs a good luck charm. He'll be yours. Now, I don't know about you, but I could use a break. How about some ice water?"

"How about iced tea? I've got lemon and some fresh

mint," she said, gesturing to a clay pot on the steps which was overflowing with the bright green herb.

"Even better. Thanks."

She handed him the tea and set a plate of homemade oatmeal cookies on the steps between them.

"Now tell me about the azaleas," she said.

"What do you want to know?"

"When did you see them? They're kind of off the beaten path."

"I live out there."

"Really? I thought all of that property was part of the old Pearson nursery. It went out of business years ago, didn't it?"

"Old man Pearson was my great uncle. I used to visit him and my aunt every summer when I was a kid. I worked on the plants, especially the azaleas. They had quite a breeding program going. Almost every variety of azalea is still out there, including a few I don't think anybody even remembers. They knew I loved the place, so I ended up with it when my aunt died."

"Very generous, considering the prices on riverfront property these days."

"Very generous. But like I said, they knew I loved it out there." He grinned at her, and again she couldn't help but notice how cute those dimples of his were and what an infectious smile he had. "It wasn't exactly prime real estate then," he continued. "Anyway, spending summers out there with them really saved me. My mom died when I was eleven, and my stepmother and I didn't see eye to eye on many things. Pretty typical, I guess. I don't know if you ever saw the house, but it's not much – just a little cottage. It's in pretty bad shape, but I'm living out there and fixing it up."

He flashed that grin at her again. "More or less, anyway. I guess you could say it's a work in progress. I want to restore the nursery eventually, start my own landscaping business. I only moved to town a year or so ago, though, and I've been cleaning up the nursery, getting greenhouses fixed, things like that." He sighed. "… and working on the house, and getting this master gardener certification."

"You've been busy."

"Yeah. But it beats the big city and sitting in an office all day—and half the night."

"Were you in Atlanta?"

"New York. I'm from a town even smaller than this one. I couldn't wait to get out of there, see some bright lights, make some big money. So after college and a few years of this and that, I applied to law school. Not long after graduation, I headed north."

"You mean I have a New York City lawyer pulling weeds in my backyard?"

"Former New York city lawyer, I'm happy to say." He took a bite of cookie. "You know, the whole time I was there I never once sat on anybody's back steps drinking sweet tea and eating homemade oatmeal cookies." He popped the rest of the little dessert into his mouth. "And by the way, these are some of the best cookies I've had in a long time."

"Thank you. I like baking, but I really shouldn't eat them. I'll give you some to take home."

Her mind returned to azaleas and the nursery. She was intrigued by the idea of the forgotten varieties, knew they would be blooming soon and was dying to see them. She hesitated for a few seconds, then continued.

"I know how busy you are, but I sure would like to see your azaleas."

He looked at her, his face serious. "This is the first time I've dealt with a bribe in the form of oatmeal cookies."

Lily grinned at him. "Well, are you taking the bribe?"

He grinned back. "Definitely," he said.

5.

Girls' Night Out

In her bedroom, Lily slid the heavy wooden window frames up just a few inches. Crisp, early evening air diffused the persistent mustiness invading her room and her privacy.

She popped a CD into the player that was housed in a converted antique linen press, opened some two-year-old bath salts she'd kept only because she liked the bottle, and slipped into a warm tub in the adjoining bathroom. She soaked long enough to shave her legs while talking on the phone with her daughters, both of whom would be home in time to help her with the party, they assured her, and couldn't wait to see Grandmother McVay's garden.

Yes, they'd heard from Howard in the form of checks to each of them along with cheery notes from Heather—on hot pink stationery with "Heather" imprinted in aqua bubble letters. "But still, Mom, it was nice of her to write."

This tiny comment was the only negative in a thus-far delightful day. It was an infinitesimal betrayal, just a twinge of hurt, but like a lone ant at the picnic, one that bites and makes you wonder, "Is this just a hint, a foreshadowing of what's to come?"

Lily shook off the niggling feeling of dread, vowed not to let this silly seed of doubt plant itself in her vulnerable psyche, and washed her hair until it was so clean it squeaked.

Make-up, new skirt, a favorite sweater in the leafy green that brought out her eyes and the warm tones of her skin, and she was ready for a night out on the town. With the girls. *At least it's not another frog date*, she told herself. Along with pantyhose, Lily had sworn off frogs.

Lily was on her front porch, locking the door when she heard the phone ringing. She would let the machine get it, she decided. If it were one of her girls and if it was something urgent they would try her cell. Lily didn't give it another thought as she headed across the lawn to the driveway where her four-year-old red jeep was parked.

She hopped in the car and had put the key in the ignition before she noticed it.

"What the …?" said Lily aloud.

Someone had scrawled an obscenity on her windshield with bright purple lipstick.

Who would do this? she wondered. Even more puzzling was: *Who would wear this color lipstick?*

Convinced this was the work of some high school girl (one in desperate need of a makeup makeover) who'd defaced an innocent car by mistake, Lily found some tissues and got enough of it off that at least it was no longer legible. She would try to take it to the car wash tomorrow. Putting it out of her mind, she backed out of the driveway and started the ten-minute trip to town where she was meeting Helen and Helen's cousin, Marilee for dinner.

In her day, Marilee had been the belle of every ball. She had predictably married well, and to the surprise and delight of her friends and family, had the sense to appreciate her good fortune. A petite, pretty blonde, she was still in love with her prosperous, down-to-earth husband, had three great, college-aged children and lived a rare, charmed life.

The only fly in this pie of perfection was Marilee's misguided determination to be a part of the business world. One creative endeavor after another (financed by her indulgent husband) had bitten the proverbial dust. She'd had a dress business, several shops—antique, gift/stationery and shoe—opened an art gallery, which was about to close, and was just beginning to show interest in yet another venture. Lily marveled that a drawer full of very clever but now-defunct business cards had not dissuaded her.

Lately Marilee's conversation was increasingly peppered with references to the Mayfair Collection, which was a line of staggeringly expensive clothes shown four times a year in the associates' homes. Passion for fashion was a must, of course, but a lovely home was also a prerequisite since a peek around the upscale premises was one of the many bonuses of shopping the Mayfair way. Marilee's spacious country French "cottage" certainly filled this requirement. It fairly oozed that sought after yet rarely attained combination of effortless perfection and homey sophistication.

Mayfair perks included fabulous clothes that could be had at an equally fabulous discount, which Marilee didn't need, and required trips to Atlanta and New York for preview fashion shows. Lily and Helen had to admit that it was right up their friend's alley.

Marilee's dismal track record did make them a tad skeptical, however. Her lack of real world experiences and refusal to come to terms with the practical aspects of her commercial endeavors had resulted in a certain perpetual naiveté. This prompted her many friends to lovingly refer to her as the deb. In addition to her other advantages, Marilee was a good sport and blessed with a sense of humor, so this didn't bother her in the least.

Minutes later, the three old friends entered a building that was one of the oldest in the historic downtown area. It had been lovingly restored, its brick floors gleaming beneath high ceilings and authentic architectural elements which had been either enhanced or added to the decor. The owners, with an eye for every detail, had filled the place with charming furnishings and some impressive artwork by local artists, achieving that homey, been-there-forever feeling. It was an immediate success and attracted an upbeat crowd of good-looking, moneyed, art-appreciating townsfolk.

After a dinner that Marilee gave a rating of five for food, but a rare ten for ambience, the three friends walked along the tree-canopied streets passing tall, inviting windows that glowed with warm lighting and convivial atmosphere. The stroll was Helen's idea of walking off the many calories she'd just consumed.

Helen was what Lily referred to as one of the diet-deluded, trying one weight-loss program after another, none of which had any noticeable effect on Helen's self-described apple-on-a-two-sticks body. Until she discovered that magical balance of carbs, fats and proteins that would melt away the pounds without too much exercise, Helen disguised her ample middle with loose-cut blouses in colors that complimented her clear blue eyes and silvery hair.

Feeling relaxed and full, Lily, Helen and Marilee discussed their biggest dilemma at present—whether to go for an ice-cream cone or a drink. Drinks won out. Not as fattening and besides, the Olive Bar was just across the street.

When they were settled at a table by the window Helen ordered three cosmopolitans.

"What are we celebrating?" asked Marilee.

"Lily has broken through her gardener's block or whatever it was and has done all this great work. From what I hear from our friend, Will, the yard will be looking wonderful for the garden club soiree," explained Helen.

"Well, thanks to you ... and Will, of course, it looks like things might just work out. Barring any natural disasters, like a tornado or Heather showing up with a few dozen plastic flamingos." She grinned, very unapologetically. "Sorry about that last part."

"She'll be there? With Howard? Wow, that should be interesting," said Marilee, smiling a thank you to the waiter for the three pink concoctions he set before them.

"Yes, but it'll ensure a big crowd," said Lily, with a grimace. "Elizabeth and Virginia will be there, though. I can always count on the twins for good backup." Her smile was genuine now at the thought of seeing her girls. She lifted her glass. "Here's to family, good friends and the end of gardener's block." They sipped their drinks in unison.

"And don't forget Will," said Helen, her voice high and teasing. "He's certainly good backup." She took another sip of her drink. "I can't wait to see Howard when he lays his beady little eyes on Will."

Marilee looked from Helen to Lily. "Who is this Will? Am I missing something here?"

Helen grinned evilly. "Will is the lovely young man who's been, uh, helping Lil's garden grow."

"Uh, oh. Somebody's been into the romance novels again. But tell me, just how young and just how lovely?" said Marilee, leaning forward.

Lily groaned, but she was laughing, too. "He's *thirty-four-years-old* for God's sake. But he is very nice and talented, and he is … Well—he is very nice looking. But, like I said, he is thirty-four."

"You know, this would make a great romance novel," said Helen, gazing dramatically into Lily's eyes. "*Love amongst the Lantana, Seduction the Second Time Around*—something like that."

"Helen, stop looking at me like that. Those bodice rippers you read have gone to your head."

"I do not read bodice rippers. I draw the line at sexual assault. But there are some really good novels out there. As I've told you before, you should try reading one. It might soften you up on the idea of love with a younger man. You're far too cynical about your love potential—that's what Catherine Smyth calls it."

Marilee frowned. "Catherine Smyth the novelist?"

"Exactly, and she knows what she's talking about. Anyway, I thought you might want to know what your gardener said about you."

"Well, I don't." Lily paused. "I'd be interested in what he had to say about the garden, or my ideas, maybe."

"Okay," said Marilee. "I'm interested. Tell me." She sipped her cosmopolitan and smiled at Lily. "Feel free to listen if you want to."

"He said Lily was very easy to work with."

"That's it?" said Marilee.

Lily lifted the glass to her lips to hide the blush of disappointment she felt.

"No, that's not it," Helen continued. "He loves her ideas, said they compliment his. He said that she wasn't at all what he was expecting—that she's a lot of fun and great looking. That's a direct quote." Helen raised her glass in salute to Lily.

"Here, here," said Marilee and did likewise.

"He said I was fun?"

"Yes. And great looking. A great looking, thirty-four-year-old guy thinks you're great looking and fun. Now, doesn't that make you feel good?"

"Yes, it really does. And I appreciate you telling me. The Howard-Heather thing and my succession of frog dates—not that I don't appreciate you trying to help, Helen—haven't done a lot for my self-confidence. But Will's just a kid. Really."

Marilee turned to Helen. "How do you know this guy?"

"Well, he inherited that old nursery down by the river—the Pearsons owned it, but it's totally run down. It'll be quite a job to get it going again. I don't think there's anything out there but a bunch of old azaleas. But as you know, that property has appreciated like crazy the last few years. And Will is interested in landscape gardening, so I guess it makes sense. He's working on his master gardener certificate through our program at the botanical gardens."

"Tell her the rest," said Lily. "He has a law degree. He's been practicing in New York. Now he's back in our little town, landscaping. How strange is that? I mean, did he get disbarred or something?"

"It is strange," Helen agreed, "To start over and abandon a career in law and take up gardening." She sighed. "Not everyone blooms where he's planted, I suppose. Sometimes you have to rip yourself up by the roots and start over in a place that suits you. I really don't know any details about what prompted the drastic career change, though. All I know is that he is very nice, if a little, oh, I don't know … just different, I guess. A bit of a loner and not very forthcoming about himself. But he's terribly knowledgeable about horticulture in general, and I've never met anyone so talented when it comes to landscape design. He's an artist, really. And he seems to like you, Lily." Helen downed the rest of her cosmopolitan and winked at her friend. "And he's certainly no toad."

"No. More like a tadpole," said Lily.

"Many younger men find mature women very attractive," said Marilee. "You hear about it a lot these days."

"Sixty is the new forty," said Helen. "That means you're not even close to forty yet."

"What does that make Will? An embryo?" asked Lily.

"Will you stop that?" said Marilee. "Men have been dating and marrying younger women forever, so why not the reverse?"

"A lot of reasons, and name one of these reverse May-December relationships."

"There's that movie star and the young hunk she dates. Now, what is her name? You know, Helen. She starred in that movie you liked so much, the one set in Paris."

"Oh, yeah. What was the title of it? *Amore* something? God, I hate not being able to remember anything."

"Tell me about it," said Marilee, rolling her enormous, brown eyes. "Anyway, this actress whose name I can't think of and her young boyfriend, whose name I also can't think of, are getting married if they haven't already."

Lily shook her head. "One person. In Hollywood."

"Well, it does happen. Especially to women who look like you," said Marilee. "You could pass for your own daughter!"

"You are both being very supportive and sweet," said Lily, "But let's face it. I couldn't hold onto a man twelve years older. He left me for someone younger than my own daughters. I don't really think I could keep a guy like Will interested even if I wanted to, that is."

"Lily," said Helen, "It wasn't you. It was Howard. He wants someone he can control. I think when you finally figured him out and stood up to him, he couldn't take it."

"That's right," said Marilee. "It's like that counselor told you, Heather is part of a pattern. You outgrew Howard, that's all. Like Helen said, his delicate ego couldn't take it, and he found someone he could dominate. I guess control means even more to him than his loss of face in this town. And we all know how important that is to Howard."

"I know you're both right. Still, I feel I should have been able to work things out. And I still don't understand the whole Heather shack-up part. It is just *sooo* out of character." Lily shook her head. "But we've talked about all of this before, and we're all tired of it, so I'm changing the subject and proposing a toast to the future."

She got the attention of the waiter, held up three fingers, and pointed to her glass.

"You're a terrible influence, Helen," said Marilee. "Keep up the good work."

Helen turned to Lily. "Speaking of the future, have you

given any thought to those two dirty little words, gainful employment?"

"Well, finally getting over my gardener's block, as we are now calling it, has inspired me. I want to do something I really love, and I love working with flowers." She sighed. "It's the gainful part that worries me. Turning a hobby into a job that pays the bills is a dream job, but one that fails a lot, I'm afraid."

"I was reading an article just the other day," said Marilee. "Now, what was it? Turn your passion into a paycheck or convert your crafts into cash? Earn interest on your ideas? Anyway, something like that."

"No offense, but those kinds of articles have gotten you into trouble, Marilee," teased Helen.

"Well, the point is, it can be done." She made a face. "Maybe not by me, but it can be done."

"I'm just kidding you," said Helen. "I admire your persistence. Really."

"Thanks, but I know I'm just one man away from the welfare line. A rewarding career is just a pipe dream for me, I guess. It would be nice to know I could support myself if I ever had to."

"You'll find your niche one of these days," said Lily.

"And remember," said Helen, "just because you haven't been drawing a salary all these years, if your net worth as a mother, wife and housekeeper were ever tallied up, you'd be a very rich woman. One man away from the welfare line ... that's ridiculous! Ask any divorce lawyer. Oh, sorry, Lily. Didn't mean to bring up a sore subject."

"I know you didn't," said Lily. "Besides, you're absolutely right. It's just that when you find yourself suddenly alone, even if money isn't an issue, well ... it's about making a whole new life."

"What about weddings?" suggested Marilee. "You're great at arranging flowers. It's about time you got paid for it."

Lily shook her head. "Weekend work, hysterical MOBs – no thanks."

"MOBs? What on earth are MOBs?"

"Mothers-of-the-bride," explained Helen.

"Oh. Good point, honey," agreed Marilee.

"I really enjoy the growing end of it more," said Lily. "I

would love to grow flowers and sell them. That would be a dream job."

"You mean like a flower farm?" asked Marilee. She looked at her gleaming silk nails and shuttered.

"One girl's dream is another girl's nightmare," laughed Helen.

"I think it would be a sort of flower farm," said Lily. "I just haven't thought it all out. The first step is to cut back on the charity work. No one believes in the merits of volunteerism more than I do, and most of the organizations I've been involved in have been worthwhile, but face it, some of them are dreamed up by bored housewives and don't impact the community that much."

"Like the Golfer's Ball," laughed Marilee. "I think that little soiree cost more money than it raised."

"Or GRITS," said Helen. "You know, Gourmets for the Return of Ice Water Teas Society," she added when Marilee looked confused.

"I heard that ice water teas are on the socially endangered list," said Marilee, smiling. "Thank God."

Lily laughed and said, "Well, the upshot of it is that I've decided to resign from all boards and committees that don't have gardening as a focus."

"Thank goodness for that," said Helen. "We need you at the botanical gardens."

"Helen, I would never drop the botanical gardens. I owe you well into my next life for all you've done for me this past year."

Helen gave an oh-what-are-friends-for wave of her hand.

"Sounds like you've turned a corner," said Marilee.

"You know," said Lily, "I think I have."

"Excuse me, girls. Time for the powder room," said Helen, sliding out of her chair.

"Me, too," said Marilee. "Lily?"

"No, I'll wait here for our drinks."

There was nothing Lily loved more than the company of Marilee and Helen, but it was nice to sit quietly with nothing to occupy her mind but jazzy background music and a cosmo-induced feeling of contentment as she watched passersby through the bar's window. She should have known it wouldn't last long.

An attractive, animated young woman came into view across the street. She wore a tight skirt and top that made the most of her tiny waist, flat stomach and gravity-defying breasts. She was laughing and gesturing to someone to hurry. The "someone" was outside Lily's view, probably having a hard time keeping up with the girl who was now hot-footing it toward the bar on heels that made Lily's feet hurt just to look at them.

The old saying, "The energy of youth is wasted on the young," drifted through her brain as she stifled a yawn, suddenly feeling the long hours she'd spent working in the yard.

As she continued watching, a familiar figure caught up with the girl. He didn't quite register at first, but then the lanky frame and dark hair curling at the nape of his neck brought recognition. It was Will.

He smiled indulgently at the girl as she turned and locked her arm in his and dragged him toward the entrance. Lily had to admit they made a very cute couple—the tall, slow-moving, dark-haired man and the vivacious little blonde. "Opposites attract," she reminded herself, but was surprised to realize that she didn't like seeing Will with the girl, and she did like it that he seemed mildly annoyed rather than charmed by her enthusiasm.

She was distracted as Marilee and Helen and the waiter all arrived back at the table at once. After the waiter had served them with fresh drinks, it took Helen all of thirty seconds to notice Will.

"Well, look who's here," she said, her blue eyes flashing.

"Who?" asked Marilee.

"Lily's gardener."

"He's not my gardener. I mean …"

"Good Lord," said Marilee. "He is a cutie, Lily. Congratulations."

"Okay, I mean he is my gardener, but I am not interested in him."

"Why not?" asked Marilee.

"Well, for one reason, I think they just carded his date. In other words, he's too young!" hissed Lily between teeth clenched into a little fake smile in case Will had noticed them and thought they might be discussing him.

"His date? You mean that little bimbo—or should I say bimbette—with the fake boobs?" asked Helen.

"That would be exactly who I mean," said Lily. "Now, will you both quit talking about him?"

Marilee was taking a sip of her drink, cutting her eyes in Will's direction. "I don't think he's interested in her," she said. "He looks bored."

At this moment the bimbette recognized a friend across the room. Squealing with delight, she dashed over to say hello. It was also at this time that Will caught sight of the three women. He smiled and started over to them. Lily noticed that Helen sat a little taller in her chair. Marilee tucked a strand of hair behind her ear, then untucked it. *My gardener certainly has a way with women*, she thought.

"It's nice to see you ladies out on the town," he said.

"It's nice to see you, Will," said Helen. She gave him that little smile that showed her dimples to their best advantage.

"Have you met my cousin, Marilee?"

"Hello," he said, grinning at her, but his attention quickly shifted to Lily. His eyes twinkled. "Now this is impressive," he said.

"What?" asked Lily, twinkling right back.

"You, here, after the work you put in today."

"Well, you're here," she teased, but then thought it sounded like him being there was the reason she was there. She felt her face get pink. "I mean, you worked harder than I did."

"I don't know about that. I just know I'm dead on my feet, and you don't even look tired. You look great as a matter of fact." He looked at her for a few seconds then seemed to remember where he was. He looked over at his date who was coming toward them. "One drink and I'm heading home."

The baby bombshell bounced up and slid an arm around his waist, pressing the large, unnaturally firm breasts into his side. "Here you are, Wills."

Did his jaw tighten a bit or was it Lily's imagination?

"Ladies, this is Jaime Rogers." He introduced them all, explaining that Helen ran the horticultural program. "Lily has the garden I was telling you about."

"I don't know much about gardening, although I actually love flowers," said Jaime, her eyes flicking to the nearby tables. "Actually, I could use another beer."

Will drained the rest of his beer and turned to his date who had lost all interest in the three women at this point. "Sure, I'll get you one, but then I've got to get home," he said to her.

"At ten o'clock?" she whined.

He looked at Helen. "I've got this early turf seminar."

Jaime pursed her pretty, little lips and rolled her eyes toward the ceiling.

"You don't have to go," he said.

"You're sure you don't mind?" She smiled sweetly at him. "There are so many people here I know. I could catch a ride, actually. Call me, okay? Nice meeting you," she said to no one in particular and took off for the far corner of the bar, evidently forgetting the promised beer.

If this bothered Will, he didn't show it. "See you day after tomorrow, Lily? Around three?"

"Sure," she said with way more enthusiasm than she'd intended.

When they had finished admiring Will as he strolled past the window and finally out of view, Marilee said, "Well, that was interesting. I wonder if they date much. I mean, she acts like a teenager."

"Maybe she is," said Lily airily. "It's really none of our business."

Marilee rolled her eyes, but didn't say what she was thinking, which was, *who do you think you are kidding?*

"Have you ever noticed how young people say actually all the time?" asked Helen.

"Actually, I have," said Lily with a little smirk.

"Oh, you young thing," laughed Marilee. "Seriously though, that boy is smitten with you," she said, sounding every bit like the southern belle she was.

"The key word here is *boy*," said Lily, but there was a noticeable lack of conviction in her voice.

6.

Familial Refuse

By 10:30 the next morning Lily had attended a quick garden club meeting, dashed by the grocery store, gotten out of her Cornbread Cookbook (5th edition, no less) Committee luncheon (she'd tried to resign but her resignation had been politely refused), had indeed resigned from the Friends of St. John's Bell Chorus Auxiliary, and started a pot of soup.

While she cooked, she thought about where photos of the garden might be. In all of her cleaning and redecorating, she hadn't come across any old pictures. It was odd, now that she thought about it. Everyone has albums or at least shoeboxes of photos they'd meant to put into albums, but there was nothing in the McVay house. She mentally wandered through each room as she chopped and seasoned. When she got to the attic, she remembered.

"That old chest," she said aloud as the last of the celery went into the pot.

She'd meant to go through it, but somehow with everything that had been happening in her life, she'd forgotten about it. In went ground pepper and mushrooms. Down went the gas flame to its lowest setting.

Lily ran upstairs then took the narrow attic steps two at a time. The trunk sat beneath the fan window that faced the street. As she started towards it, she thought she heard the doorbell so she climbed onto the chest to look out of the window. Parked below was a shining, black, just-washed Hummer.

"Damn!"

Except for Howard, Heather, or the ghost of her dead

mother-in-law, this was the last person Lily wanted to see. At the thought of Mrs. M., a familiar cold draft swept up the stairs through the open door.

That noxious smell of stale perfume further befouled by acrid setting solution, more pungent than ever, rode the icy air into the room, and settled on everything like a musty cloak. Holding her nose with one hand, Lily watched as Dwayne Bond got into his machine and hummed off down the street.

She stood for a moment, admiring the bird's eye view of her lovely neighborhood and was surprised to see another car cruise slowly up to her house and stop. It was a convertible driven by a blonde woman she was unable to recognize from her attic perch. Suddenly the woman took a bag of trash—fast food wrappers from the looks of it—and tossed it onto Lily's front yard.

"Damn!" Lily said again. What was that about? But she was determined to stick to the task at hand, so she put the sexy litterer out of her mind and climbed down. Still holding her nose, she tried to lift the chest's heavy lid. It wouldn't budge.

There were some keys in that dented brass cricket box of Mrs. McVay's which was … where? She looked around the attic. There it was on a shelf of the hideous étagère from the parlor/ den. The third key did the trick. The lid creaked up. *Voila!*

The mother lode of familial refuse—stacks of albums and boxes of letters and yellowed baby clothes, two silver monogrammed baby cups, their bottoms dented from being banged on the antique high chair nearby. *It's hard to think of any of the McVays as ever being babies*, thought Lily, picking up a sterling silver baby spoon in Mrs. McVay's Rose pattern. The spoon fell from Lily's fingers and clattered onto the floor, the sound breaking through her reverie.

The soup. How long had she been sitting there? Lily grabbed an armload of stuff from the chest and hurried downstairs. Pushing a pitcher of roses out of the way, she placed everything on one end of the kitchen's pine table.

That's when she noticed the answering machine's light blinking impatiently and remembered the phone ringing as she'd left the night before. She pressed play. Nothing. It was the phone freak again.

She was about to hit the erase button when a woman's muffled voice said, "This is a call for Mrs. McVay. Mrs. Rosemary McVay. I know she's there."

Even as muffled as the voice was, Lily knew she had heard it before—a woman's voice yet with a strange, childlike quality.

Heather? Could be, but she didn't think so. Besides, even Heather would be above such a juvenile prank, wouldn't she? Or maybe foraging through the McVay attic had put her imagination into overdrive. Maybe it was just a persistent telemarketer working from an old list. That happened all the time. That had to be it.

She gave the soup a quick stir and went back for another arm load of letters, hurrying out of the oppressive attic. The cloying atmosphere was inescapable, however. As a matter of fact, it seemed to be following her and dissipated only after she'd opened all the doors and windows and turned the ceiling fans to their highest speed.

As Lily made her final trip into the attic and retrieved the last box of letters, it dawned on her that the pervasive funkiness could in fact be more than just years of sprayed, dabbed and spilled perfume and the stench of too-frequent permanent waves that had leeched into the very walls.

What if the suddenly chilled air was more than an old house's predictable draftiness? And what about the times she jokingly talked to Howard's dead mother's portrait and was overcome with the creepy feeling that it heard her? Was the old lady a natural part of the house's long memory, or was she somehow still here in a very unnatural way? And what about the phone message?

"Do do dee do, do do dee do," Lily sang, trying to tease the edge off of this idea that had been playing around the recesses of her brain for months.

Whenever inklings of Mrs. McVay dogging her from the grave surfaced, Lily questioned her decision to accept the house and the garden project as a divorce settlement. Had she put pride before sanity?

"You'll never be free of the McVays as long as you're in that house," Helen had warned again and again.

"Ridiculous," Lily said aloud, shaking her head. But she knew it wasn't ridiculous. The house and its "ghosts" were getting the best of her.

She felt the prick of tears, and willed them to come, but as usual, they would not. What was wrong with her? She knew the house, her relationship with her mother-in-law, the divorce, the garden—it had all been too much. But she couldn't even cry. Not once, since she and Howard separated had she shed a tear. Her friends and daughters were impressed by her remarkable composure, but Lily did not need the marriage counselor to tell her that this inability to cry, to really grieve the loss of her marriage, was not at all normal.

I'm not afraid of ghosts from the past as much as I'm afraid of the ghosts of my future, she thought. *Or am I quite simply, going nuts?*

Lily stirred the soup again and sat down at the table. A cloth of lacy sun/shadow fell across its surface from the tall window and open French doors. The azaleas nearest the house had popped into bloom, and the sun released their faint aroma.

(Everyone will tell you that azaleas have no aroma, and Lily had been assured it was something else she was sensing—some nearby honeysuckle or unseen jasmine vine, perhaps, but Lily was convinced it was the light bouquet of the azaleas she was enjoying).

Glass-fronted pine cabinets showed off her mother's blue and white china, a reminder of the modest, homey kitchen of her girlhood when her parents were still living. The smell of the soup on the stove top mingled with the soft fragrance of roses. A favorite abstract highlighted the single bare wall. Her daughters' framed photographs smiled at her from the tiled counter top. Now, for this moment, at least, the house was hers and she felt at home.

Lily forced away all thoughts of Mrs. M's discontented spirit and started in on the stack of McVay memorabilia. By lunchtime she'd separated personal correspondence, long-defunct legal documents and the like, and photos into neat piles. The letters and documents were placed into large, zippered plastic bags to be perused later. Next she narrowed the most useful pictures down to a dozen or so that covered almost every view of the spectacular back garden.

It was just as she remembered it—with one exception. In the oldest photo, a man in overalls with blonde, almost white, hair stood with his hand on the shoulder of a small boy. She recognized the boy as Howard. The man and the boy grinned at one another as if sharing a secret joke while they posed beside a lovely, circular pond. Water splashed from an urn held by a kneeling maiden in its center.

It was difficult to tell exactly where in the garden the fountain was located, but a section of brick wall could be seen behind it, so Lily was fairly certain it had been in her back yard at one time. Why would Mrs. McVay have gone to the trouble to remove such a lovely pond and statue that so perfectly complimented her garden?

Lily closed her eyes and imagined the splash of the water, saw sunlight reflecting on the constantly moving surface. If only another, similar pond and statue could be installed. It would be just right. Just right, but impossible on her budget.

She groaned then reminded herself that there was good news—her memories of the garden and more importantly, her vision for its restoration were right on track. She couldn't wait to show Will.

Lily's moment of tranquility was interrupted by the simultaneous clamor of lawn mower, buzz of weed eater, and roar of leaf blower coming from the front yard. It was Herbert Adams' Azalea City Lawn Service with his crew of yard men and enough equipment to tend a small farm.

"The pine straw! I almost forgot," she said aloud.

Compared to her rear garden, the front was miniscule, taking Herbert and his men only minutes to "service." If she didn't hurry, she could miss them. As it turned out, she didn't need to worry.

A persistent breeze had strewn the fast food wrappers all over her front yard. (Lily had totally forgotten about the blonde litterbug in the red convertible.) Thanking Herbert for cleaning it up, she busied herself showing his men where to put the pine straw, and Lily put the odd occurrence of the trash-tossing blonde out of her mind.

By the time Will came through the back gate, pine needles blanketed the beds along the porch and beneath the azaleas. The day before, she had weeded out beneath the hydrangeas and freed them of honeysuckle and stray jasmine vines. A small mountain of leftover straw was piled beside the shed. Next to it was a pile of aspidistras, roots intact.

"What's all this?" Will stopped midway through the yard. He stood with his long arms outstretched looking as happy as an aphid in a pansy bed.

"This," said Lily proudly, "is the entire street's pine straw and," she continued with a flourish, "Mrs. Pringle's discarded aspidistras, all donated by my extremely nice yardman, Herbert Adams. He even had his men put the straw in those beds for me."

"You and Mr. Adams do very good work," said Will. "The aspidistras are just what we need under the magnolia."

"That's exactly what Herbert said," said Lily.

"They'll be a pain to plant around those roots, but we can do it. Those things will grow anywhere."

"Also, I found paint leftover from the house to spruce up the shed. I thought a window box and a Bermuda shutter on its little window would brighten it up. Oh, and I found some old pictures. They're in the kitchen. Which reminds me I need to check on my soup." She started up the steps, then remembered her manners. "Will, would you like to stay and have some chicken soup when we're done?" It was the least she could do, after all his help.

"That'd be great. Thanks."

Will hauled in some topsoil and the two of them went to work under the magnolia tree. The exertion made conversation impossible, but the silence was easy, enjoyable even.

They worked well together, and after a couple of hours the trim on the shed had been scraped, readying it for fresh paint, and a thick ring of the long, tropical–looking leaves encircled the base of the old tree. They looked terrible.

"It seemed like such a good idea, too," Lily said.

Will walked over and threw an arm around her shoulders.

"Where's all that optimism you had earlier?" He looked at Lily's skeptical expression and laughed. "Don't worry. I've got some shiny new ones that will camouflage these. It'll look fine for your party," he said.

He gave her a small hug of encouragement and left his arm there a little longer than was necessary. He got the hose and gave the new bed a good watering. He took a long sip from the hose, and held it out for Lily.

She couldn't remember when water had tasted so good.

7.

Why me, Lord?

Lily switched on the radio. They had their soup with lots of French bread at the kitchen table, but they were still hungry, so Lily filled two of her favorite blue and white bowls with vanilla ice cream and a few homemade cookies. She drizzled a bit of amaretto over the ice cream and served it with coffee. When they were finally full, Will pronounced the meal "outstanding."

"This is a great room," he said, looking around. "It's just like you, you know?"

"Thanks." *What a nice thing to say*, she thought. "It's my favorite room in the house. Would you like to see the rest of the place?"

Will showed a surprising amount of interest in the changes she'd made and was very complimentary about all of her ideas. He asked questions about everything—from stains and paint colors to hardware and light fixtures. When they got to the parlor, however, the first thing he commented on was the portrait over the mantle.

"I assume that's Mrs. McVay. She looks pretty intimidating."

"She is definitely that. I mean was definitely that."

"I'm surprised you keep her up there."

"I tried to give her to Howard—he's my ex-husband." Lily sighed. "But he said she belongs here."

"Do you always do what you ex-husband tells you to do?" he asked.

"No, of course not," she answered a bit too quickly.

Will continued to stare at Mrs. McVay for a while, his hands jammed self-consciously in his back pockets. *Even her picture intimidates people*, thought Lily.

She looked at Will's strong profile, the tanned skin already full of laugh lines, and hoped Mrs. McVay could read her thoughts: *Do you have any idea what he and I are doing to preserve your memory? Why do I get the feeling that you're still disapproving of everything I do?*

Mrs. McVay continued to glare at the two of them.

Lily narrowed her hazel eyes at the portrait. "After the party, I think I might just donate her to the Garden Club, to hang in their headquarters. They would love to have her, and I think she would be happy there."

"You talk about her like she's still here," said Will. He shook his head, a wry smile playing across his features then looked directly at Lily. "I guess the past is hard to get rid of sometimes, isn't it?"

Lily sat on the arm of the sofa and looked back at him thoughtfully. "Yes, it certainly is." She smiled. "I've about decided that the trick is to simply leave it in the past where it belongs. Sort through it as best you can, then move on and don't look back. Once the soiree is over, I plan on doing exactly that."

"Good. A crazy old lady once told me the past can only follow you if you let it. I think she's right," said Will.

"Thanks to you, I think I'm going to be able to put the McVays to rest."

"Thanks to me?" He looked a bit panicky, and she realized how her comment sounded.

"I mean because of the garden."

"Oh, I see."

Will sat in the club chair opposite her. "You know, you're one of the few people who hasn't asked about my past. I ... Well, I appreciate it."

"Oh, I'm as curious as anybody," she said. "I just know how it feels to be under the town microscope."

"Because of your divorce?"

"You know the whole sordid story, I guess."

He looked a little sheepish. "Yeah. You know how small towns are. That may be the one thing I prefer about big cities. Not as much gossiping going on. They're all too busy."

"I hate to admit this to you, Will, but New York is one of my favorite places."

"That's because you live here."

"You're probably right. It always makes me appreciate small-town living when I get home from a big city."

Will was quiet for a while, then said, "Since you were nice enough not to ask, and since I know your story—I admit, I was curious and I asked about you—I'll tell you a little about myself. Besides, some of the stuff going around about me is worse than what happened."

He leaned forward, rubbing the tops of his knees with his palms. Lily figured he was trying to decide where to begin or maybe just how much he wanted to tell her.

"I was in way over my head in New York. Not so much where the work was concerned, but when it came to firm politics and personalities. I was the original babe in the woods. They recruited me hard and made all over me when I first got there. And I believed it, thought I was Teflon man or something. I ended up in some pretty big trouble, got involved with someone I had no business being involved with, just about got myself disbarred. Your basic first-year associate's nightmare."

"I'm sorry," said Lily, and she meant it.

Sitting there with his long arms resting on his knees, shaking his head, Will looked like an oversized little boy who'd lost his new puppy. It was all she could do not to go over and console him. A *lot*.

"But you didn't get disbarred. Why didn't you start with another firm somewhere else?"

"My reputation was pretty well shot. But the real thing was, well, when everything went to hell and I got fired, I felt kind of relieved. I couldn't wait to get back home to the nursery. Every good memory I have growing up happened there. Fishing, sailing, working with my aunt and uncle and reading the books they bought for me. They were great people." Glancing up at Mrs. McVay, he said, "They saved me from my stepmother." An embarrassed grin worked its way across his face. "And her from me, I guess."

"They sound like wonderful people," said Lily, remembering her own sweet parents.

"Yeah, they were. Looking back on it, the only disadvantage was that there weren't many other kids around. It made me kind of a loner, I guess. My aunt used to tell me that I was an old soul. She also said that I should always have my hands in the dirt."

"Now that was good advice. You definitely inherited a green thumb from somewhere."

"All I know is I'm starting to feel like my self again. I was never suited to big city living, but needed to get all that big shot stuff out of my system to know it."

So there it was, but with precious few details. Lily was dying to ask exactly what it was that he'd done. Who was the "someone" he'd gotten involved with? After he'd complimented her on her lack of nosiness, she didn't dare pry.

"Well, I'm glad it all worked out for you. New York's loss is definitely my gain," she said, grinning at him.

He grinned back at her. "You sure are easy to be around, Lily McVay," he said.

The air suddenly became chilly, and Lily rubbed her arms to warm herself. She thought she detected a faint mother-in-law aroma, but Will didn't seem to notice, so she didn't mention it.

Instead she said, "Why don't I show you the pictures of the garden? They're in the kitchen."

"It's pretty much how I thought it would be—and should be again," said Will when he'd finished looking over the photos. "I wonder what happened to the pond and fountain."

"It's a shame they're gone," said Lily. "I can't figure out exactly where in the garden they were. And why would Mrs. McVay get rid of it? It was the *piece de resistance*, as they say."

"I think it's still there. The pond, anyway."

"What do you mean? Where?"

"You know that patch of dead stuff in the middle of the yard? I think the statue was removed, but the basin is still there. Someone planted shrubs in it, and they died. Maybe they couldn't get enough water or something. We'll find out when we remove them. It'll be a dirty job, though."

"Are you sure you want to get into that. You've done so much already. We can just take out the dead bushes and fill the space with impatiens or something."

"Impatiens? No way. Like you said, it'll make the garden. Besides, it'll be good advertisement for me when I start landscaping for profit. Lots of people will see it at your party."

"Okay then. Just remember, I gave you an out, and you didn't take it."

In spite of her excitement at solving part of the mystery of the fountain, Lily stifled a yawn.

Will flashed that grin at her. "Out late again last night?"

"No. Not late." Actually, she had fallen into bed exhausted before nine o'clock, but she didn't see any reason to admit this to Will. "I am tired, though," she said.

"Why don't I take these pictures with me," said Will, putting their dishes in the sink—something Howard rarely did. And Lily could not help but think how nice it was to have Will in her kitchen.

"Sure," she said. "I'm going to sit here and go over these letters for awhile. There might be something else about the garden in them."

He started for the door, then stopped. "You still interested in seeing my azaleas?"

"I was afraid you'd forgotten."

"How about Thursday? Right after we look for that pond? And I'm cooking fish for supper if you're interested."

"Great. What can I bring?"

"Just yourself. See you Thursday."

After he left, Lily decided she was in too good a mood to immerse herself in the McVay past. Heading up the stairs to the luxury of a hot bath, she took a deep breath and sighed gratefully. The aura of Mrs. McVay and the old lady/abandoned beauty parlor smell was blessedly absent. Maybe her dearly departed mother-in-law had decided to haunt Heather and Howard for a change. Lily envisioned Heather sniffing the air in her plush Chicago hotel suite and wrinkling her pug nose.

"Nice thought, anyway," Lily said, pulling off her clothes.

Looking in the mirror, Lily decided that the hours of yard work were definitely a benefit to her body. Her arms seemed firmer, and she'd definitely dropped a few of the excess pounds she'd gained from all the self-pity snacking she'd indulged in. However, her coppery hair and fair skin looked tired and had seen too much sun. Vowing to double up on the sunscreen and wear a hat from now on, she found a tube of the new conditioner her hairdresser had recommended for her "color-treated" hair.

"I don't see how they expect anybody to read these tiny directions," she grumbled aloud, reaching for her cute round reading glasses that for some reason made Lily look like a nearsighted owl, and holding the tube under the light.

"Hmm, twenty minutes under a shower cap."

Finding one of the clear plastic ones they give out at hotels, she applied the white goop, and donned the cap. When she looked back in the mirror, it was quite a sight.

"No matter how bad things get, never get a job in a cafeteria," she told her unsettling reflection, thinking that none of those food-serving women cruelly forced to wear plastic caps ever looked as bad as she did.

She went to turn on the water in the tub for a nice soak when she noticed that the soap dish was empty. She'd gotten some at the store that morning, but left it on the kitchen counter.

"Damn." She covered herself—well, almost—in a terry wrap, slapped the Velcro tabs together and headed back down the stairs. It was just as well she'd forgotten the soap because the radio was still on.

Aretha Franklin was getting started on Chain of Fools. Lily found the soap, but turned the music up and decided to indulge her tired, overworked muscles in a splash of wine. Before she knew it, she was singing along with Aretha. Seconds later, she was dancing with Aretha.

Before the song was half over, she *was* Aretha, belting it out, the bar of soap her microphone. She couldn't sing like the fabulous Ms. Franklin, but she definitely had better moves. Twisting her hips and stretching her arms over her head, she felt the taut muscles in her back relax.

"Chai-ai-ai-ain of foo-ools." With her back toward the porch, she moved closer to the door, taking a step with each beat, rolling the stress out of her hips and legs. "Chai-ai-ai-ai-ain." She swung herself around in a circle facing the yard and—

"Will!"

He was standing at the door, transfixed, a weird little smile plastered on his face. As she stood there staring back at him, she remembered her visage in the mirror, then added to this vision her no-holds-barred Aretha impersonation. Could she be imagining his face there, like she was imagining Mrs. McVay's unwelcome presence?

Please, God, let me be insane, she thought. But no such luck. He was there, in the flesh. Her next emotion was fury at him for catching her, and before she knew what she was doing, she had snatched the door open. She stood there, clutching her little terry wrap together, snatching at her owl glasses, which were stuck to the shower cap and refused to come off her face.

"Uh, I'll have the turnip greens and the succotash, ma'am," said Will. The cafeteria worker image was obviously not lost on him. As soon as he got the words out, he dissolved into howls.

"Oh, my God!" she screamed, but then started to laugh, too. They were both laughing so hard, she was afraid she'd break out of her Velcro, and he would lose his balance and fall down right there on her back porch.

When he could breathe again, he wiped his eyes and said, "I'm sorry. I forgot the pictures. I thought you'd still be here—you know, looking through the letters." He started laughing again. "You said you were going to look through the letters," he repeated.

She grabbed up the envelope of pictures and handed it to him, staring him in the eye. "You ever tell anyone about this, and you're a dead man."

"I swear," he said, holding a palm up and stifling a chuckle. "I'm really sorry." He took the pictures and mercifully, he left. But as she shut the door behind him, she heard his laughter echoing in the night.

Lily poured the rest of her wine in the sink as "r-e-s-p-e-c-t" started from the radio.

"Shut up, Aretha," she said.

8.

Azaleas and Fried Fish

The pond was right where Will thought it would be. With the help of a shovel and his strong back, the dead shrubs came up easily, bringing mounds of hard-packed dirt with their roots.

The two gardeners were more like two kids finding buried treasure. They soon exposed a circular rim of old bricks a couple of inches high. More digging revealed the depth of the fountain to be about three feet. The pipe that had run to the statue and the platform on which it had once stood were still intact. What had become of the statue itself remained a mystery.

"Good work, Sherlock," said Lily.

He was grinning like crazy at her (was he picturing her in her shower cap and reading glasses, dancing like one of the fools in Aretha's song?), but all he said was, "Thank you, Watson. And now, are you ready to see some weird azaleas?"

"I can't wait," she said, forcing the Aretha memory from her head and grinning back at him. "But I've got to clean up first. Give me fifteen minutes."

She was surprised that the mention of a shower didn't prompt some remark about the spectacle she'd made of herself several nights before, but he didn't mention it. Lily was impressed. She wouldn't have been able to resist the temptation to tease him if the situation were reversed.

Twenty minutes later they were on their way, windows down. "A little l-i-t-e country," as Will called it, playing on the truck's radio. About the time they got to the end of Lily's street, Lily glanced in the rearview mirror and noticed a shiny, black Hummer pulling up in front of her house. Further down the street, keeping its distance was a red car, possibly a convertible.

Could it be the sexy litterbug? Was it worth involving Will in a confrontation and explaining the whole sordid story of the phone freak to get a glimpse of someone who may or may not be the phantom trash tosser? Lily decided it was not. She put all unpleasant thoughts out of her mind, thanked the fates she had narrowly escaped Dwayne Bond and focused on the road ahead.

Before she knew it, the town was fading into pine, scrub oak and patchwork farm land, its squares dotted with cows or striped with new corn. Brick farm houses, at odds with the natural beauty around them, looked as if they'd all been constructed by the same uninspired builder. Many had permanent produce stands that marked the seasons by their content, and were wisely situated under the nearest big pecan or oak to catch the shade. Hand-painted signs advertised: Peaches—better than Chilton County, Silver Queen Corn, home-grown tomatoes, and the occasional Bible verse or team slogan, Roll Tide being the most prevalent.

As they got closer to the river, which emptied into the bay, which ultimately became part of the Gulf, the landscape grew lush and smelled of pine and water.

Before Lily knew it, they were headed down an oyster shell-covered drive that curved through palmettos, wild azaleas and moss draped oaks. These gave way to the classic Southern Indian azaleas, those huge evergreens from China and Japan that had found the perfect home in the fickle Gulf Coast climate. They lined the drive the rest of the way to the house, most in full bloom. But there was nothing that resembled a nursery anywhere in sight.

Will seemed to read her thoughts and said, "I'm going to run in my place first and grab a quick shower."

He smiled at her for a second, and she thought sure he was going to say something about her recent performance, but he simply stopped the truck in front of a rustic, one and a half-story house on short pilings. The place was typical of what used to be "camps" along the river. Most of these cottages or camps had been updated and expanded as the price of waterfront property soared.

Will was wisely following the trend. His house was set back from the water, just before the property began a gentle slope to the wide part of the river. A weathered board and batten exterior, wrap-around porch and high, pitched roof suited the climate and casual living. A single dormer window indicated an abbreviated second story.

One side of the porch was given over to lumber and sawhorses, but the other held rocking chairs like the ones Lily remembered from her childhood. The seats and backs were woven, the arms wide enough to accommodate a plate of fried chicken and a glass of iced tea if you were careful.

"Make yourself at home," said Will. "I need that shower, then I'll show you around."

Lily looked toward the river where a small dock with built-in benches beckoned. A sailboat mast was visible through the trees. Lily had sailed quite a bit when she was young, and she wondered what kind of boat he had. Her curiosity about Will's renovations won out, though, and she followed him inside.

One large room dominated the front of the house and faced the river. A fireplace flanked by windows accented one end, a stairway with a landing the other. The floors were wide heart pine desperately in need of refinishing. The room's main furnishings were a computer desk piled high with books and papers, an overstuffed mildew-colored sofa, three fishing rods, and a freshly painted green picnic table which sat at the stairway end of the room.

This "dining area" opened into a tiny disaster of a kitchen, which opened onto a screened section of porch. Lily assumed a single bedroom and bath filled the other corner of the rectangular bungalow.

She'd barely had a look around before Will emerged, scrubbed clean and looking incredibly handsome in a faded polo shirt, wearing a pair of fresh but wrinkled jeans. Lord, he looks young, thought Lily in spite of the shadow of a beard on his face. But he grinned at her like she was the best thing he'd seen all day, and Lily decided that his smile was the best thing she'd seen all day, and maybe she would just enjoy it.

"Now for the guided tour," he said. Gesturing grandly

toward the sofa, he stated, "The living room." Then he moved to the picnic table. "Dining room," he said with a small bow. "And now for the kitchen." He walked into the tiny space. "Would you like a beer before we begin the second phase of the tour?"

"Yes, thank you," laughed Lily, attempting and failing to mimic his serious tone.

He stuck a beer into a faded purple hugger that said "Geaux Tigers" in gold letters and handed it to her.

"Are you an LSU graduate?" she asked.

"Yes, ma'am, and proud of it," he said. "You?"

"Roll, Tide." She raised the hugger in salute.

"Ah, the University of Alabama. And also very proud, I see," he said and shook his head in mock sympathy.

She rolled her eyes in response and followed him back across the living room into a still-steamy hallway that smelled deliciously of masculine soap. He stood back so that she could look into the bedroom, which was larger than she'd expected. An unmade, cannonball bed, a pine dresser and a rocking chair that was obviously meant to be on the front porch didn't come close to filling it up. Large, double windows on two sides were uncovered.

The bathroom was also surprisingly large with a window that looked out into woods that encroached on the house. The medicine cabinet's door sagged open. There on the bottom shelf was a box of tampons and a black hair clip.

"Well, unless you need to use the facilities, that's about it," he said, his tone noticeably less cheery. He knew she'd noticed the cabinet.

And so what if he did? she thought. *Why would he care? And why do I?*

"The azaleas await," she said finally, smiling and matching his earlier tone.

"Yes they do," he said and looked at her as he had when he'd come into the living room after his shower.

It was a look Lily was getting very attached to.

They walked away from the river along a path through woods dappled with late afternoon sun. The air was scented with the crisp smell of pines and the soft aroma of spring flowering everywhere. When they came to the nursery proper, it was all

Lily could do not to groan out loud. There was a tattered shed and a roofless greenhouse overgrown with weeds. A mound of clay pots had been reduced to rubble. Someone had obviously used them for target practice.

"This is the bad news," he said, suddenly looking tired. But then he brightened. "Now for the good news."

He led the way between the two dilapidated structures into a clearing, and it was an onions-to-orchids experience. Rows of freshly potted plants sat beneath shiny new sprinkler heads. About a third were in bloom, the delicate pinks, purples and reds dazzling in the slanting rays of the sun that rippled through pine boughs overhead. Through the sides of a large greenhouse, tables of seedlings and hanging baskets were visible. A golf cart and trailer were parked nearby.

"Good Lord, did you do all this?" asked Lily, grinning with excitement at the transformation.

"Not exactly. I've had a crew out here helping me."

"Was this in the same shape as the first buildings we saw?"

"Worse. But this is where most of the azaleas were, so I wanted to get to it first, sort everything out before they started blooming so I can tag them. I'd really like to see this town covered in azaleas like it used to be when people came from all over to see them."

"That would be great," agreed Lily. "It's such a shame we've lost so many."

"It's a shame all right." Will shook his head, and Lily could see that this was really important to him. "There aren't many places in the world where azaleas bloom like they do here," he continued. "But I've talked to your friend, Helen at the botanical gardens, to the chamber of commerce, to several beautification committees and to some private owners of commercial property. They're all behind getting this town back in shape, azalea-wise."

"How did it happen? Losing the azaleas, I mean?"

"When the big box stores came in, everybody started buying things they saw there, including azaleas bred for northern climates. Those azaleas were a disappointment here. And people bought other things as well that are great up north, but can't take our heat and rainfall amounts. Also, people got smaller yards. These giant Southern Indian azaleas take up a lot of room—like in your yard. Smart planting and pruning can avoid that, and we've got lots of smaller varieties now." He smiled and scratched his head. "Sorry. I'm starting to sound like one of the lectures from the Master Gardener Program. Come on. I'll show you."

Will unhitched the trailer from the golf cart, and they set off. Azaleas and camellias, some as big as trees, were all over the property. Lily recognized many, but was amazed at the variety of size and color. There were azaleas with ruffled blooms and a variety the color of strawberries in cream, some with tiny buds that Will assured her would bloom well into May, extending the typically short season. They had been bred by Will's aunt.

There was an acre that had been tilled and was ready for planting.

"Don't tell me you're growing vegetables, too," said Lily.

"Zinnias. If I get around to it. My aunt grew them every year and sold them at the farmer's market and from a little stand out on the highway. She had me make a big, hand-painted sign that said 'Petals' and hang it on the front of the stand. People left money in a box nailed to the wall and took bouquets of flowers—mostly zinnias arranged in painted coffee cans and mason jars."

"What happened to it? The flower stand, I mean."

"Hurricane got it. By then my aunt was too old and sick to fool with it anyway." He frowned and shook his head, suddenly looking much older. "What do you think the chances are of the honor system working in this day and time?"

"I would say pretty good. We have a lot of nice people around here, you know."

"Now that you mention it, I have met some very nice people lately," said Will flashing the grin—the one that made her feel she might just melt into a puddle right there in the golf cart.

As promised, Will fried up fresh fish. He'd gotten a casserole of cheese grits from Pumpernickel's, the gourmet take-out shop, loaves of hot crusty French bread from the bakery, and made a very tasty green salad. It was warm enough to eat outside, so they took their plates and glasses of a crisp pinot grigio onto the porch. Afterglow soon gave way to candle glow as the night closed in around them.

Their conversation was easy and light. They shared the same sense of humor and laughed easily together, bringing out the best in one another. By the time the meal was over and their wine glasses empty, the soft night air was thick with an almost magnetic attraction—very physical and entirely mutual. Aware of the increasing sexual tension, Lily steered the conversation back to the neutral ground of gardening, and she and Will shared the dreams of their respective futures.

The idea of raising flowers and selling them was shaping into a real plan for Lily, and Will's enthusiasm and suggestions furthered her resolve to make it happen.

"You could use that acre we saw this afternoon. I'm kidding myself thinking I've got time to do it, and I'll be seeding it soon. I know you're busy with your garden, but after the party, you'll have plenty of time."

"It sounds like you'll be doing all the work."

"Tending it, and dealing with the business end is the real work."

"This is a very tempting offer," admitted Lily. *Why on earth am I hesitating?* she wondered.

"I've already talked to people who'll buy as many as we can deliver," Will continued. "And I tell you what. I'll get my workers to throw together a new stand out by the road. I've still got the old Petals sign. We'll see if your faith in the honest natures of our neighbors is deserved."

"Speaking of faith in people, how do you know I'm someone you want to work with? You really don't know me that well."

"I've gotten to be a pretty good judge of people, I think. I know you're a hard worker." He smiled. "And one hell of a dancer."

Lily groaned. "Just when I thought that was all behind me!"

"You didn't really think you could live that down, did you?"

"I may have to kill you after all, Will."

"Don't worry. As long as you behave, your secret's safe with me. Remember, I'm not opposed to blackmail—on a small scale, of course."

"It's very generous of you, and I'm definitely thinking about it," she said. "It would be nice for your aunt—for her memory, I mean."

"Yeah. She'd like this idea," agreed Will. "She would've liked you, too." He looked at Lily. "You remind me of her in a lot of ways."

"You were very fond of your aunt, right?"

"Very fond," said Will.

9.

What are Friends for?

Lily had spent most of the past weeks toiling in the garden alone since Will was tied up with the nursery, and she amazed herself with all she'd been able to accomplish. The downside was that she was becoming acutely aware of how much more enjoyable her labors were when Will was around. The garden was assuming "project" status again. The work was starting to feel like … well, like work.

Another entry on the positive side was that Howard was mysteriously but blessedly absent lately (more business trips with the executive assistant, Lily guessed), giving her a respite from his and Heather's interference.

There was also the fact that Howard still didn't know about Will. The few times he had stopped by, Lily was alone in the yard. She didn't have the mental energy to get into it with Howard about charity and how McVays simply did not accept it and all that baloney. So she took full credit (or blame, when it came to the ultra-critical Howard) and didn't mention her able-bodied help.

Howard's absence also gave her plenty of time to enjoy a quick weekend visit from her daughters. Having the girls at home and having them to herself without Howard and Heather to contend with made her realize just how much she missed them.

Though she was determined not to make them feel guilty about her being alone, she had to ask, "Do you ever think about moving back here?"

"I do," said Elizabeth, who had returned to graduate school

after trying on a couple of careers.

This didn't surprise Lily. Elizabeth had always been the mama's girl, the homebody. Virginia, on the other hand, was much more the adventurer. But she had recently parted ways with yet another young man, and seemed restless, was calling home more often, so Lily told herself it was a possibility.

"What about you, Virginia?"

"I think about it. I can't imagine being away from Sissy." (The pet name they had called each other since they could talk.) "If she moves back, I might have to, too."

Lily didn't press the point. The fact that it was a prospect was more than she'd hoped for. She turned the conversation back to the garden, asking her daughters' opinions on the improvements.

Elizabeth and Virginia loved every change Lily had made and were brimming with unique ideas for the garden party. Their enthusiasm and youthful perspective on livening up the soiree energized Lily's sagging determination to see it through.

"So, Mom, tell me about this guy, Will, who's been helping you," said Virginia.

"Well, he's very nice," began Lily.

The twins' identical eyebrows rose instinctively as they looked at one another and then their mother.

"I'm sure he is nice," said Elizabeth, "but that's not what I meant." She grinned at her sister. "You wouldn't be interested in this guy, would you?"

"No," Lily said too loudly and too quickly. Clearing her throat nervously, she added, "He's just been so helpful—more than he needs to be. That's all." She waved a hand dismissively and said, "He's just a young guy—in his thirties. Just very nice. And an excellent gardener."

She turned her comments to Will's horticultural abilities, careful not to mention any positive, personal traits, such as kind, interesting, funny, good looking, sexy, etc.

"So, have either of you heard from Howard?" asked Lily, more to change the subject from her gardener than anything else.

She wished she hadn't asked. They'd both had a few brief notes from Howard with postscripts in the form of bubble letters and happy faces from Heather. And Heather had called them a few times, just to chat. As it had before, the knowledge that Heather was involving herself with her daughters upset Lily. Heather had Howard. Wasn't that enough?

The vague premonition of Howard and Heather and Elizabeth and Virginia as a family with Lily left out in the cold was needling the periphery of her delicate resolve, making her doubt she might be able to turn things around, that she could have a normal life again. It even obscured the hopefulness she'd felt when the girls mentioned moving home. Home with her? Or home with Howard and Heather? She knew she was being dramatic, ridiculous even, but she couldn't help herself.

Lily made a half-hearted attempt to shake off the panicky feelings, but once the girls had left her alone in Mrs. McVay's house, she gave into self-pity, and her feelings of uncertainty grew into mountains of dread.

Instead of reveling in the impressive amount of progress she had made, she saw only an overwhelming amount of work to be done, an impossible job. What had she been thinking?

Though pots of healthy, new aspidistras sat nearby, the ones she and Will had planted under the magnolia looked awful. Looking at the new ones, knowing how difficult it would be to get them in the ground among the web of magnolia roots just made her tired.

The beds behind the shed were still full of vines that needed to be tied up or dug up or chopped down or something. But what? She was too tired to make a decision.

The sad excuse for a pond with its exposed pipes and chipped, dirty bricks was like an ugly sore. It mirrored the feeling in the pit of her stomach when self-doubt and pessimism suffused her, causing recent and old wounds alike to fester, and leaving her feeling they would never heal.

It was all Lily could do that night to go through the bedtime routine of washing her face, brushing her teeth and falling into bed and wouldn't you know it, just as her head hit the pillow, the phone rang. *Please don't be the phone freak,* Lily thought, but somehow she knew that's exactly who it was.

"Rosemary McVay is there, you know," said the muffled, little-girl voice. "She hates y—"

Lily noticed her hand shaking as she hung up the phone. Why was this nut doing this to her? Who was she? Where had she heard that voice before? But she was too tired to think and drifted into an uneasy sleep.

She dreamed that she was furiously weeding her flower beds only to have the weeds return as soon as she'd pulled them. Honeysuckle vines were everywhere, choking the azaleas and hydrangeas and camellias, threatening to take over not only the yard but the house—even Lily herself if she stood still long enough. She dreamed that while she slaved away in the yard, sweaty and dirty, Mrs. McVay, Howard, Heather, and her daughters, all attired in white linen, sat on the porch—like a family, drinking lemonade and ignoring her.

Dream? *It was a nightmare, just like that infernal garden*, she thought the next morning as she woke up exhausted. When she went out front to retrieve the morning paper, there was a fresh layer of trash strewn across the lawn. The phone freak/litterer— it had to be the same person, right?—had struck sometime during the night. Surely there weren't two people who hated her this much. Her mood went from bad to very bad.

Two cups of coffee didn't help. They only gave her a case of the jitters. She choked down a piece of toast and headed out into the backyard. And where was Will anyway? Maybe he'd had enough. Maybe he wasn't coming back. Helen would send someone else, but the thought of finishing the garden without Will …

She looked around her at all that was left to be done and couldn't think where to start. Hearing the earnest call of a cardinal from a limb in the magnolia tree, Lily walked over to see if she could get a glimpse of her favorite bird. Maybe the sight of its lovely red feathers would perk her up. Looking into the gnarled, old branches, she heard a rustle in the leathery leaves above her. That's when it hit her. Literally adding insult to injury, the cardinal decided to relieve himself at that moment, splattering her tired face.

"Damn bird!" Lily screamed at the bird who simply fluttered away to another less unpleasant perch. Tears of frustration stung the backs of her eyes, but would not come, denying her even that relief.

The terra cotta frog she had given Mrs. McVay all those years ago grinned stupidly at her. Wiping the bird poop off of her face with the hem of her T-shirt, Lily yelled, "Damn frog!" She walked over and kicked it as hard as she could. It landed in the day lilies with the unmistakable sound of cracking crockery.

"Hey, don't take it out on him."

It was Will, with his incredible sense of timing, who had come through the back gate in time to witness the whole sordid scene. Lily was mortified at being caught once again in an unflattering moment. Will had observed her not only losing her temper but taking it out on an innocent bird and an inanimate frog.

"Oh, great. Now you show up!" She stomped into the house, and just in case he hadn't noticed that she was angry, slammed the door before going to the kitchen sink to try and clean the bird droppings from her face and hair.

She heard the door open, felt him come up behind her. He took the dish towel out of her hand, ran it under the water and gently wiped her face.

"Damn birds," he muttered, wiping her hair. "Damn frogs."

"I can't believe I broke our good luck charm," she said, the nearness of Will calming her down. "I feel terrible about it. I love that old frog and his stupid grin. Kicking him was childish."

"True," said Will, "But understandable, under the circumstances." He dabbed at her hair. "Besides, I think he can be fixed," he said softly.

"You do? Really?" This made her feel much better.

"Yeah. And cracks add character. He'll look all the better for it." He put the dish towel on the counter, but did not move away. "Lily, what you've managed to do with this place is amazing. You're amazing. To tell you the truth, I'm relieved to see a little anger from you. You'd have to be a saint to keep on the way you've been, working your ass off, trying to please that … ex-husband of yours. Everybody gets discouraged. I know I do. Sometimes I want to get on that little boat of mine and not look back, sell the river property and all the headaches that came with it. Seeing what you've accomplished, how you're turning things around in your life when you got such a—a raw deal … It's kept me going when I wanted to chuck the whole nursery idea."

"Really?" She was feeling immensely better.

"Yeah. Really. This garden of yours is too much for two people, much less one doing it herself." He grinned at her. "If you weren't so pretty, I'm not sure I'd have even volunteered to help you. Anyway, I'm sorry I haven't been here much these past weeks. I guess I let you down."

"No, you have your nursery business and your house to work on and your gardening classes. We both have way too much on our plates right now."

Lily tried to explain to him how she was missing her girls, how upsetting it was to have Heather wheedling her way into their lives, how she hadn't slept, had foolishly skipped breakfast.

Will listened sympathetically. When she was finished, he surprised her by wrapping his arms around her. They stood like that for several minutes, not speaking. Lily thought she might faint, it felt so good. How long had it been since someone had held her like that? It was just what she needed, but she had to admit there was an added benefit. It was Will holding her. The feel of him against her, the smell of him, his strong arms around her, just the sound of his breathing, knowing he cared—nothing and no one could have made her feel any better.

Finally he stepped back. "I hope that was okay. Me hugging you like that. I guess it was kind of …uh, inappropriate, you being my boss and everything."

"What? No, it—it was very sweet." She smiled at him. "It was exactly what I needed. Thanks."

"My pleasure," he said and grinned at her in that teasing way he had. "Besides, there's just something about a woman with bird crap in her hair."

"Oh, my God. I'd almost forgotten about that."

But it made her laugh.

"I tell you what," said Will. "You go wash your hair and I'll fix you something to eat. Do you like scrambled eggs?"

After a shower and a tasty two-egg omelet, Lily felt like a different person. She and Will tackled the aspidistras and he showed her how to tie the vines up with all-but-invisible fishing wire. He found some spackling compound and mended the frog's bottom where he was cracked. As Will set him back on the steps, Lily marveled at the fact that both he and Will were still smiling at her.

Will had just left for his class on landscape design and Lily, still in her work clothes, was sitting on the back steps when the doorbell rang. She went to the door and found Helen and Marilee standing on her front porch holding wine and the familiar brown and green bags from Pumpernickel's.

"We're here to celebrate your gardening progress," said Marilee. "Besides, I owe you."

"You do? For what?"

"You have inspired me—you and an article on time management I read. It was called, *Make Your Time Your Own*, and it was great. You both should read it. Anyway, after thirteen tedious years I have dropped my membership in the Chantilly Club."

"No!" said Helen in mock horror.

"Well, it wasn't easy. The membership is already dwindling."

"No surprise there," muttered Helen.

Marilee bit her lip and frowned at her cousin. "Bitsy Jean— you know she's the one who got me in the Chantilly club to begin with, well, she was just elected president. She made me feel like a dog."

"They say timing is everything," teased Helen.

"Something I've never been known for." Marilee shrugged then grinned like a child who's just gotten away with the whole cookie jar. "But I stood my ground. I am officially an ex-Chantilly Club member. I mean last month's seminar was on researching the history of your china pattern. I was a history major and everything, but really. And next month—two hours on how to brew the perfect cup of tea. I just couldn't do it. Bitsy Jean or no Bitsy Jean. Besides, I'm going to need all my free time for a little enterprise I'm considering."

Helen groaned, but Lily had to laugh. "What now?" she asked.

"I'll tell you later. But first, the garden. I can't wait to see what you've done."

"First the wine," Lily corrected her. "It's just what I need. We've been working all afternoon."

"We?" said Marilee.

"Will and I. You just missed him."

Helen sighed. "Now that's a shame."

Marilee winked at her friend. "Timing's everything," she said.

As Lily led her friends down the wide center hall toward the back porch, she felt a chill and caught an unmistakable whiff of stale perfume and fresh perm sneaking out of the parlor. She shuddered.

"Are you okay?" asked Marilee. "You look like … well, like you've seen a ghost."

No, just smelled one, thought Lily, but since neither Helen nor Marilee seemed to notice, she said, "I just need to take a break. Your timing happens to be perfect."

They went to the kitchen, opened the wine and headed out to the porch.

"Lily, I don't believe it!"

"Such a transformation!"

The exclamations went on as they walked down the steps to get a closer view.

"Is that the same shed that was here?" asked Marilee. "And where did you find that great pot?"

"It's amazing what leftover gray and white paint from the house and a little gingerbread trim around the door did for it. I found that big pot in the flower bed. It has a piece missing, but I just turned the bad side toward the wall. Besides, the cascading petunias and asparagus fern will hide it. Will got the iron window box and bench wholesale," explained Lily. "But it's the same, old shed."

Helen took in the newly-weeded beds lined with fresh pine straw and the lush lawn. "The grass is really coming back," she said, turning in the direction of the old shed. "And when did you get this done?"

Clematis and jasmine vines intertwined gracefully on an arbor that broke a hedge of unclipped boxwood, the clematis in full bloom, the jasmine just beginning. Beyond this, behind the renovated shed, was a small lawn bordered with herbaceous plants. Freshly-painted black wrought-iron chairs and a table sat in its center. An old Cherokee rose covered the back of the shed, spreading onto the brick wall, scenting the entire area with its white blossoms.

"It's like a separate, secret garden," exclaimed Marilee.

"Most of this was here," explained Lily. "It just needed to be cleaned up. Will had his crew from the nursery paint the furniture and fix the gate. I painted the shed and arbor myself, believe it or not. This afternoon we pulled the vines out of the crepe myrtles and hydrangeas by the wall. The vines were twenty feet long, at least. And we wove them through the arbor. We tied the rose to the shed wall with fishing line. You can't even see it." Lily looked around the lovely little space and sighed. "Will is so clever," she said.

Marilee grinned at Lily's enthusiasm and winked at Helen behind their friend's back.

"Will says you're the clever one," said Helen.

"Oh, no, it's Will," said Lily, moving back through the arbor in the direction of the old oak. She pointed back toward the porch. "Look how he filled in these old aspidistras with shiny, new ones. I never thought anything would grow under that magnolia." She grinned at her friends. They walked over to the formerly debris-clogged fish pond by the wall.

"I didn't even know this was back here," said Marilee. "It's beautiful with the water lilies and hyacinths floating around."

"Thanks. We stuck ferns all around the back to hide the bare areas next to the wall. That was Virginia's idea. She and Elizabeth were here for a quick visit this past weekend. They loved everything. And I'm feeling downright optimistic about things. I think it's really coming together. You know, I think even Howard's mother might approve."

"It's incredible," said Helen. "I think Mrs. McVay would love it, although I still don't understand why you care about pleasing her. She was awful to you, Lily, and you were a wonderful daughter-in-law."

"Well, I feel like it will settle something between us if I can restore this garden. There's a lot to settle, though, I admit. As much as she loved Elizabeth and Virginia, she never thought I was right for Howard, and blamed me that there were no McVay heirs."

"But it was Howard who didn't want any children, right?"

asked Marilee.

"Yes. He said his stepdaughters were enough. I couldn't tell his mother that, though."

"So you took the blame," said Helen. "Lily, there's such a thing as being too good."

"Don't give me too much credit," laughed Lily. "I was just trying to keep the peace. It wasn't worth getting into it with Mrs. McVay and Howard."

She heard the phone ringing on the porch, and since the garden tour was completed, she went to answer it.

"Hello?"

Nothing. It had to be the phone freak again.

"Anyone there?" said Lily sarcastically.

The muffled woman-child voice said, "Mrs. McVay, please."

"Who is calling?" asked Lily.

"Mrs. McVay, please," the voice repeated. "She's there, you know."

Lily calmly hung up the phone, but Helen and Marilee could tell by the look on their friend's face that something was wrong.

"Who was that?" asked Marilee.

Lily paused a moment, then decided the time had come to confide in her best friends. She had hinted at her admittedly irrational ideas in her conversations with Helen, but hadn't quite laid it all out on the line before now. If they thought she was insane, well, there was nothing she could do about it.

"I've been getting these prank calls for weeks now. At first the person would just sit there, breathing. Then she started asking for Mrs. McVay. But not me, Howard's mother."

"She?" asked Marilee, her eyes huge with excitement. "Heather! It has to be Heather! That little—"

"I don't think it's Heather," Lily said.

"A telemarketer," said Helen. "With an outdated list."

"That's exactly what I thought," said Lily, "But just now after she asked to speak to Mrs. McVay, she said, 'She's there, you know.' And I've heard that voice somewhere before. It's a child-like voice. But I just can't put it with a face or a name. Something weird is going on. I thought it was just my imagination, being in this house and everything, but now I'm not so sure."

Lily told them about the strange chill that came and went with no discernible cause and the pervasive old-lady smell that was literally haunting her. She confessed that she often talked to her dead mother-in-law's portrait.

A look that said *you do what?* passed quickly over Marilee's face, but she said nothing. But Lily had gone this far with her true confessions, so she added that at times the portrait seemed alive with condescension and criticism.

"The other strange thing is that no one else seems to notice any of it—except maybe Howard, and he's not talking.

"I think if I can get this garden back together, Howard's mother might finally be able to rest. And frankly, give me some rest," she added. "I guess you both think I've gone crazy." She sighed and said, "Sometimes I think I have, too."

"I don't think for one minute you're crazy," said Marilee. "Stressed, maybe, but certainly not crazy. I'm not too sure about the ghost thing, though." She bit her lip, frowning. "But that's just me," she added quickly. "Stress can't explain the phone calls. Are you sure you heard correctly? You said the voice was muffled. I mean maybe it's all a lot of coincidence." She reached over and patted Lily's hand. "I guess it doesn't help that Mrs. McVay is buried across the street."

"No, it doesn't," agreed Lily. "What do you think, Helen? You're being awfully quiet."

"I think Mrs. McVay's haunting you alright, in one way or another. And I think the first thing you have to do is change your phone number, maybe get an unlisted one. The next and most important thing is to sell this place and get out from under the McVays once and for all. Finish the garden if you have to, get through the garden club party, and then move on for heaven's sake. Get on with your life."

"I agree, but everything seems so unfinished, I can hardly think that far ahead—to selling the house. I mean, I intend to, but I have to get the garden done and have the soiree first. It all comes back to restoring the garden. This is where all the answers are. It's hard to explain, but I just know it. But who is calling me? And why? If I change my number, I may never find out."

Helen sighed. "I don't know, but if it's so important for you to get to the bottom of what was going on with Mrs. McVay and her garden, you really should talk to Maisy Downey. She's been living back there forever. I bet she knows a lot about the McVays."

"Oh, I don't think so," said Lily. "They didn't have much contact. I don't think she would know anything. Besides, she's such a nut, I don't know if I'd believe her anyway."

"You should give her a chance. She's just a character." Helen started to chuckle. "Remember when she told you you'd die of boredom if you married Howard? She might be a nut, but she sure had Howard and the McVays pegged right."

"What about the fact that she dresses up like a gypsy and reads fortunes at her parties?" Marilee asked.

"The spooky thing is that she seems to know what she's doing. I mean she has a knack for really seeing things, I've heard," said Helen.

Marilee rolled her eyes, shook her head, and resumed her Maisy reminiscences.

"What about the time she showed up at the club in a bikini?" she said. "She had to be seventy if she was a day."

"Lord, what made you think of that?" laughed Helen.

"Oh, I don't know." Marilee grinned evilly. Maybe all that gray, Spanish moss hanging out of the oak tree."

"Thanks for that visual," said Lily, giving Marilee a little slap on the arm.

Helen was howling with laughter. When she caught her breath, she said, "I'm telling you, Lil. Maisy may be outrageous, but she doesn't miss a thing. Besides, it's time you two started acting like neighbors."

"I agree," said Marilee. "What have you got to lose?"

"What little sanity I have left? Okay. I'll think about it. If I ever get through back here."

Lily turned toward the fountain base that sat like a wart on the yard's lovely face. "If we can do something with that eyesore, I think we'll have it made."

"I hate to say it," said Marilee, "But maybe you ought to just fill it in again with plants. It looks like quite a job."

Lily frowned. "I'm beginning to think you're right. I'm running out of time and money. It would just make this garden perfect, though—just like Mrs. McVay had it originally." She shook her head and sighed. "But I feel like Will has gone above and beyond the call already, and there's no way I can do it myself."

"Don't be too sure," said Helen. "After seeing all you've accomplished this year, I don't think there's anything you can't do."

"Helen's right. Forget everything I said," said Marilee. "And we can help. Right, Helen?"

"Right."

"Don't say another word," said Lily, "Or I'll start crying. Everybody should have friends like you two."

"Besides the fountain, everything looks great," said Helen, changing the subject back to gardening. "Just like it used to be. I remember coming here as a child. This was always the quintessential southern garden in my mind—the oak with its Spanish moss, the unstructured shrubs, the feeling that the plants are growing right before your eyes, and the smells—not just the flowers, but even the trees and the dirt are fragrant in this humid air."

Marilee sighed. "It's true. But I think you've been writing too many articles for the botanical gardens newsletter, Helen—or reading *Affair in the Azaleas* or something.

"I happen to be reading *The Tycoon's Tryst* which is very well written and has nothing to do with flowers."

Changing the subject, Lily said, "Let's get another glass of wine and see about our supper. I'm starving."

Minutes later they were seated around the table on the porch, eating squash soup and crab quiche.

"Hope you don't mind take-out," said Marilee.

"Are you kidding? This is delicious," said Lily.

"Sure is," agreed Helen. "Besides, as my mother used to say, 'I've never had a bad meal out.' Now, tell me, Lily. What does Howard think about the garden?"

"He hasn't seen it. He and Heather must still be out of town."

"If he hasn't figured out what an idiot he is already, this should enlighten him." Helen waved her fork in the general direction of the yard. "Heather could never pull this off. Lord, I don't understand what he sees in that girl."

"I think Howard has decided he doesn't like girls with brains," said Lily.

"Then Howard doesn't really like girls, does he?" said Helen.

"Very well put," said Marilee, raising her glass in salute. "But really, Howard's just fallen for a young set of boobs like so many men before him." She shook her head and rolled her eyes in disgust. "The expression, 'no fool like an old fool' has been around a long time. And for good reason."

"What causes it?" asked Helen. "The old fool syndrome, I mean."

Lily sighed. "It's probably not the young girls they're chasing so much as their own youth—the same thing that causes women to get face lifts and spend hours at the gym, I guess. Maybe it's some surge of the psyche's version of adrenaline, a last gasp to combat old age."

Helen laughed. "Hold that weird thought while I get dessert."

"Let me help," said Lily, getting up stiffly from her chair.

"No. I'll help," said Marilee. "You've done enough work for one day, Lily."

Lily relaxed into her chair and enjoyed the early evening air. Spring, with its astonishing freshness and renewal was her favorite season. But it wasn't just the transformation of seasons she was feeling. It was something personal, too. She thought about the "old fool syndrome" and how the concept was slightly more manageable now that she'd given it a name.

She even toyed with the notion that maybe she shouldn't be so hard on Howard and others of his ilk. Instead of snickering at the victims of OFS like cruel adolescents making fun of one another's acne, shouldn't she react with a little compassion? Was empathy the Clearasil for the soul that Howard and so many other similarly afflicted mortals needed if they were to navigate this puberty of middle age? She took a sip of her wine and thought about it.

Hell, no! That kind of attitude might help Howard, but I need to stay mad for a while longer if I'm ever going to get to the other side of all this.

She breathed deeply of spring air, took in the amazing beauty of the garden. Though she could still see the lovely yellows and pinks, the white blossoms seemed to glow in the gathering twilight, and she noticed lightening bugs twinkling in the bushes. Yes, she was still angry, but like the fireflies in her azaleas, there was a flicker of light at the end of this tunnel.

Helen and Marilee returned with small squares of tiramisu on Lily's blue and white china. Marilee set a plate before Lily, sat down, ran her fingers through her hair, then clasped both hands together. This was a gesture of excitement that Helen and Lily had witnessed many times—usually just prior to the announcement of Marilee's latest foray into the business world.

Sure enough, she said, "I've decided to join the Mayfair Group!"

Helen and Lily searched each other's faces for a clue as to what on earth the Mayfair Group was.

"You know. The Mayfair clothing line." When she saw recognition in her friends' faces, she raced on. "I was approached by Mary Largely Darling herself! She thinks I'll be perfect for the job."

"Wait a minute," said Helen. "Who is Mary Largely?"

"And how on earth did she get that name?" said Lily, who, after growing up in the south thought she'd heard it all as far as bizarre appellations were concerned.

Marilee looked from one of her friends to the other as if trying to decide which inane question she should answer first.

"Mary Largely Darling is only the top field marshal at Mayfair. My suite mate from college, Laura Jane Jones—you remember her, don't you, Helen? Anyway, Laura Jane grew up next door to Mary Largely and now sells Mayfair in Savannah, and she told me that Mary Largely has made more money than anyone else. It is really a compliment that she called me personally. I've heard she almost never does that." Marilee paused and gave a slight shudder. "She's also very formidable, I hear."

"Not an unusual character trait in a field marshal," muttered Helen.

"Or it could be a reaction to going through life named Mary Largely," said Lily. "I hope she's thin."

Helen rolled her eyes and said, "I'm sure there is no such

thing as a large Mayfair associate."

Marilee smiled at her plump cousin. "Beauty comes in all sizes, Helen." Coming from anyone else, that statement would have been patronizing, but Marilee was sincere. "Well, now that you mention it," she continued in a confidential tone, "there is a little story about that."

Lily and Helen leaned closer.

"According to Laura Jane, Mary Largely is from a very old, prominent Georgia family. The first daughter of each generation is named after the first Mary, who was a duchess or something, and Lord, you know there's nothing that thrills southerners like finding royalty nested in the family tree somewhere. Anyway, each Mary is given her mother's maiden name which results in a double name. For example, Mary Largely's mother was Mary Tully and her grandmother was Mary Buck. You know how all the debutante selection committee members love a double name."

Helen rolled her eyes again. "As long as it's not Wanda Fay or something like that."

"Exactly," agreed Marilee. "Anyway, Mary Largely was not only the first daughter, but the only daughter of Mary Tully. As you can imagine, she was terribly over-indulged." Marilee sighed and shook her head. "She was lazy and became addicted to sweets. By the time she hit puberty, she weighed in at over two hundred pounds." She paused to let this visual sink in then pressed on. "Her name became a liability, to say the least. You can imagine how much fun she had in high school."

Marilee looked like she might cry. Helen was chuckling while Lily was doing her best not to laugh.

"Y'all are going to feel bad when you hear the next part. Mary Largely was stood up for the prom by her own nerdy first cousin."

"You're right. That is sad," said Lily.

"The boy was probably pressed into service by his well-meaning mama," said Helen.

"I think it was something like that," said Marilee. "Anyway, Mary Largely took a fistful of Mary Tully's sleeping pills. Due to her weight, I guess, the result was just a mercifully good night's sleep, which was just what the poor thing needed. The whole episode was a nightmare, but do you know it shocked her into action? By the time she started her sophomore year at Agnes Scott, she was a size six and has never gained the weight back." Marilee collapsed back into her chair. "Laura Jane says the experience made her tough. I think 'mean as a cottonmouth' were her actual words. So you see, it's very important that I get on the good side of Mary Largely Darling."

"And how are you going to do that?" asked Helen.

"Well, I'm going up to Atlanta in a month or so. It's the first show to preview the fall clothes."

"Fall clothes? It's not even summer yet," said Helen.

"I know," agreed Marilee. "It's crazy, but it's just the way they do things. And in answer to your first question," she continued with exaggerated patience saturating her voice, "I'll just have to impress Mary Largely with my enthusiasm for Mayfair. They're having a big fashion extravaganza and reception." Her hands went through her hair again. "And guess what?" Marilee was leaning across the table, a huge grin on her face. "I can bring two friends!"

"You're talking about the two of us, I suppose," said Helen.

"Of course! Who else would I take? I mean, what are friends for?"

Lily looked out at the pond still half filled with dirt and debris, its antiquated plumbing exposed to the world and thought about all she had left to do. She looked at Helen who didn't own anything without an elastic waist-band and who was now running her fingers through her own short, silvery hair. Unlike Marilee, it was not a gesture of excitement. Going to Atlanta for a fashion show was the last thing either of them wanted to do.

Thinking they had surely misunderstood, Marilee said with even more enthusiasm, "I can take both of you!"

Oh, what the heck. I'll be in desperate need of a break by then, thought Lily. "It'll be fun," she said. "Right, Helen?"

"Oh, yeah," said Helen, with only a trace of sarcasm.

10.

It was a Dark and Stormy Night

Lily had just popped several frozen heath balls into her mouth when she became aware of a distant ringing. Her cell phone. In her purse. But where was her purse? Oh, yes. In the dining room.

Sure enough, the leather hobo bag was ringing away on Mrs. McVay's Empire Revival mahogany dining table. Stubbing her toe on one of its claw feet, she dug through the overpriced purse with its pockets and compartments all of which had been added to avoid just such a moment of frustration as this.

Lily snatched at an unzipped makeup pouch, dumping the contents into the black hole of the bag, found the roll of antacids she'd bought after her last conversation with Howard, discovered a penlight key chain, a midget umbrella, and finally the phone. *Be prepared*, she thought, the motto of every Boy Scout and woman over fifty.

"Hewwo."

"Hey, Mom. This is Elizabeth. You into the chocolate again?"

Lily laughed. Her daughter knew her too well. "How do you know it's not carrot sticks I'm eating?"

"Because I've just been into the Oreos. It's got to be a genetic thing. Anyway, Virginia wasn't sure if I should call, but I just had to warn you."

Lily felt the heath balls grow hard in her stomach. "Warn me? What's going on?"

"Dad called. He and Heather … Well, they are engaged. Sorry to be the one to drop this bomb on you. Mom? Are you still there?"

"Yes. I'm just really surprised. I never thought he would—"

"I know. Virginia and I can't believe it either. When he called, Heather got on the phone and said they were going to come to grandmother's—I mean your house to tell you in person. I didn't want her to catch you off guard. I don't know if it's spitefulness, her coming along with Howard to tell you or if she's really a total idiot. Probably both. She's a spiteful idiot. And she wants to be our buddy. That's what she said, 'We're going to be best buddies.'"

It disturbed Lily to think she could react with such delight upon hearing these unkind comments from her daughter. So instead of offering an opinion of Elizabeth's assessment of her soon-to-be wicked stepmother, Lily simply said, "I have a feeling Heather has plenty to keep her busy." *Like husband-stealing, spending Howard's money and social-climbing,* she thought to herself. "I wouldn't worry about it too much. It'll work itself out."

"I should be consoling you, Mom. Sorry."

"You are consoling me—by caring enough to call. When are you two coming home?"

"Not until right before the garden club party. I'm swamped at school, and Virginia is traveling so much with her job, there's just no time right now."

An hour later, Lily had caught up on her daughters' lives and given Elizabeth a report of the local happenings and gossip. She told her daughter about Marilee's latest venture, but did not mention Marilee's and Helen's assessment of grandmother McVay's presence in the ancestral digs. She described the latest improvements to her garden, but was careful to share only professional details about her gardener.

The news of Howard's impending marriage was a shock—sort of. Since being bushwhacked with the news of their affair, she had learned to always expect the worst. As depressing as it was, it was rather offset by the guilty pleasure she took in the knowledge that Heather was making no headway in her campaign to win over the twins. Shock. Sadness. Relief. She was full of too many emotions, and they all seemed to be at war in her brain. What she needed was a good run and some fresh air to clear her head.

The phone rang again, but Lily decided to let the machine get it. She heard her own voice playing a brief message as she changed into her running shoes. "This is the McVays. Please leave us a message."

She hadn't changed it when Howard left and told herself it was for safety reasons. Wouldn't want anyone to think she was living there alone, now would she? As she grabbed her key and headed to the front door, she heard the strange, muffled voice of the phone freak.

"I'm calling for Rosemary McVay, please. I know she's there." Then Frank Sinatra started to sing about how he'd done it his way. He was still singing as Lily ran out of the front door.

It was humid and still and she could smell rain. She'd only gotten half a block down the street when distant thunder announced a much-needed downpour.

By the time she got to the narrow end of her block the wind had picked up. She decided that exercise was more important than staying dry, so she turned the corner and increased her speed down Pine Street where Maisy Downey lived. She passed other joggers and walkers who obviously felt the same way, taking their chances that the weather would cooperate just a little longer, determined to get their exercise in.

Soon Lily was in front of Maisy's house with its row of Formosa azaleas and was reminded how Maisy had put mannequins in them for the city's azalea parade and how it had delighted the children. *Crazy old thing*, she thought, but remembering put a smile on her face as she ran.

The pleasant memory vanished however, as she turned the corner and ran along the high iron fence of the cemetery. Out of habit, she slowed her pace as she approached its open gates. She had a clear view of the McVay mausoleum sleeping peacefully beneath a very old magnolia tree there in the gathering dusk.

She stopped, catching her breath and moved just inside the entrance to get a better look. Someone had placed a large bouquet in front of the crypt's little door. Street lights, which had just come on, caught on gold and silver ribbons intertwined with Bird of Paradise, Tropicana roses and glitter-covered greenery. It was monstrous and had Heather written all over it. Lily was sure there would be a card—ensuring that Heather would receive credit as the devoted future daughter-in-law—but she had to see it for herself.

It was a bit spooky roaming around a cemetery in the growing darkness, and not something she would normally do, of course, but curiosity got the best of her. She had to read that card before the rain got to it. Besides, there were still people on the street. She would be fine.

The flower arrangement, which turned out to be the scariest thing in the grave yard, was even more horrible up close. Lily imagined the spirit of Mrs. McVay bouncing off the walls inside the tomb and felt just the tiniest bit sorry for her as she bent close to read the inscription.

Sure enough, the card, prominent on its plastic stick, read *With Love, from your future daughter-in-law, Heather*. Written in bubble letters with a smiley face at the end. As Lily stood staring at the atrocious bouquet, pondering the bizarre-ness of the moment, a bolt of lightening came out of nowhere and struck a nearby tree, severing one of its limbs. It fell to the ground with a crash. As if this wasn't loud enough to wake every dead person in the place, it was accompanied by a deafening clap of thunder.

At first she thought she had been struck by the lightening, but then decided it was the loud clap of thunder that had knocked her to the ground. Actually it had frightened her so badly that she'd jumped and tripped over the irregular stones around the mausoleum's perimeter. As it began to sprinkle, Lily found herself crumpled against the front of the building having narrowly missed landing on the offensive Heather-posy.

Lying there against Mrs. McVay's final resting place, she had a vision of her mother-in-law and her with one thin wall of mortar separating them. It was a terrifying image.

Oh, my God! What if it was Mrs. McVay's angry spirit that had caused the lightening? Lily had done it now, making fun of Heather's flowers on the old woman's grave.

"I've got to get out of here," she said aloud, trying to push herself up. But she was stuck. At least her foot was. She couldn't see what was holding it in the dark and the shadows, but she just knew it had to be Mrs. McVay literally reaching out from the grave.

"Let go!" she screamed. "Please let me go!"

"What the hell?"

Lily looked around to see Maisy Downey and two other very old ladies holding umbrellas. They were all staring at her.

"Lily McVay?" said Maisy.

"Yes, it's me. I'm stuck. To Mrs. McVay's grave."

"That's a pretty nerve-wracking predicament, all right," said Maisy. "Hermione, do you have your little flashlight?"

The flashlight was produced, and Lily was embarrassed to see that it was not the withered hand of Mrs. McVay that had her, but the ornate hinge of the mausoleum door that had the loop of her shoestring held fast in its grasp.

She quickly unhooked it and stood towering over the diminutive Maisy and her two umbrella-wielding friends, feeling even sillier because of her size and their level-headedness in rescuing her.

"Thanks. I guess I let my imagination run away with me. Cemetery in the dark, thunder and lightening and everything."

"Not to mention those flowers," said Maisy.

Her friends shook their heads. "Tsk, tsk, awful," they agreed.

"Are you sure you're alright, dear?" asked Hermione.

"Oh, yes. Just embarrassed."

"Don't be," said the other friend, who introduced herself as Frances before reading the card from Heather. She, like the rest of the town, knew the whole story.

"So Howard is marrying that little piece of work." She looked down at the bouquet. "Well, Rosemary, it's no less than you deserve," she said to the woman interred in the mausoleum. She reached up and patted Lily's shoulder. "It'll never last, you know, Howard and ..." She looked at the card again, nearly poking Lily in the eye with her umbrella. "Howard and Heather. It'll never last."

"What does she care?" said Hermione. "She's got that cute, young gardener mooning over her. Will, isn't it? Maisy, isn't your cute gardener named Will? I could tell the way he was talking about our Lily, here—remember at your house the other day when you were asking about Rosemary McVay's garden, all he could talk about was Lily? He's real taken with her."

"Really?" said Lily, before she realized that she was smiling. "I mean, that's great because he has been such a help. With the garden," she added quickly.

The sprinkle was becoming a steady rain, and Maisy said, "Well we'd better go before we all get struck by lightning or drown."

Lily thanked them all and when they'd exited the cemetery grounds, hurried down the street to her house where she was greeted by the remains of someone's (the sexy blonde in the convertible, maybe?) pig-out at the Dairy Queen. Wrappers, bags, a milkshake cup and a few leftover fries decorated her front yard.

Maybe tomorrow she would stake out the Dairy Queen and see if the red convertible showed up. Maybe not. It would be too dangerous. I mean, Lily could eat her weight in DQ fries. She gathered up the trash and let herself into the house. The insistent, blinking light of the answering machine caught her eye when entered the kitchen.

"Enough, already!" she said aloud, and pressed *erase*. Tomorrow she was getting an unlisted number.

By the time she finished her shower, steady rain had become the anticipated downpour—the kind that promises to continue off and on throughout the night. It was exactly what the garden needed.

Lily flossed, brushed, put on her favorite cotton nightgown, and opened the windows a bit to hear the rain on the banana leaves beside the house. Then she snuggled into bed with Jay Gatsby for perhaps the tenth time. (Her book club, The Bayside Bibliophiles, was doing F. Scott Fitzgerald this month.) She'd just been reintroduced to Nick Carraway, the narrator, when the phone rang.

"Oh, no not the phone freak," she prayed out loud. I mean after all she'd been through that evening, what could be worse? She picked up the phone as if it might bite her.

"Hey, Babe. Bond here."

"Who?"

"Bond. Dwayne Bond. Listen, my plans kinda fell through for next weekend, and I thought, hey, maybe we could make up for lost time, you know?"

"Lost time? I don't understand," said Lily.

"Well, we got off on the wrong foot on our first date, Babe."

"You mean our last date," said Lily, who was too tired to beat around the bush with the car wash king.

"Listen, the ex and I were just talkin' that night at her house. She's kind of lost it since our divorce, called me right before I picked you up, went all hysterical-like. I just thought I could kill two birds with one stone, so to speak. Thought we'd drop by her place, all behave like reasonable folks then we'd be on our way. Should've known better."

"I'm sorry, Dwayne, but—"

"Listen, it isn't often that ol' Dwayne gets to take out a Cadillac like Miz Lily McVay and then he goes and screws it all up. Let me make it up to you."

"I'm sorry, Dwayne. I'm kind of seeing someone right now," she lied. But it worked, and she finally got rid of Dwayne Bond. Another good reason to get an unlisted number.

No sooner had she put the phone down than it rang again.

"Lily, this is Will." She heard music and voices in the background. "Hope I'm not calling too late. I tried earlier, but I guess you were out."

"Oh, no. It's not too late." She wasn't about to tell him she'd been jogging around the cemetery in the rain with three old ladies (four, if you count her deceased mother-in-law.)

"I was wondering if you could do me a favor."

"Anything. I think I owe you into the next century."

"Helen told me that you used to sail. I'm having some trouble with the boom on my boat. I have to be under sail to fix it and need someone on the rudder while I fiddle with it."

"Some favor. I'd love to. I haven't been sailing in forever."

Familiar girlish laughter now joined the music and voices.

"What?" said Will. "I'm sorry. I'm having a hard time hearing. Just a minute. Hey, can you keep it down a little?"

The laughter and voices subsided a bit.

"I said I'd love to."

"Great. I have to work at the nursery in the morning and have a plant path class tomorrow afternoon," he yelled. "I could pick you up at three-thirty. We can grab something to eat after, if you want."

"Okay. See you tomorrow."

Lily hung up the phone and was again enveloped in the serenity of her bedroom which seemed all the more serene after the noisy conversation she'd just had. She had an idea that the laughter she'd heard was the effervescent Jaime. If so, while Lily kept company with the imaginary Nick Carraway, Jaime was out with the very real Will.

But Lily was lying on crisp linens, breathing rain-fresh air, listening to raindrops drumming on the banana leaves. Jaime was likely sitting on a barstool breathing second-hand smoke while listening to a second-rate rock band. *Thank God it's Jaime and not me*, thought Lily.

Doesn't that tell you something? admonished the voice of reason. You and Will are almost a generation apart. Except for gardening, what do you have in common? And the fact that he called you when he's out with Jaime – he wouldn't do that if he was interested in anything but a friendship, right?

But the words of Maisy's friend, Hermione, were louder: … *all he could talk about was Lily. He's real taken with her.*

Instead of dwelling on the sweet little old lady's words, instead of listening to the little pragmatist in her head, Lily simply opened her book and returned to West Egg, home of the great Jay Gatsby.

11.

Porch Traffic

The next morning Lily fairly levitated out of her bed as the realization hit her that sailing meant she would be expected to wear a swimsuit. Anxiety about the phone freak and getting an unlisted number were quickly replaced by direr concerns. Like being seen by Will in a swimsuit, never mind a five-year-old one with a bleach stain in the back!

She was in good shape for her age. People told her that all the time. But that does not mean good shape in general, she reminded herself as visions of Jaime and Heather in bikinis tap-danced across her vulnerable middle-age psyche.

Ha! Middle-aged if I live to be a hundred. I'm flattering myself saying I'm middle-aged, she tortured herself.

Finally, after two cups of coffee and an extended pep talk with herself, she calmed down. In the first place, this was not a date. It was another pseudo-date. *Not a date … Not a date …* she repeated like a mantra. And after all, Will had seen her in shorts and a T-shirt or tank top countless times.

There wasn't that much left to reveal. "Just upper thighs and back flab," she groaned aloud. Well, there were no improvements she could make to her body at this late date. There was, however, the matter of swimwear. She grabbed her keys and mentally geared herself up for that futile quest—a flattering swimsuit.

After all, it was sort of a date. And there was a dinner involved.

She was racing out of the door (she had only six hours in which to find a stylish, youthful, concealing, flattering, appropriate-for-sailing suit), when who should pull up but everyone's favorite lovebirds, Howard and Heather. Howard had the decency to wear a pained expression, but the future Ms. McVay bounded out of the car, grinning like a jack-o'-lantern.

She was carrying a large gift bag done up in pink and white. Lily figured it must be a consolation gift in the who-gets-Howard competition. But Lily was hardly able to give the package a second glance because of Heather's hat. It was a wide-brimmed, black straw affair. The crown was done all over in plastic shrimp, crabs, and fish floating in a nest of Spanish moss. Faux okra and tiny bottles of Tabasco sauce completed the chapeau tableau. Then it dawned on her. The Mad Hatters' Annual Seafood Boil!

Howard had obviously bribed someone to get Heather into the Mad Hatters Club, which "owed its effectiveness to its selectiveness" and was almost impossible to get into. Lily realized that there was a spot available only because she had recently tended her resignation. It was just like ever-efficient Howard to accomplish two chores at once.

First of all, Heather was dangerously close to exploding with happiness over being the newest Mad Hatter, and in being replaced by Heather, Lily had been properly chastised (in Howard's twisted reasoning) for dropping out of the Hatters. Knowing that the Hatters' unofficial slogan was "we're effective because we're selective," Lily figured Howard must have called in every social favor owed him to pull this off.

Lily chose to ignore the gift as well as the hat and informed Howard that she couldn't invite them in because she was on her way to an important meeting, which wasn't a lie since her newest bathing suit was five years old and had a bleach stain on the back. Heather's face fell. She'd obviously hoped for an extended torture session.

"Howard and I were hoping for a tour of the garden. I can't wait to see what you've been doing back there. This is our contribution," she said sweetly, holding out the bag. She adjusted the seafood topper, but Lily didn't bite, though it was hard to ignore.

"Lily, I wanted to get your input on my mad hat!" she said finally. I know you were in the Hatters for … gosh, forever, and I just got in. Howard says they get very upset if your hat is lacking

in creativity. I want to make a good impression. For Howard."
She smiled sweetly up at him from beneath a dangling crab
claw.

That same uninspired idea of plastic gumbo fixings on
a bed of moss had turned up on six different hats at the first
Mad Hatters' Boil thirty years ago. The members, who would
be ready to boil Heather on general principles, would not be
amused at this sub-par effort.

"It's perfect," said Lily.

Lily dug through the pile of tissue, finally retrieving a box that
held a set of very large copper wind chimes. As she held them
up, the pipes clanked and clattered beneath two intertwined
H's, sending birds, squirrels and a few cockroaches scurrying
for safety.

"Oh, my," said Lily.

"Heather had it made especially for the soiree," said Howard,
looking at his watch. For the garden, you know."

"I thought we might hang it on Mother McVay's back porch
where everyone can enjoy it during the party," said Heather.

The suggestion was met with an uncomfortable silence, for
neither Lily nor Howard, to his credit, was able to summon any
words in response. Finally, Heather poked Howard in the arm.
He cleared his throat.

"We have some news, Lily. Heather and I are getting
married."

Even though she'd known what was coming (*thank you,
Elizabeth*) it was quite a shock to hear Howard speak the
words.

She managed to congratulate them and even heard herself
say that she hoped they would be very happy.

Heather, oblivious to Lily's discomfort or possibly because
of it, chattered on about a destination wedding, and how she
couldn't wait to tell the twins that she wanted them to serve as
her maids of honor.

"Won't that be adorable? Identical maids of honor!"

She and Howard were headed to the airport, she babbled
breathlessly. On their way to Bermuda to scope out places for
the nuptials and honeymoon.

Howard started to blush at this last part, checked his watch once more, and Good Lord, look at the time. They would miss their plane if they didn't get going. He hustled a very self-satisfied Heather into the Lexus and made his getaway down the street.

Lily felt the hot tears pricking at the backs of her eyes and welcomed them, needed them to pour out of her, but as usual they would not. Instead, she was left standing alone and dry-eyed on Mrs. McVay's front porch clutching the ugliest wind chimes in the county and feeling like she'd just been slapped.

12.

The Pseudo-date

By the time Will showed up at her door, Lily had found the closest approximation of a flattering swimsuit (yes, it was black) in the city (with an hour to spare) and was wearing it under a pair of denim shorts and a green, fitted T-shirt that just happened to be the same color as her eyes.

Leather flip-flops exposing a fresh pedicure, a baseball cap with her shining coppery ponytail pulled through the back, sunglasses, and an oversized bag of essentials completed the ensemble.

Will was similarly attired, and it occurred to Lily that this was the first she'd seen of Will's exceptionally cute legs.

She grabbed her bag from beside the door and stepped out onto the porch. The vision of Will, wearing an old pair of shorts, a faded, blue T-shirt, and a grin that could melt your heart was definitely the best thing to grace her front porch that day. He looked so good that he almost erased the specter of the prospective honeymooners and their hellish wind chimes.

"Nothing like a prompt first mate," he said, taking the bag from her and steering her toward the running truck.

Lily laughed. "Promptness is about all I can promise. It's been awhile since I've sailed."

"I'm not worried," he said. "Once a sailor, always a sailor."

It was just after five when they sailed Will's vintage nineteen foot boat, the Recess (named during Will's law school days) under the old drawbridge, exited the mouth of the river, and entered the choppy waters of the bay. A good breeze had sprung out of the southwest carrying the impatient warmth of summer laced with the last coolness of spring. Thanks to Daylight Savings Time, they had several hours before dusk.

Lily took the tiller while Will attacked the malfunctioning boom with a wrench and a can of WD-40. He had her alternately steering into the wind, filling the sails and coming off the wind, allowing the sails to flap loosely. It was great practice for her rusty sailing skills. Just when she was beginning to feel relaxed enough to notice the wind in her hair and the late afternoon sun dancing on the water, Will stowed his tools in a large tackle box.

"All done," he exclaimed, obviously proud of himself.

"Already? I was just starting to get the hang of it."

"She's all yours," he said. "I usually have to do all the work on this boat. Now that I have an able-bodied crew, I think I'll have a beer and take in the scenery. Would you like one?"

"Maybe later. I don't want to jeopardize my first mate position."

"Oh, I don't think you have to worry about that," he said, grinning at her.

After an hour of skimming across the bay, the sun grew warm on their skin. Will took off his shirt, revealing predictably great abs—and a farmer's tan. His arms, face and neck were several shades darker than his chest and back, but this was barely noticeable due to the complete lack of anything other than muscle anywhere on his body. Besides, the dark hair on his chest, which Lily decided was just the right amount, was all she could think about at the moment.

"I've always been a redneck at heart," he said, grinning self-consciously. "Now I've got the tan to prove it."

"Me, too," said Lily. She hesitated only a second, all the insecurities about her body surfacing momentarily. She fought them back and took a deep breath. *It is what it is*, she thought and pulled off her shirt. Unlike Will, she had been vigilant with the sunscreen. However there was a faint hint of the same tan lines as Will's from her hours in the garden.

Will laughed. "That's a pretty good tan for a redhead, I guess, but there's no way it qualifies you for redneck status."

"You rednecks are such snobs," teased Lily, throwing her shirt at him and getting out of her shorts.

"That suit definitely doesn't qualify as redneck swimwear," said Will, checking out her new purchase.

"Thank you. I think I'll take that as a compliment."

"You're welcome. It was given as one. I hope it's not just for looks, though, because I'm ready for a swim."

"Sure," said Lily, though it was a little early in the season and late in the day for swimming as far as she was concerned.

Will dropped the anchor, grabbed a couple of flotation cushions and went overboard. Lily climbed hesitantly onto the side of the boat.

"How's the water?"

"Cold. Feels good, though. Come on in before you fall in." He patted the extra cushion.

Lily, being the good sport that she was, jumped in.

"Cold is an understatement," she sputtered, but after kicking around for awhile, she warmed up. "You're right. This feels great. It's been ages since I've been swimming."

"Best exercise there is. I try to swim in the river every day. It gives me a second wind after working on the nursery all day." He paused. "Speaking of the nursery, have you thought any more about getting into the zinnia business?"

Of course she'd thought about it. It would be a perfect way for her to see if her business plan would work without getting overextended financially. Still, she hesitated. Where was the "voice" when she needed it? What if things got weird working with Will everyday? She couldn't deny that she was very attracted to him, which was ridiculous, she reminded herself for the zillionth time.

If she gave into her feelings, she was bound to get them hurt. No, crushed was more like it. But what was the alternative? To go back to living in an emotional vacuum? But what happened to becoming an independent woman? Doing it on her own?

She didn't want to start depending on another man when the remains of her marriage were still warm. Besides, she had taken enough charity from Will. Good grief. You sound just like Howard! Finally, "the voice" kicked in. *You're over analyzing again, Lily. Everything has risks attached, if not financial then emotional. Take a chance, for God's sake!*

Lily wasn't sure whether it was really the voice or pure

rationalization, but she cleared her throat and said with determination, "I have been thinking about it. A lot. I don't want to take advantage, because you've helped me so much already, but if your offer is still good, then, yes, I've decided it's exactly what I want to do."

"Great. Because it's all planted and we already have orders. You'll just have to harvest the flowers, keep the stand stocked, and make deliveries and keep up with the paperwork."

"Oh, is that all?" she teased.

They talked about the business end of zinnias, watched a couple of grinning dolphins playing not twenty feet away, discussed the finer points of the McVay garden, and placed bets on two kids racing their boats around the bay. Lily entertained Will with stories of Marilee's business misadventures.

They watched as two parents tried again and again to get their young son up on a pair of beginner skis, moaning along with them each time he fell. Finally the dad looked at his watch and began pulling the tow rope into the boat.

"One more time, okay?" the boy yelled.

The dad looked at the mom who gave the boy a thumbs up. "You can do it, Jason. Just hang on. Don't let go for anything!" she called to him.

The boat took off, the boy wobbling this way and that as he was dragged through the foaming wake. When Lily was sure his frail arms would give out, he stood up, that unmistakable grin of a first-timer on his face.

His dad turned toward the boy and with his free hand balled a fist and brought his elbow into his side as proud as any professional athlete. The mom clapped her hands over her head so the boy could see.

"Way to go, kid," yelled Will, and Lily realized that she, too, was cheering.

They laughed at themselves for getting so caught up in the child's triumph and traded first-time-I-got-up-on-skis stories.

"There's nothing like growing up around the water," said Will. "I didn't realize what I had until I moved away for awhile."

"So no regrets about leaving the big city?"

He ran a hand through his wet curls, then made a fist,

squirting water up through his fingers. He watched the water for a few seconds and looked back up at Lily.

"Truthfully, I have a lot of regrets. Not about leaving, but the circumstances." He smiled at her. His white teeth flashed against his suntanned face, but the dark blue eyes still held traces of that regret. "I'll tell you all the gory details one of these days, but not today. We don't want to get into swapping war stories on a day like this."

"I agree," said Lily, "Besides, I've been spending entirely too much time in the past lately. The present is a lot more interesting."

Will smiled at her. "It certainly is."

The breeze had picked up, turning Lily into one big goose bump. They climbed into the boat, and she wrapped a beach towel around her shivering shoulders.

"You look like you could use a bowl of gumbo," said Will, pulling his shirt on. "With this wind, we should be back in no time."

He raised the anchor and headed for the bridge. By the time they cleared it, the sun was beginning to set. The sky was purple and orange and red on blue. The scene rendered again in an impressionistic reflection of itself on the choppy bay. The sky to the north was bruised to a threatening blue-black.

Will motioned toward it. "Looks like we might be in for a thunderstorm. The nursery could sure use it. I just hope it can hold off till we get back."

Will's house wasn't too far up the river. With the stiff breeze, the return sail was quick, as promised. A few large drops fell as they put the boat in order, but they were safely inside before the downpour. Will flipped on the front porch light and one lamp inside, which sent a warm glow over everything. He insisted that Lily have first crack at a hot shower.

The medicine cabinet was free of all feminine paraphernalia, she noticed. What is going on with the Will-Jaime relationship anyway? Deciding not go there because it would surely ruin her date—if that's what this was, she hopped into the shower. The steam released the piney, masculine smell she'd noticed on her first visit.

It's just deodorant and soap, for God's sake, she told herself, but it was making her positively light headed. *I've been celibate entirely too long,* she reminded herself again, turning off the water. She twisted her wet hair into a rubber band, applied a minimal amount of makeup, tugged on jeans and a long-sleeved white shirt and turned the bathroom over to Will.

Now that she was warm again, Lily checked out Will's home improvements while he took a shower. On the plus side, the floors had been stained and finished to perfection, bringing out their hidden patina, and a great looking suede arm chair had been added to the "living room." The bad news came in the form of a mounted trout hanging on the wall above the front door.

"Hey, what do you think of the floors?" Will asked from the doorway.

"They're really beautiful."

"Glad you approve. You know your stuff when it comes to doing this kind of thing." He grinned at her. "Ready for that gumbo?"

But when they stepped out onto the porch, the rain began pouring off the roof in sheets.

"Sorry, I haven't replaced the gutters yet," said Will. "Man, what a downpour. This is what my uncle used to call a toad strangler."

"Do you have an umbrella?"

"Nah, don't believe in 'em."

In spite of her growling stomach, Lily had to laugh. Howard would never have been caught so unprepared, and would have been completely turned off by the toad strangler comment, immediately classifying Will's uncle as redneck or déclassé or a hundred other unkind references. Lily was just sorry not to have made the old man's acquaintance.

"Guess we better wait a few minutes," said Will.

Lily curled herself into one end of the mildew-colored couch (mentally picturing it slip-covered in white canvas) and watched the rain through the large, still-bare windows. It was quite nice being warm and dry in the lamp's soft glow while the rain poured outside. Just when she didn't think she could be any more content, Will handed her a glass of wine.

"Hope you like red," he said, sipping from his own glass.

"It's all I have."

"In that case, I like it just fine," said Lily.

"Ah, the joy of a woman who's easy to please," he said, smiling at her. "They're getting to be an endangered species, at least the ones I've run into lately."

"Welcome to our world. You men have just had it too good for too long," she teased, keeping the conversation light although she meant every word she was saying.

"I hope you haven't lumped me into that group. I happen to be a fairly easygoing guy."

Lily tasted her wine and pretended to think about it.

"You know, you are very easy to be around. I am hereby excluding you from the impossible-to-please category."

They sat talking until the drumming on the roof subsided. Will set his empty glass down and stood.

"Ready to go?" he said, holding out his hand.

Lily placed her hand in his like she had on the first day they'd met. But instead of letting go once he'd helped her up, he held on, looking at her, a question crinkling the corners of his eyes. A smile played around one side of his mouth. He looked— mischievous was the only word for it. It was a look as old as sexual attraction itself, and one that few women could resist, especially in a handsome man they had become very fond of.

There were many reasons Lily should have breezed past him and out of the door. These raced through her head as if quickly making room for the long list of reasons to "just go where the feelin' takes you" as Marilee might have put it. Based on her previous dating fiascoes, number one on the list was "I might never get this chance again in this lifetime." The rest were based on pure infatuation and couldn't really be put into words.

Her decision must have registered in her face because Will pulled her to him, let go of her hand and slowly ran his hands along her back, her waist. When he pressed himself against her, she melted into him, her arms sliding around his neck.

"Lily," he whispered. She felt her skin grow warm, felt his breath on her face. His lips touched the corner of her mouth.

"Will! Will, open up! We're getting wet out here!" Female voices were accompanied by laughter and banging on the front door.

Will looked toward the door, which was directly behind them. He made no move to answer it.

"Come on, Will!" The knocking continued.

"You have to answer it," said Lily. She was so disappointed, she thought she might cry.

Will smiled at her. "I can't open it like this."

It didn't take long for the mood to pass, so to speak, and Will finally opened the door.

Jaime and her friend stumbled in.

"Oh," she said. "Didn't know you had company. Uh, have we met before?"

It occurred to Lily that Jaime had most likely overheard Will asking her to have dinner with him and knew exactly who she was.

"Jaime, this is Lily McVay," said Will coldly. "She has the garden I've been working on."

"Oh, yeah. And we met at the martini bar. This is my friend, Kate."

Lily and Kate murmured how-do-you-do's.

Jaime seemed just a little irritated, though she was making an effort to hide it. "So, what is this? A garden meeting? I mean we can come back another time."

"Oh, no," said Lily, relieved that Jaime and Kate hadn't witnessed the almost-kiss. "We're all through talking about the garden, I think."

"You know, I had a few more things to go over with you, Lily. Sorry, girls. Another time?"

"Oh, sure," said Jaime, waving a hand nonchalantly. "I should have called first."

She gave Will a good-natured peck on his cheek and bounced out the door with a confused-looking Kate close behind.

"I don't guess we could take up where we left off," said Will.

Hell, no, we can't take up where we left off. You're putting the big move on me while your girlfriend is at the door? There is no way I'm getting involved in this!

"We were on our way to get gumbo, as I recall," she said. "I'm starving."

Will took her to a seafood restaurant that hung out over the bay where they had heaping, steaming bowls of the promised gumbo and lots of crusty French bread.

The conversation returned to boats and plants, and the most romantic ten minutes in the last twenty years of Lily McVay's life faded away into the night.

13.

Somethin' to Talk about

Marilee called to say she had bought some adorable gardening gloves and a great hat that were absolutely going to waste and insisted on coming by to help Lily in whatever capacity she was needed in the garden.

Marilee, who never ceased to surprise her friends, proceeded to put in several hours of hard work weeding, planting annuals, and rearranging the porch furniture into a much more functional configuration that Lily would never have thought of.

While the friends worked, they talked about the garden progress, and tossed around ideas for the soiree. Lily was surprised, but relieved that her friend hadn't wanted to know all about "that cute, young thing, Will." Finally Marilee mentioned she was worried about Helen.

"You know she's been borderline diabetic for over a year. Missy Grogan, her gynecologist really gave her a hard time the other day. You know, about her weight and her cholesterol and all that. Of course, Helen just got on another one of those crazy diets of hers."

Lily groaned. Helen's cabinets and refrigerator were full of low-fat this and sugar-free that. She'd read every diet book there was. In between diets, however, Helen ate huge portions of everything. To make matters even worse, shopping for diet books and romance novels was her only form of exercise.

"What's the new diet?" asked Lily.

"She can't eat or drink anything unless it's green. She won't stick to it, though—you know how she does. And her latest romance novel? You won't believe this. It's called *Loving*

Large. On the cover there is this pretty, but uh, fairly plump woman encased in a flowing garment. She's in the arms of this incredibly handsome, shirtless guy who's getting ready to kiss her. It's terribly sexy." Marilee sighed and got a faraway look in her eyes. "He had these full lips that were parted so that you knew it wasn't going to be any little, old wimpy kiss."

"Really?"

"Cross my heart." Marilee sighed again, this time with a deep frown. "Helen is not only my friend, but she's family, and she's very conflicted right now. It's the right time for us to step in."

"Conflicted how?"

"*Loving Large*, by Caitlin McCoy is right there on her bedside table next to *Living Green*, by Harvey Green, PhD. I think it's high time we had an intervention."

"An intervention? Are you serious?"

"As a broken heel in the Miss Cotton Ball pageant. Listen, I think she might pay attention if we both talk to her. You know how I feel about all this pressure on women and girls to be thin. It's ridiculous. Some people are just meant to be curvy. When I was young, people appreciated a voluptuous figure." Marilee realized she'd hopped on another train of thought and paused. "Anyway, the point is, when a person's weight starts affecting her health, well, that's something else again. Helen's eating habits are out of control. She says she's going to change her evil ways, but do you know she asked me to take her to the Dairy Queen for a farewell Dixie Dog?"

"She didn't. You didn't take her, did you?"

"Well, she would've taken herself if I hadn't. Oh, and by the way ..." Marilee chewed her bottom lip for a second or two, then affected her most nonchalant demeanor. "Not that you really care, but for what it's worth, I saw Will in there with that little bimbette-from-the-bar, Jaime what's-her-name. Oh, and honey, you might want to know that everybody's talking about you dating some young guy—has to be Will they're alluding to." Marilee grinned. "I just hope Howard's heard it. It will drive him crazy!"

Lily's brain was spinning from information overload. Finally she shook her head and said, "First and certainly more important, is Helen. I think you're right. Somebody's got to talk to her." She sighed. "It won't be easy, though. She loves her crash diets almost as much as she hates exercise. But Helen is going to get diabetes over our dead bodies. A farewell Dixie Dog? Good, Lord."

"I know. It's really getting scary," said Marilee. "Well, how about tomorrow afternoon. She gets off early on Thursdays."

"Sure. We'll have our food intervention tomorrow afternoon. Where?"

"Helen's. I'll set it up."

Lily looked at her friend. "It's for her own good, right? I feel like we're ambushing her."

"It has to be done, Lily. Besides, Helen is always telling you to be more assertive with Howard and everything. And if I had a dollar for every time she advised me about my career choices, I'd be a wealthy woman."

"You are a wealthy woman, Marilee."

"Oh, you know what I mean. Helen will receive our advice in the spirit in which it's offered. She'll know it's because we care about her."

"I hope you're right. Now, concerning the second piece of information ... I wouldn't mind Howard thinking I'm going out with a younger man. I'm pretty sure he wouldn't like it a bit. But, Marilee, what if Will has heard the rumor? He's been pretty scarce lately. Maybe that's why."

"Well, he's the one who took you sailing and to dinner. He knows how people talk around here." Hesitating just a few seconds, she added, "But what is going on with him and Jaime?" She smiled at her friend. "I think you're getting mighty attached to your gardener, not that I blame you. But be careful, sweetie."

Lily explained that as part of her latest defense mechanisms against: a. making an ass of herself, b. getting her barely mended heart broken, or c. contracting Old Fool Syndrome, which was really the same as a., she'd made up her mind once and for all about Will.

He was simply one of those cute womanizers who come in all ages who are addicted to the thrill of turning any and all women on—and the ensuing attention the grateful females lavish on them in return. Men who truly enjoy the company of females, they're sincere in their interest, but hopelessly obsessed with the constant yet ever-changing attention of fresh admirers. Sad but true. There.

"Wow. You sure have him pegged," said Marilee, who had listened to all of this with a quizzical, glazed look in her big, brown eyes.

"I think I do," agreed Lily. "Finally!"

She and Will would be gardening buddies. Only. Whew! It felt good to have that sorted out. Now she could move on and think about things more suited to a woman her age, she explained. There were more important matters that she had been neglecting.

"Like what?" Marilee wanted to know.

"Like making a hair appointment. Auburn highlights and gray roots are not a good combination. Like purchasing a new pair of reading glasses. They're all over the house, but I can never put my hands on any when I need them. And getting a massage. Boy, could I use a massage. My garden might be flourishing," she said, "but my back suddenly feels like it's eighty-years-old."

After Marilee left, Lily decided to give her aching back a few minutes rest. There was a nice, little breeze floating across the back porch. She reclined on Mrs. McVay's wicker chaise and thought about her conversation with Marilee.

14.

The Banshee next Door

Swimming in the cobalt depths of Will's eyes, Lily heard her own breath quicken, felt her skin grow hot. His arms tightened around her, his strong chest muscles pressing eagerly against her breasts through the delicate lace of her gossamer gown. She studied the delicious curve of his lips as they parted and drew closer to her own.

"Lily, I know you're old enough to be my, uh, aunt, but I'm in love with you," Will said, pulling her to him. He buried his face in her hair, and finally, ever so softly, his lips brushed hers.

"Ooo. Help meee."

Lily practically flew off the chaise. She'd been dreaming so deeply that for a moment she didn't know where she was. Oh, yeah. The back porch. *Good Lord, what time is it?* she wondered. A quick look at her watch told her it was three o'clock in the afternoon. A few minutes' rest on the porch sofa had turned into a two-hour nap.

"Oooo. Help me, please."

"What in the hell is that?" Lily muttered, infuriated that whatever it was had interrupted the best dream she'd had in years.

Was it coming from the cemetery? *That would be a logical solution*, thought Lily illogically, *since it sounds like a demented banshee.* She expected to see the spirit of her dead mother-in-law swooping over the garden wall from her resting place across the street. *No, that can't be it. Banshee swooping takes place after dark.*

Besides, she now realized, the noise was coming from the direction of Maisy's house. Crazy Maisy was obviously in some kind of terrible distress.

Lily tried to shake the sleep out of her head while she went over the basics of CPR she'd learned from an inebriated fire fighter at last year's Annual Five Alarm Chili Cook Off. Every time she got to the mouth-to-mouth part, however, her recently interrupted dream filled her head.

A woman was dying and all she could think about was sex! *What is wrong with you?* "the voice" screamed as she flew through the gate, jumped the boxwood, and hurtled the hybrids as the terrible wailing continued.

"What are you doing?" she yelled, startling Maisy, whose hand fluttered to her chest.

"What are you doing? Trying to give me heart failure?"

"But I heard you screaming. I ..." Lily didn't finish because she'd finally noticed the earphones Maisy was dislodging from her ears. Lily could hear the music coming from them. "Help me, please," cried the singer.

Maisy looked at the earphones then at Lily's mortified face, and burst into a fit of cackling laughter.

"I was ... I was ... Believe it or not I was singing," she gasped.

Lily had to laugh, too, and that, as they say, was the beginning of a beautiful friendship.

She thanked Maisy again for the helping her in the cemetery.

"I hope none of you caught cold," she said.

"Oh, no. We all came over here for a hot toddy. Hermione says it's the most fun she's had in days."

Lily could tell Maisy was having some difficulty stifling a chuckle. Luckily, Lily had recovered enough that she now saw the humor in it all, so she and Maisy had another good laugh over the "twilight rescue from the mausoleum," as Lily referred to it.

The conversation inevitably got around to a discussion of why it had taken them so long to connect. Maisy apologized for her "rude remarks about poor Howard" when she'd first met Lily all those years ago and even admitted it stemmed from early reservations about her own marriage.

"I've always been too outspoken for my own good. A form

of self-preservation, a therapist once told me," she said. "And proud. Too proud to apologize after I shot my mouth off about Howard like I did." She reached over and turned the music off. "Now let's have a look at your yard. There's only so much I can see peeking through the gate or from my upstairs balcony."

It turned out that the vista from Maisy's balcony hadn't always been an obstructed one. Before the trees filled it in she'd seen a lot of what went on over at the McVays'.

Howard had been a boy and Maisy the teenaged bride of the equally young Dubbie Downey when she became the McVays' backyard neighbor. Everyone thought Dubbie Downey, with all that family oil money, had been taken for the ride of his life. He was naïve, quiet and unassuming, both physically and socially—the antithesis of the stereotypical Texas oil man. But despite early misgivings, Maisy really loved the diminutive, mild-mannered millionaire and had kept Dubbie happy if exhausted.

They'd raised four sons, who had in turn given them seven granddaughters. The Downeys had traveled, partied, and thanks to Maisy's tireless spirit, had partaken of more adventures than Dubbie could've dreamed of on his own.

Lily gave Maisy the garden tour and amazingly, Maisy gave suggestions only when asked. Until they approached the pond, that is. The area including the intricate, scarred brickwork around its perimeter was approximately ten feet in diameter. Lily and Will had scrubbed and bleached until it was almost free of the years of accumulated dirt and plant debris.

They'd wisely left enough that the brick kept its old world look and blended into the surroundings. Sadly, the still-dirty interior of the pond, the bare platform in the center and the ugly protruding pipe obscured any improvements to what had once been the garden's piece de resistance. For now it remained the garden's eyesore.

"I remember the statue that used to be on that pedestal," said Maisy. "You can't find them like that anymore."

"I know," said Lily. "I've looked everywhere. Everything in my budget is hideous. Even the ones way over my budget are awful."

"I know where you can get exactly what you're lookin' for,"

said Maisy. "It's called Les Jardins. A friend of mine owns it. He'll give you the Downey discount if you mention my name. I'll give you his Web site. You'll find what you're lookin' for," she repeated. "There's just one problem. It's in Atlanta. And they don't ship."

"I'm going to Atlanta soon. Helen and I are going with Marilee to this clothes thing. I'll check it out."

When Maisy had inspected and complimented every bush and bloom and improvement to the McVay grounds, she accepted Lily's invitation to share a glass of tea on the back porch and filled Lily in on life with the McVays.

Mrs. McVay hadn't allowed Howard to consort with the rowdy Downey boys and their older cousins, which left Howard alone in his back yard listening to the yells and laughter coming from over the garden wall.

"One time I was at the gate, you know, coming over to get Howard. One of my boys had invited him to go to the movie with us. I could hear Howard crying, and heard old McVay say, 'Those people are not like us, Howard. You're better than that.' It really hurt my feelings, Lily. Believe me, that's the last time I came over here—until your wedding reception. I only came to that because I liked you right off, and I suppose I felt bad about that crack about Howard." She shook her head. "Couldn't stand the idea of you married to Howard, though."

Lily raised her eyebrows as if to say, *are we going to get into all that again?*

"That's another fault of mine," said Maisy. "I have a hard time minding my own business." She grinned at Lily, and her weathered face crinkled into a thousand wrinkles. "I'm working on it, though."

If you haven't gotten a handle on it in over eighty years, I don't think it's gonna happen, thought Lily.

She kept this observation to herself, of course, and merely said, "Would you like to see the house? I've made a lot of changes."

Maisy was equally complimentary of Lily's changes to the interior of McVay house. "You've really got a knack, Lily," she said again and again. "Of course, I was only in here once. I used the john at your wedding party."

"I definitely remember this room," she said as they entered the den/parlor. "It's beautiful now. I can't believe it's the same room. Before, the décor was horrible—nothing but old McVay." She smiled up at Lily. "Now it's nothing but you. What an improvement!"

Lily noticed a sudden chill in the air, which seemed to bring out the stale perfume-perm odor. To her surprise, she saw that Maisy was rubbing her arms and wrinkling her nose. She glanced at the portrait of Mrs. McVay. The old lady looked more menacing than ever.

"Maisy, do you smell that?"

"Lord, yes. What in the hell is it? Smells like Chanel gone bad—gone bad in an abandoned beauty parlor."

Her eyes fell on the portrait above the mantle. A bony hand flew to her mouth. "Oh, oh. It's her. That's the way old McVay and this house of hers used to smell. I hate to tell you, Lily, but you're being haunted."

Lily was so relieved that she hugged the tiny lady so hard she thought she might break her. "Oh, Maisy, I'm not crazy."

"No, I don't think so. Of course, could be, we're both crazy." She gave this idea a few seconds thought then shook her head. "Nope. We're not gonna think that way."

"What about Sinatra music?" She told Maisy about the phone calls with musical messages from "Ol' Blue Eyes."

"No, I don't know anything about that. Something else is going on there, I'd bet. You don't know it, but a pretty gal like you can cause a lot of jealousy. There are a lot of nut cases out there, Lily. That's something else you're going to have to get to the bottom of."

"And you don't think it's possible that the house is drafty and has absorbed the odor? That's Howard's explanation—that all old houses are musty and drafty."

"My house is old, and it might smell like a couple of old folks live there, but nothing like this. Besides, it's mostly in this room. And where's that chill coming from? It's warm out. Nope. Something else is going on in this house." Maisy looked at her watch. "It's after five," she said. "And you look like you could use something stronger than iced tea. Come back over to my house. I need to check on Dubbie. I fix a mean margarita, if I say so myself."

Twenty minutes later they were sipping a couple of very mean margaritas beneath the clematis. Maisy had kicked off her shoes and propped her gnarled old granny toes (decorated with hot pink polish) up on a low table. Because of the afternoon heat, she'd tied her shoulder length, platinum hair into a high ponytail, adding a large, pink bow the same shade as her toenails. Dubbie snored, mouth wide open, margarita untouched, on a nearby sofa.

Lily sat back and recounted the whole story. Not once did Maisy ask why on earth Lily was knocking herself out to please a dead woman who had treated a kudzu vine with more kindness than her own daughter-in-law. Instead, as Lily finished her tale, both women grew quiet, thinking.

Lily took a long sip of her drink and said, "Maisy, how is it that you were aware of Mrs. McVay's presence? No one else except maybe Howard who refuses to discuss it, seems to feel the chill or even to smell that musty odor."

Maisy waived a claw-like hand dismissively. "Oh, I don't know, honey. Maybe it's just because I'm so old—closer to the other side than most. I'll be over there with old McVay sooner not later, you know."

Lily had the distinct impression Maisy was trying to change the subject. For some reason, Maisy didn't want to answer the question. The skeptical look on Lily's face caused Maisy to laugh.

"Okay, I'll tell you the truth. I've got a gift—or curse is more like it sometimes. Got it from my Granny Lulu, but that's another long story. If I explain, you're gonna have to keep it under your hat. I'm already this close to being committed." She held up a bony thumb and forefinger less than a half an inch apart.

"But the fortune-telling at your parties …"

"That's a way for me to do a little good, use my gift. Everybody thinks it's just for fun. You know, the best place to hide is in plain sight. So I dress up like a gypsy, don't get too specific, try to steer folks in the right direction. Believe it or not, even though they think it's all a big joke, they pay attention to the advice I give them. I throw in enough silly hocus-pocus so most of them don't suspect."

"Most?"

"Every now and then somebody gets suspicious—usually somebody you might call intuitive, but they've walked in my size five-and-a-half's, so they leave it alone."

"But why me? I don't have any gift."

Maisy cackled. "Oh, you've got gifts, baby, just not that one." The hundreds of laugh lines suddenly collapsed in on themselves as Maisy turned serious. "I don't know too much about haunts and the like, but I've been to enough scary movies and read enough paranormal stuff to guess old McVay can't or won't move on because of unfinished business. You say old McVay died leavin' unresolved issues between you two. That's psycho lingo for something hanging over your head—learned it from my therapist."

Maisy swallowed the rest of her margarita in one undignified gulp. "Yep. You've got to get to the bottom of it. For your own sake. Like I said, I saw and heard more than I should've from that balcony up there. I'm not going to say more. Lord knows I've made a fool of myself enough times to keep me from spreading gossip and speculating on other people's business. Besides, I've got a feeling you have to unravel it in your own way, and when I have a feeling, well, I've learned to pay attention. You go back and look through everything. You'll figure it out. I will say this. I think it all goes back to that buried pond."

As Lily got up to go, thunder rumbled, rousing Dubbie. He seemed surprised to see Lily. Though Maisy had explained who she was before he'd fallen asleep, he said, "Dubbie Downey. Pleased to meet you, young lady."

He struggled to rise from the sofa, so Lily hurried over to him. "Please don't get up." She bent over him and shook his hand. "I'm Lily McVay."

"Lily … Lily," he said, searching for the memory. "Oh, yes, this is the young lady Will is so taken with. Right, Maisy? Now, where have we met before?"

"We met a long time ago at my wedding party."

"Wonderful party," he said. "Had a great time, didn't we Maisy?

Lily doubted he remembered it at all. She was sure the thousands of parties he and Maisy had attended over the years were one big festive fog to the old man.

"I'm glad you enjoyed it," she said, but Dubbie Downey was snoring again.

Maisy shook her head. "Sorry about that. The housekeeper fixes his supper at four o'clock, and Dubbie just can't stay awake after that." She grinned at Lily. "Puts a crimp in the nightlife, I can tell you that."

"He seems like a very nice man," said Lily sincerely.

"Oh, he's the best, been putting up with me for almost seventy years. Still puts the blue in my sky, as they say. I'm lucky to still have him—even though he has gotten a little fuzzy-headed. What he said about Will, he wasn't mixed up about that, though. Will thinks a lot of you."

"We do work well together. You can't imagine how he's helped me—in the garden, you know."

"I know exactly. It's exciting, having the attentions of a younger man. Enjoy it. Does wonders for the complexion. Just keep the Kleenex handy."

"What?"

"There's a good chance he'll make you cry."

Lily started to object, to insist that theirs was a professional relationship or at the most a rapport between gardening buddies. Instead she smiled at the outrageous old woman and said, "Maisy, do you know how long it's been since I cried?"

15.

Digging into the Future

She didn't know whether to blame Maisy's confirmation of paranormal shenanigans, the old lady's general quirkiness, or the mean margaritas, but Lily's head was spinning as she climbed the steps of the back porch.

A thirty-minute jog was what she needed, but thunder rumbled in the distance. Her usual routine took her around the perimeter of the cemetery, and the memory of trotting along in the gathering darkness, thunder menacing above the silent graves was a little too fresh. Of course, she wasn't about to let Mrs. McVay scare her away from the flat, tree-shaded streets that were perfect for a short run, but maybe she would confine her jogs to daylight hours for awhile.

This evening, she opted for a cool shower and a light supper. She threw together a salad of crisp baby romaine, tomato, and crumbled blue cheese. Tasty, but definitely not enough after the day I've had, she thought. She made a cheddar cheese omelet, toasted an English muffin, and washed it all down with a tall glass of iced lemon water.

Feeling very good about the relatively low-cal feast, she found a few heath balls she'd overlooked in the freezer and popped them into her mouth. They would provide the energy and comfort needed to dig back into the box of McVay memorabilia, she told herself, hurrying to catch the phone.

"How's it goin', babe?"

Lily groaned inwardly. "Hey, Dwayne," she said.

"I got a couple a tickets to a Buffett concert."

"Jimmy Buffett?"

"Yes ma'am. I'm a parrot head and proud of it."

Jimmy Buffett, yes, thought Lily, *but Dwayne Bond, the parrot head? No way.*

"Sorry, Dwayne. I'm kind of seeing someone."

"That kid? The gardener? Honey, I hate to break it to ya, but the boy is hot on the trail of some little blondie. Now what d'ya say?"

"Good-bye, Dwayne." And she hung up.

The phone rang again immediately.

"Give old Dwayne a chance."

She hung up.

It rang again.

"Now look, Dwayne."

"You witch!" said the slurred, muffled voice of the phone freak/DQ litterer. "Rosemary McVay hates you. She won't be happy until you're in that little grave house with her!"

Make that drunk, dumb (little grave house?) phone freak-slash-litterer, thought Lily, but still, it frightened her. This was the first time the woman had really threatened her. Who was she? And where had Lily heard that voice?

She put Dwayne's comments about Will and Jaime out of her mind. Well, almost, by concentrating on these questions. But the other questions eventually surfaced. What was Will up to? Why did he act so interested in her if he was really interested in Jaime? *You've already decided all that, remember?* She chided herself.

But she knew Will was sincere. They did have a special relationship. They did. But what kind of special relationship? A very special friendship. *I've got to stick with that scenario until I find out what is going on with Jaime,* she decided. *Otherwise I'll drive myself crazy!*

Lily checked the locks, turned on all the outside lights and took a quick shower. She rechecked the locks and headed for the kitchen where she could spread the McVay papers and photos out on the table.

First she sifted through the stack of pictures Will had returned to her on his last visit. She kept going back to the photo of a young Howard standing next to the fountain. It was a clear picture, but the sun cast lacy shadows over the scene, which is why it had been so difficult to make out the first time she'd studied it. Now instead of the fountain, she scrutinized the boy.

Howard was dressed rather formally as in the other pictures she'd seen of him. And like earlier shots of him before the age of eleven or twelve, Howard was wearing a funny, self-conscious grin. Photos after this time usually had her ex-husband sporting a sour, troubled expression, which Lily had always chalked up to a rough puberty. (After all, her cousin, Bootsie Jean, hadn't smiled once in the presence of her family between puberty and her sophomore year in college.)

This being one of Howard's biggest grins, she took a closer look. She got up and rummaged through the junk drawer—okay one of the three junk drawers—in the kitchen until she found the magnifying glass Helen had given her when she turned forty.

Howard was indeed happy here. By adjusting the glass, she could clearly see the fellow he was leaning against. The man was wearing overalls and looked vaguely familiar—a younger version of someone she knew. The man had his hand on Howard's shoulder in a paternal way and looked at Howard with a father's pride. But it wasn't Howard's father. For one thing, Mr. McVay would not have been caught dead, much less on film, in a pair of bib overalls.

Who is this man that Howard feels so happy and comfortable with? Lily wondered. *The square jaw, the prominent nose, the white-blonde hair—it's all so familiar, but who …?*

It came to her in a flash. Jake Johnson, Mrs. McVay's old gardener. Except it was not old Jake, but a much younger, barely recognizable version of Jake. It had to be. What other overall wearer would've been allowed such fraternization with a McVay? It was odd that Howard had never spoken of Jake when they'd clearly been so close.

Lily put the picture aside and started in on the correspondence. There were letters from Howard to his parents from Vanderbilt and from summers abroad. The envelopes were all addressed to Mr. McVay. The letters began rather stiffly, "Dear parents." They were extremely short and directed to his father. There was not one comment that even remotely spoke to his mother. Lily knew that college-aged guys were not known for their letter-writing skills, but she could almost feel the coolness towards her mother-in-law flowing from the yellowed papers. She picked up the picture of happy Howard, the boy, in her right hand and the letter with its formal salutation in her left.

She was beginning to doubt pubescent angst as the basis for the sad transformation of her ex-husband. After all, most adolescents negotiated puberty successfully, emerging with their personalities more or less intact. (Even Lily's surly cousin, Bootsie Jean had survived the experience and grown into the most delightful adult.) Howard McVay, on the other hand, seemed to have never regained his boyish charm and love of life.

What happened to you, Howard, to turn the boy in this picture into the young man in these letters? And what will it solve when I find out? Lily didn't know the answer.

She was certain, however, that it would be disturbing, whatever came out of this Pandora's Box of the past. But the box had to be opened because Lily knew as surely as she knew anything that digging into the McVays' past was the way out of her own past and into her future.

16.

Real Women don't Eat Salad

Lily and Marilee pushed through Helen's back gate.

"Yoo hoo!" yelled Marilee so cheerfully that no one would dream she was planning a food intervention.

They found Helen on her patio deep into *Loving Large*, her latest romance novel. On the table next to her were a salad and some grass–colored chips and next to this unappetizing concoction was *Living Green*, her latest diet book.

Marilee motioned toward the romance tome with its sexy cover. "Hey, aren't you supposed to be eating bonbons with that?" she asked.

Lily shot her a look. It was not exactly a good opener for a food intervention in her opinion.

"Very funny," said Helen, "But I've been on this rabbit food for a week now—everything green—not even carrots are allowed. The low-cal dressing is even green. I think I'm starting to turn green."

"Oh, my God, Helen. I think you are!" said Marilee.

Was it the reflection of the shrubbery behind her, or was Helen's skin and hair actually taking on a greenish hue? Lily wasn't sure, but she was convinced now, more than ever that the time was ripe for a major discussion with her friend.

Helen sighed. "I don't mind telling you, I'm getting discouraged." She picked up the paperback and gazed at its intoxicating cover. "Do you suppose Delphine here is worried about her cholesterol?"

"She ought to be worried about her blood pressure—woo, that's some hunk getting ready to plant one on our large heroine," said Marilee.

"Well, I guess you either starve yourself and turn green and live a long, miserable life—or live it up and die young," said Helen sadly.

Self pity was simply not in Helen's repertoire of emotions, and it upset Lily to hear it. It was time to get tough.

"With high cholesterol and high blood pressure and/or diabetes, you're apt to live a fairly long miserable life," she said.

"Have you ever noticed," said Marilee, "that it's the overweight people's kitchens that are filled with diet food and diet books? And I hate to say it, but it's usually stuffed in with all the unhealthy things they eat when they go off the rabbit food. You don't see much of that stuff—the diet foods or the junk—around people who are at a healthy weight."

"That's because people like you don't need diet food, Marilee."

"Look, Helen," said Lily, "You're not going to stay on Dr. Green's diet forever are you?"

"Hell, no. Just until I lose the twenty-two pounds. Twenty-two pounds in twenty-two days. That's what he guarantees."

"Well, what happens when you go off of it?" asked Lily.

Marilee made a face. "If I'd been eating that stuff for twenty-two days, I'd eat everything not green I could put my hands on."

Lily held up the two books. "Neither of these is the answer. Helen, you give us advice all the time—good advice that we appreciate, well, most of the time anyway. The point is, today we are giving you advice."

"An ultimatum is more like it," said Marilee. "But it's because we love you, and like Lily says, you're getting diabetes over our dead bodies." She paused here for effect, reminding Lily of Howard. "You are going to start eating healthy, regular food, smaller portions. You are going to start eating breakfast—a low carb, low fat, but delicious breakfast. No more lite lattes or mid-morning snacks."

Helen looked guilty when Marilee mentioned the snacks.

"And you are going to meet us every afternoon, Monday through Friday, for a long, brisk walk," Marilee continued.

"Oh, and I've signed you up for a yoga classes at the Y. They have them all hours of the night and day. You are to attend a minimum of three times a week."

"Helen, it's what Marilee and I do, more or less," said Lily. "I know it's easier for you to gain weight, but I promise you, if I didn't exercise and really watch what I eat, I would have a weight problem."

"Same here," said Marilee. "I've tried those diets. When I inevitably get off of them, my eating habits are worse than ever. I crave everything I shouldn't have. When I allow myself to have what I want in small portions, it works better. I promise."

Helen let out a giant sigh. "Sandy pretty much told me the same thing last night. When you hear it from two friends and a husband, I guess you have to pay attention. Okay. I'll try it for six months."

Marilee stood up. "Well, let's get going."

"Where?" asked Lily and Helen at once.

"Shopping. There's nothing like a new pair of walking shoes to get you in the mood to exercise. Then to Health-Mart. They just got in the prettiest vegetables. Then to the bookstore. We've got to get something to replace *Loving Large*!"

17.

Position Number Eighty-seven

"Thank you, honey. See you tomorrow?" Maisy's crackled voice floated through the curtain of Spanish moss above the newly repaired gate. It now swung easily on its hinges, as Will came through it.

"I'll do my best," he called over his shoulder, a bit halfheartedly, frowning and obviously tired. When he saw Lily, he smiled, and stood looking at her as if seeing her for the first time, and she knew he'd missed her, too.

The next hour was spent hosing out the inside of the pond, then scrubbing it with an old broom. Lily said a silent prayer as Will opened the valve. Someone up there was paying attention. Miraculously, the water flowed easily down the pipe.

"Now all we need is to get a new pump, see if the plumbing to the statue that we have to replace works, add some plants, and you'll be in business," said Will.

"I will, won't I?" She looked around her at the twisting paths, herbaceous borders, and grass beneath the low oak and magnolia limbs dripping with moss. "It's beautiful, isn't it?"

"Yes, it is," he agreed, his eyes twinkling at her. He wasn't looking at the garden.

Lily smiled at him.

"Will, you have done enough work for one day. Sit here. I'll be right back."

A few minutes later she handed him an icy beer.

"To celebrate the miracle of the functioning plumbing in the pond," she said.

Lily hosed off the last of the dirt along the bricks around

the pond and watered plants while he sipped his beer from the steps and watched her. Before long, he'd stretched his long legs out, eyes closed, reclining against the steps, reminding her of that first day when she'd seen him on Maisy's patio. And to think—she'd almost left before even giving him a chance.

Just when she decided that he was asleep, he said, "Hey Lily, mind if I have another beer?"

"Anything you want."

"Really? Now that's an interesting offer."

Lily laughed. "I'm talking about food and drink. Speaking of which, I think I'll have a beer, too."

Seconds later he walked over to her with the beer as she turned off the hose.

"Thanks," said Lily, taking a long sip from the icy bottle. "Let's sit in the secret garden."

"Sure," he said. "Where is it?"

"That's what Helen and Marilee call it. That little area behind the shed. And, by the way, they love everything we've done."

"Glad to hear it. Of course Marilee doesn't look like she's ever pulled a weed in her life."

"Oh, you would be surprised." She told Will about how Marilee had shown up in her new hat and gardening gloves and the surprising amount of work she had done. "Never underestimate the deb," laughed Lily.

They walked beneath the arbor.

"Oh, great," she moaned. "Look at this."

The Cherokee rose they had so artfully tied to the wall lay in the bushes. The fishing line had come untied at one end, and the whole thing had come down.

"Not a problem," Will assured her. "We'll just tie it back up with a better knot this time. But first let's finish our beers."

Lily was so thirsty she chugged hers down, then had another with Will.

"This garden is turning us into alcoholics," she giggled. "It's a good thing we're almost through."

"Working on this garden with you is what is keeping me out of AA. We've been having serious problems with the new sprinkler system out at the nursery. I've been trying to live in my house while redoing it, and Maisy keeps thinking of things for me to do. She's having a big party for Dubbie's birthday, you know. Thank God, it's after the soiree."

"I know. I'm invited. Dubbie's a sweet old thing. So fragile though. Frankly, I'm amazed he's still alive."

"Well, he was the last time I looked. I used to think Maisy was going to kill him, dragging him to parties and doing crazy things, but I think the excitement is what keeps him going."

"She was complaining about having to cut back on her social life."

"I don't know about that. The first week I worked for her, she picked him up from the hospital—he had some heart procedure—and took him to a cocktail party. Had his dinner jacket in the car."

They were still laughing and telling "Maisy" stories when Will attempted to tie the rose back to a screw high in the garden wall.

"Here. I'll hold the vines while you tie the line." He pulled the line taut, and the rose obediently returned to a close approximation of its original position. Lily couldn't reach the screw, though. She got a clay pot, turned it over, and placed it between him and the wall.

He looked skeptical as she stepped up on it, but said nothing.

"Can you get it?" He breathed the words into her ear. She felt his chest against her back, the rest of him against the rest of her. She couldn't move, couldn't speak.

"Lily? You okay?" But his voice croaked out the question, and the breath in her ear intensified.

He gently turned her to face him and searched her eyes. Lily thought she might just keel over into the hydrangeas. Instead she returned his gaze, and, propelled by some uncontrollable force of desire or instinct or downright horniness, kissed him right on the mouth. She did it gently but with a passion she didn't know she had.

And he kissed her back, also very gently, but with a passion she didn't know anyone possessed. Like that evening at his cabin, the feel of him against her made her light-headed and she melted into him. Unfortunately, this slight shift in position was enough to throw her off balance, and she slipped from her precarious perch atop the pot. Will tried to catch her, but was not exactly steady at this point either, and the two of them ended up in the hydrangeas, Lily on top, her left breast squarely in his right eye.

"Lily!"

The voice was definitely not Will's, and besides, it did not come from under her chest. She twisted her head around, pulling her hair on one of the hydrangea's woody stems. Framed there under Mrs. McVay's arbor, looking like the bride and groom (or bride and grandfather-of-the-groom) on a wedding cake stood Howard and Heather.

"What in the hell is going on here?" yelled Howard, completely destroying the illusion.

Heather simply stood there wearing a little white sundress and a very big smirk. Lily tried to get up, realized Will's shirt was somehow caught to something on her shorts, and that one very sore arm was lodged under his head.

She finally disengaged herself, stumbled to a standing position, and said as if the whole horrible scene were a perfectly natural occurrence, "Will, I'd like you to meet Howard and Heather."

Will got himself to a sitting position, and said, "Uh, nice to meet you. Sorry for not getting up, but my pants seem to be caught on this bush."

Heather flashed him her hundred-watt executive assistant smile while Howard turned as red as one of Maisy Downey's American Beauty roses.

"Just what in the hell is going on here?" Howard repeated.

"Calm down, Howard," said Lily, turning a bit pink herself. "We were just attempting to tie your mother's Cherokee rose to the wall where it belongs."

He looked at the beer bottles on the bistro table, then glared at her and Will. "It looks more like you were just plain tying one on to me." He gestured behind him. "Good God," he added, his obvious disgust increasing, "And what have you done to this garden? This is not at all what we discussed." He turned to the grinning Lolita clone at his side. "You were right, Heather. I should've turned this entire project over to you."

"What?" she put in dumbly. She was so busy giving Will the

once-over, she hadn't heard a word. Multi-tasking just wasn't her thing, you know.

"Now, you look here, Howard. Will and I have worked hard to restore this yard to the way your mother had it—"

"You mean you hired him?"

"Not exactly."

"He" was now standing, but looking a bit like a cornered animal searching for a way out of this dreary, little domestic drama. He ran his fingers nervously through his hair and bent over to retrieve his LSU baseball cap from the hydrangeas. Heather's grin went into mega wattage.

"Don't tell me he's on loan from Helen. Lily, I specifically told you McVays do not take charity."

Will cleared his throat, and they all looked at him. Or I should say Howard and Lily looked at him. Heather hadn't taken those big, baby-blues of hers off Will yet.

Lily noticed the muscles in Will's jaw had tightened, and his sweet, blue eyes were narrowed and dark. He suddenly looked very intimidating—and incredibly sexy.

"I've got to get going," he said.

Howard and Heather almost fell into the boxwood trying to get out of his way. Howard had the decency to wait until they heard the driveway gate clang shut before he resumed his tirade.

"I hope you know what this means, Lily. You have not held up your end of our agreement, and if I'm not mistaken, I may have grounds to take back my family's home. It was some kind of misplaced guilt that made me relinquish it in the first place."

Heather was bobbing her head up and down in agreement. "Temporary insanity," she proclaimed.

"And I'm just glad it was me and not your daughters who walked into this page out of the Kama Sutra," growled Howard.

Kama Sutra? Judging from their past sex life, Lily was surprised he'd ever heard of it.

"I mean, getting it on with the yard boy? Good God, Lily." He stared at her with revulsion.

It was all quite over the top, even for Howard, and even

Heather had the sense to look uncomfortable at this pile of hypocrisy.

Howard stormed back into the main part of the yard, Heather and a limping Lily behind him.

"I want this pond buried, do you hear me?" He growled the words at Lily. "I got rid of it once, and I won't look at it now."

"I kind of like it," said Heather. She turned to Lily. "You could get a mermaid statue spitting water or some little boys peeing, you know?"

"That's enough, Heather," said Howard. "I'll meet you in the car."

Heather walked up the steps into the house. Not through the gate to the driveway, but through Lily's house, which meant they had come in through her house without her permission. It was just too much. It was also just enough to fill her with righteous indignation and uncharacteristic bravado.

"Let's get this straight, Howard. You're trespassing here. This is my house now, and you know I earned every bit of it, the way you treated me and my daughters who you're suddenly so worried about."

His shocked expression gave her the courage to go on. "There was nothing in our agreement as to how I was to restore your mother's garden. I'm trying to do it as a tribute to her, Howard, not to you and certainly not to Heather, who we both know your mother would definitely not approve of." Lily gestured wide with her arm. "This is how it was when the garden was in its prime. It was the obvious choice—to put it back like she had it. I am shocked that you're not pleased."

"Get rid of that damned pond or you'll hear from my lawyer." It was as if he hadn't heard a word she'd said.

"Howard, if you show up here again without calling first, you'll here from my lawyer."

Howard headed for the back door, then changed his mind and left through the driveway gate.

Lily sank onto the back steps. She was exhausted, sore and full of scratches. Thanks to Howard and the beers she'd scarfed down, she had a headache and indigestion. She'd finally gotten to kiss a non-frog, and like most other things, Howard had managed to ruin it.

She closed her eyes, remembering the kiss. She sighed and a smile crept across her face as she replayed the scene in her mind. The tension drained from her neck, easing the headache until a loud burp escaped her. It jolted her out of her reverie but sure made her feel better.

18.

Road Trip

"Oh, my God. Will!" she said aloud, hurrying into the house.

She picked up the phone and punched in his number.

"This is Will. Leave a message."

"Hi, it's Lily. I'm so sorry you got involved in all that today. Please give me a call when you get in."

But he didn't call that day, that evening or the next day. Or the next. She and Helen and Marilee were scheduled to leave the following day to attend the Mayfair extravaganza in Atlanta, so she tried once more.

"Hi. This is Lily. I don't blame you for avoiding me after being subjected to Howard and all that." Her voice sort of trailed off at this point. She didn't want to bring all that up again. "I just wanted to let you know that I'll be out of town for a few days in Atlanta. Maisy told me about a place where I can get a statue for the fountain. Of course I don't know how I'll get it home if I'm able to find one. They don't ship. Anyway, I'm sorry about the other day, and I understand if you've gotten busy. You've done way too much already. Anyway, I guess I'll talk to you when I get back."

Good Lord, I was rambling like an idiot! Someone needs to invent a recorder that can be erased when an idiot caller realizes she's babbling.

Feeling worse than ever, Lily started packing her suitcase, throwing in the closest things she could grab. She tossed in some recently-purchased lingerie with a sigh. It would be totally wasted on Marilee and Helen. This depressing thought was interrupted by the ringing phone, which was right by her hand, but she didn't want to seem too anxious in case it was Will, so she let it ring three times.

"Hello?" she answered with as much nonchalance as she could muster.

"Lily? This is Marilee. Were you expecting someone else?"

"No. Why?"

"I don't know. You sounded a little peculiar or something. Listen, all three of us are invited to a cocktail party tomorrow night, so pack accordingly. I've pulled out everything I own. I just don't know what to wear. It's going to take hours for me to decide," she mock groaned. "So I can't talk. We'll have plenty of time for that tomorrow." Marilee was practically singing this info, she was so excited. "See you in the morning. Nine o'clock sharp. Bye."

As soon as she put the phone down, her cell began to ring. She let it ring twice then answered with what she hoped was an appropriately casual, "Hello."

Frank Sinatra serenaded her with the haunting strains of It Was a Very Good Year. The irony of this was not lost on Lily. It had been a very crappy year. She turned off the cell and tossed it onto the bed. "I've about had it with phones," she said aloud. She picked it up again and punched in Virginia's number.

"Hey, sweetie. It's me. Just wanted to let you know I'll be in Atlanta for a few days and I won't have my phone with me. If you need me, call Marilee or Helen. Love you."

She left an identical message with Elizabeth. At least she would have a couple of days without worrying every time a call came in, she told herself.

Sure enough, Marilee's big, silver Mercedes pulled up in front of Lily's at nine sharp. A sleepy-looking Helen was in the front passenger seat.

"That's all?" Marilee whined at the sight of Lily's small overnighter and skinny garment bag. "At least it's more than Helen. I guess she's planning to go to the cocktail party in her underwear, because that's all she has room for in that so-called suitcase she brought.

"I travel light, that's all" said Helen. "Wash and wear and wrinkle-proof, that's the only way to go."

"You brought a wash and wear cocktail dress? They're gonna

kick me out of the Mayfair family before I even get started," she moaned, but a little smile was playing around the corners of her mouth.

"What?" said Helen. "I'm not going shopping, if that's what you're thinking."

"Not shopping-shopping, like wandering around the mall or anything. I was thinking we might find you a Mayfair dress. You can be my first customer."

"You might as well give in," laughed Lily.

"Oh, well, as long as I don't have to go into a store, I guess my wardrobe could use a little help. Besides, thanks to you two, I've lost five pounds."

"Five pounds in a week?" said Marilee. "That's great."

"And I'm feeling better, too," said Helen. "I'm even not loathing my yoga class. I've only been three times, but it's gotten downright tolerable. And since we started our afternoon walks around Lily's neighborhood, I've been sleeping through the night for the first time in months."

"I'm so proud of you," said Lily. "How are you doing with the non-diet diet?"

"Pretty well, but that's been the hardest part. Sandy's eating healthy with me—no barbeque or snacks, lots of veggies and fruit, whole grains only, protein shakes for breakfast. We're getting used to it. I think I'm going to be able to stick to this routine pretty well."

"Well, you definitely need to reward yourself with a new outfit, then," said Marilee.

For the next hour, they discussed clothes in general, the Mayfair Collection in particular and suitable attire for the upcoming Garden Club Soiree in great detail. The latter brought them to the subject Lily had been hoping to avoid: Will and his involvement in her latest confrontation with Howard.

After several lame attempts at changing the subject of "the great embarrassment," which is how Lily now thought of the recent humiliating events, she gave in and told all to Helen and Marilee. Sharing the emotional burden with her friends made her feel immensely better, of course.

"The Kama Sutra?" Helen was laughing so hard, she could hardly catch her breath. "And he didn't even notice Heather ogling Will?"

"No," said Lily. "He was too busy doing his impersonation of a horse's ass."

"But how could he not like the garden?" asked Marilee between chuckles.

"Really," said Helen. "It's ridiculous! After all, the goal was to restore it. That means put it back like it was. Which is exactly what you did."

Lily shook her head. "I don't know. The pond seemed to upset him as much as anything. He said, 'I got rid of it once. I'm not going to look at it now.' But he won't have to look at it. It's my yard now. I guess he means at the soiree when he'll accept the posthumous award given to his mother."

"Why would he care if the pond is there at the party?"

"I don't know," Lily said again. "It makes no sense—but then, we are talking about Howard, after all. Howard the snob who ran off with Heather, the office help who's young enough to be his daughter. Who knows? Maybe he just wants me to fail. Or maybe it's because I got outside help—gardening charity. He said that McVays don't accept charity, they give it."

"He didn't," said Marilee, looking completely exasperated.

"Oh, yes. He did. But the big question to me is what did he mean, he got rid of the fountain once. Why? When? Maisy hinted that the solution to the whole, strange puzzle of Howard and his mother and the garden has something to do with that pond and fountain—and the missing statue."

"Maisy?" said Helen. "You have been talking to Crazy Maisy?"

"Oh, I almost forgot to tell you both. It's the other development in my own personal soap opera. Maisy and I are now officially friends."

"Well, good for you," said Helen. "It's about time."

Lily related how she'd raced over to her neighbor's at the "sound of the banshee" intent on saving the poor woman's life and had ended up befriending her instead.

"She came over for a tour of the garden. That's when she suggested that I search further into the McVay memorabilia I found in the attic. She knows something she's not telling me, but she did say the pond was a key factor in it all."

"So you think Crazy Maisy holds the clue to the mystery of the missing fountain, huh, Nancy Drew?" teased Helen.

Lily ignored her.

"Howard may not like charity, and he may not be crazy about his mother's taste in fountains," said Marilee. "But I'll tell you the real problem. It's Will. It's because he couldn't stand to see you with Will. God, Lily, I still can't believe you kissed him like that. Lordy, just hearing about it is the most exciting thing that's happened to me in ages."

"It's just like *The Centurion's Kiss*," said Helen. "I swear, Lily, this would make a great romance novel."

Lily just rolled her eyes.

Marilee was laughing. "What would you call it, Helen? *The Gallivanting Gardeners*, or how about *The Horny Horticulturists?*"

"*The Cradle Robber's Revenge?*" added Lily, getting into the spirit of things. Laughing about it put her situation in a better, more manageable perspective.

"Anyway, as I was saying," said Marilee, "Howard is just plain old jealous."

"You mean even though he didn't want me, he can't stand the thought of anyone else being with me?"

"I'm not so sure Howard doesn't want you. He just didn't want the new and improved you, a woman who stands up for herself. But yes, Howard can't stand the thought of anyone else being with you. Especially someone like Will. I sure would like to have been a fly on your garden wall when Howard found you in the bushes with the hunky gardener."

"Me, too," said Helen, starting to giggle again.

"There's one thing that isn't so funny about this, though," said Lily. "I'm afraid Will didn't see the humor in it at all. I tried to call and apologize for everything, but I ended up having to leave messages."

"You mean you haven't spoken to him," said Helen.

"Nope. He hasn't returned my calls."

"Damn that Howard," said Marilee. "He won't be happy until he's ruined everything for you. Not that he could ruin the uh, thing with you and Will." She puckered her pretty features into a frown. "What is the thing with you and Will, Lily? I mean you had a date ..."

"Sort of ...," said Lily. "More of a pseudo-date, really."

"And you did kiss him," said Helen.

Lily sighed. "I think what Will and I are, is over. Not that there was anything, anyway. I mean he is just—"

"Thirty-four," said Helen and Marilee at once.

"Look Lily," said Marilee, "You've got to get past this age thing. I admit that it's unusual, but obviously there's some big attraction going on. I mean, the guy didn't have to cook dinner for you."

"I practically invited myself to see his azaleas," Lily reminded her. "He kind of had to show them to me."

"Easy to do without dinner and a bottle of wine," said Marilee.

"And he did invite you out on his boat," said Helen.

"He said it was a favor, that he needed someone to sail the boat while he worked on it. I don't know what's going on with him. I mean, we really get along. And there is this ... attraction." Lily sighed. "Maybe I'm imagining it after all. I keep remembering the almost-kiss in his living room. Sometimes I think I dreamed up the whole thing. I mean is it possible that I'm so love- and sex-starved that I stumbled into him and my poor emotionally malnourished brain turned it into romance? Am I imagining Will's attraction to me just like I'm imagining Mrs. McVay's presence in my house?"

"Don't forget. Maisy felt it," said Marilee.

"But like Maisy said, there is the possibility that we're both nuts," said Lily.

Y'all aren't nuts," laughed Helen. "Maisy may be outlandish, but she's got a tight grip on reality, and you—you're the sanest person I know, Lily."

"Hey, wait a minute, Helen," said Marilee. "Remember you and I share the same gene pool."

"Lily, you're one of the two sanest people I know," Helen corrected herself.

"Men," said Marilee. "Face it, ladies. If we haven't figured them out by now, it probably ain't gonna happen. And like you said, Lily, this is a different generation." She threw up her hands. "God only knows what makes them tick."

Lily sighed. "Believe me. I've given it plenty of thought." She hesitated.

"And?" said Helen.

"I had about decided that Will is just one of those charming men who love the attention of women regardless of age, and it's a kind of a hobby, getting a rise out of us relationship-deprived females. But then I had a second theory. I think he wants to spend time with me—and not just as my gardener, but he knows I'm way too old. That's why he doesn't want to call our little outings dates. He's embarrassed."

"Lily," said Helen, "I know Will thinks very highly of you, and anybody can see he's attracted to you. He lights up at the mention of your name, dreams up excuses to talk about you. I don't think your age is a factor. At least not in the way you think. The only thing is ..."

"What?" said Lily and Marilee at once.

"He is still seeing Jaime Rogers. I asked him about her—you know, in an off-handed way, and he said they were just friends. But I don't know. Look, I think this flirtation or whatever it is, is just what you need. The thing is, like Marilee said, we think about these things differently than younger people. They're so cavalier towards sex and relationships and all that. I think Will is a good guy, but—"

"I know," interrupted Lily. "There's a lot we don't know about him—other than the sketchy fess-up when we went sailing that day, which he promised to elaborate on and never has. And you don't want me to get hurt."

"Exactly," said Helen.

Lily pressed her lips together in resignation. "Well, it doesn't matter now, because I think Howard scared him off."

"Good Lord, Lil," said Helen. "Will was a lawyer. He knows how these things work. I can't believe your little domestic drama shocked him that much." Helen sighed. "And since you brought it up, I have reason to believe that our cute, little lawyer-cum-landscaper has a few weeds in his own garden, if you get my meaning."

"I think you know something, Helen," said Lily. "Come on, I can take it. What have you heard?"

"He's gay," said Marilee.

"What?" cried Lily and Helen at once.

"What on earth makes you think that?" said Helen.

"I'm guessing. I thought that was what you were going to say," said Marilee. "But think about it. He's into flowers. Really into flowers. And remember how he was so interested in Lily's colors and fabrics and everything when she showed him around Mrs. McVay's—sorry, I mean Lily's house?"

"Well, the little bimbette we saw him with—uh, what was her name, Lily?"

"Jaime."

"Yeah. Jaime didn't look much like a guy to me."

"But he didn't seem very interested in her," said Marilee. "He was more interested in talking to us. Gay guys love middle-aged women, you know."

"Hmm," said Helen. "You do make a pretty good argument." She turned to Lily. "Do you think it could be true?"

Lily sighed. This latest idea was seriously depressing. Of all the obstacles to a relationship with Will, this was one she definitely had not considered.

Gay? Will, gay? She turned the thought over in her mind. Finally she said, "I've been out of circulation a long time, and I know I've led a sheltered existence, but I do have gay friends, and I do know when a man is attracted to me. No, I don't think Will is gay. As a matter of fact, I would bet my last petunia that Will is as straight as they come." She grinned. "Poor choice of words, but you get my drift."

"I certainly do," said Marilee, grinning back at her friend. "Forget I ever mentioned the whole gay thing. Okay, Helen, I interrupted you. What have you managed to dig up on the gardener?"

"I didn't say anything because it's nothing but a rumor. Several rumors as a matter of fact, but they all have a central theme, so there's probably at least a common kernel of truth." She sighed, obviously trying to decide where to begin. Lily sat, literally, on the edge of her seat waiting to hear.

"There's a woman at the center of it all, of course," said Helen.

"There always is," said Marilee shaking her head sagely.

"This woman was the boss' daughter, or maybe even his

wife according to one version. Will was engaged to this woman, ooorrr," Helen drew it out, "He was married to her, oooorrrr," she drew it out further, "He is still married to said woman."

"Still married," Lily murmured. "Oh, my God. That's almost as bad as gay. I mean worse than gay. Much worse than gay."

"Okay. We know you wouldn't go after a married man," said Marilee. "Knowingly, anyway," she added.

"There's more," said Helen.

"Children," said Marilee. "I bet he has a bunch of little children."

"No children," said Helen. "At least not that I know of."

"Whew," said Marilee.

Lily looked very relieved.

"It seems he left the law firm in New York under some kind of shady circumstances. I don't think he was disbarred or anything, but he won't exactly be getting any letters of reference from his former employers either. Of course, if the part about him running off with the boss's wife is true, that's not surprising."

"Where did you hear all this stuff?" asked Marilee.

"You know I never reveal my sources. Let's just say here and there. The interesting thing, what with our village grapevine being as efficient as it is, is that everybody seems to know all about Will helping Lily and showing her his uh, azaleas and taking her sailing and everything, but the big rumor concerning our girl here is that she's dating Dwayne Bond." Helen made a face. "Sorry, Lily. If I hadn't fixed you up with him …"

"The car wash king?" cried Marilee.

"The one and only," said Lily, glaring at Helen. "Why would anyone think I'm dating him?"

"It seems he's told a few people he's crazy about you and well, the folks around here put two and two together—"

"And came up with five," interrupted Lily.

"I wonder if Will's heard the rumor?" said Marilee quietly.

"It doesn't matter," said Lily. "People are going to talk, no matter what." She sighed. "And that goes to show you that Will's marital status and employment history are just one big moot point because he doesn't think of our relationship as anything but business. The fact that he hasn't mentioned me to anyone proves it. I'm such an idiot—or old fool, I think is the standard term." She groaned. "Besides, the whole thing with Will is just so … inappropriate. Why couldn't he be fifteen—even *ten* years older?"

"It's just a little different, that's all," said Marilee gently. "Things aren't always a perfect fit, you know. Also, you don't choose who you fall in love with like you decide which kind of car to buy. It's not a rational thing. You can't help what you feel."

"No, you can't help what you feel," agreed Lily, "But you can help what you do." She rolled her hazel eyes and shook her head. "I can't believe I kissed him. I cost myself a perfectly good gardener. For one kiss." She thought back to Will's muscular body against hers, remembered the passion in that one short kiss, and felt her face flush. She suddenly leaned as far forward as the seatbelt would allow. "You know what? I think it was worth it." A few seconds later she slumped back into the luxurious leather. "I should've waited until we had the fountain back together, though." She sighed. "I guess timing has never been my strong point."

"Oh, hush," said Marilee. "You're being too hard on yourself. For God's sake, it's the twentieth century."

"Twenty-first," said Helen.

"Twenty-first century. Thank, you, Helen. Lily, you're single, he's single. It's not a big deal. Good Lord, the way I hear it, everybody is having sex with anybody these days. And you're worried about one kiss?"

"True. But we were working together. He could sue me for sexual harassment."

"Remember, it's your word against his," said Helen.

"Just hope you get a woman judge," added Marilee. "No woman would convict you once she's seen Will."

"Another excellent point, Marilee. And you know what? I'm not going to waste one more minute of our trip worrying about this."

"That a girl," said Helen.

"Smartest thing you've said all day," agreed Marilee, "Not that I'm not getting one heck of a vicarious thrill out of it all."

By the time they pulled into the Four Seasons Hotel in downtown Atlanta, Lily had forgotten all about Dwayne Bond,

Howard, Will and "the great embarrassment."
    Well, almost.

19.

Good Guys and Bad Guys

That night over Black Russians, which were Marilee's aperitif of choice, (honestly, vodka *and* chocolate?), she explained her calendar was booked with various meetings. These were to be held in a building near the famous Mayfair warehouse where last season's fabulous fashions could be picked up for a song—if you happened to be an associate of a bona fide Mayfair associate, that is.

One had to have the prestigious black and silver card in her possession to gain admittance to this inner-sanctum of very high style at seventy-percent off. Marilee would hand her temporary card (bearing her hastily printed name followed by Mayfair Ass. and signed by none other than Mary Largely Darling) over to Helen and Lily for it's virgin shopping expedition.

"The cocktail party is in our hotel's Georgian Room. It starts at six, followed by dinner and the fashion show." She explained this for perhaps the tenth time, segueing into her "business voice." "Tomorrow will be a very busy day. We'll need to get an early start in the morning. My meeting starts at nine. I'll park near the warehouse, and y'all can use the car when you're done. I'll grab a cab back to the hotel when I get out of my meetings."

"Don't forget Les Jardins," said Lily. "I need a statue in the worst way."

"I haven't forgotten. We're doing that day after tomorrow, right?"

"Right. Marilee, you're being very organized," said Lily, genuinely impressed.

"I'm trying to be. It isn't exactly my strong suit, as you know, but I think I can pull this Mayfair thing off." She chewed the nail of her index finger. "Don't you?"

"Sure you can," said Lily. "Nobody knows clothes better than you, and you're a born salesperson. I bet you could sell Mary Largely a polyester pantsuit and a plastic headband to match."

"I appreciate that," said Marilee, smiling at the image of M. L. Darling in polyester and plastic. But then the smile turned into a frown, and she bit her lower lip, evidently needing a tad more reassurance. "I didn't have much luck with the gallery, remember."

"By Christmas, every debutante and her mama will be running around in Mayfair," Helen assured her. "You're a natural for this."

Marilee grinned and relaxed into her chair, her confidence and good humor completely restored.

They spent the next hour discussing spring fashions. Actually they listened to Marilee educate them on the subject, but they didn't mind. A second round of Black Russians would have made a lecture on IRS forms a pleasantry.

The next morning, eight AM sharp found the three women back in Marilee's gleaming silver Mercedes propelled toward the world of "couture that's pretty damn haute," as Helen put it.

"Boy, this place is deserted," said Helen, looking around downtown Atlanta.

"It's a good thing I got here early. We have our pick of parking places," said Marilee, flipping her new yellow and lavender Mayfair scarf over one shoulder. "In another hour we wouldn't be able to find a space this close to the warehouse. There it is, right there, and my meetings are in the building next to it."

She pointed to a block of tall buildings as she pulled into a corner parking lot just down the street. A Mutt-and-Jeff couple of young guys approached the car with a roll of tickets.

Marilee rolled down the window of the Mercedes and smiled. "Should I park it or will you?"

Jeff smirked and elbowed Mutt who peered into the car as if he'd never seen females before and shrugged his shoulders.

He spoke to Jeff in a language totally foreign to the women then turned to Marilee and said with an enormous grin, "Ten dollar, please. All day, twenty," and handed Marilee a ticket torn from his roll.

"Twenty dollars!" yelled Helen, but Marilee had already whipped a couple of crisp tens out of her lemon yellow Mayfair bag. She handed them to Mutt as she slid out of the front seat. Helen and Lily hopped out as well.

"Oh, I guess you keep these," said Marilee, tossing the keys to an astounded Mutt.

The keys sailed up in a lovely arc, the Mercedes emblem on the key chain catching the early morning sun before they landed safely in Mutt's outstretched hand. Marilee turned on her fabulous new Mayfair heel and headed toward her future.

The Jeff half of the parking duo suddenly ran up behind them, pointing back toward the car and speaking animatedly in his strange tongue.

Marilee, who was used to being harassed by men, gave him a stern look and instructed her friends to "just ignore him."

Since Marilee would be cabbing it back to the hotel she gave Lily the parking ticket, and the three friends parted ways at the corner.

Marilee quickly made her way to Mayfair headquarters where a kindly doorman who couldn't have been a day under ninety directed her to the lavishly appointed Mayfair Salon. She clipped a silver tag bearing her name in black calligraphy to the yellow silk of her Mayfair sweater and was granted entry to the world of "intercontinental fashion with American flair."

At this moment Helen and Lily were having a more down-to-earth experience. After proceeding from one locked door to another, they noticed a discreet sign informing them that they had indeed found the outlet of all outlets—the Mayfair Second Season Apparel Warehouse.

"Uh, oh," said Helen.

"What?" asked Lily, squinting to read the small print on the sign. "Mayfair Warehouse, second and third floors. Open Monday through Friday, 10 to 6." She stared at Helen. "And this is Saturday." Lily turned and slumped against the locked door. "I can't believe this. What are we going to do?"

"First, we're going to find Marilee and strangle her with her new five hundred dollar scarf, then ..." said Helen. She stopped mid-tirade. A strange look came over her face, and she smiled. "What am I talking about? This is a good thing. I hate shopping for clothes! We can go to the museum, the bookstore, have lunch—"

"Go to the botanical gardens," interrupted Lily. "Let's get the car."

The two friends retraced their steps, getting lost only twice along the way.

"Lord, I feel like I've been down Alice's rabbit hole," said Helen as they finally made their way to the front of the building.

What had been a deserted street was now full of cars and pedestrians, erasing the "twilight zone" feeling they'd had since they'd pulled into the parking lot.

But when they got to the corner, it became apparent that something was not quite right.

"Is this the same corner?" said Helen.

"Yes. There's that big Coca-Cola sign, and I remember that brick wall covered in vines over there," said Lily.

"Then where's the car?" they said in unison.

"And where are those guys who parked the car?" said Helen.

Three other young men also of obvious mid-eastern origin were now issuing tickets and directing drivers into parking spaces. They were not collecting anyone's keys or parking any cars themselves.

Lily stared at her friend with a stricken look on her face.

"What?" said Helen, the gravity of the situation not having dawned on her.

"They stole the car! Those guys stole Marilee's brand new zillion-dollar Mercedes, that's what!"

"Omigosh. You're right. That's why that guy chased after us. He was trying to tell us not to leave the keys with his friend."

"I hope I'm wrong, but that's the only solution I can think of."

They raced across the intersection to the probable scene of the probable crime and descended on the new attendants who spoke only slightly better English than their predecessors.

After a lot of pig Latin, and sign language that was getting them nowhere, Lily remembered the ticket in her purse. This got the replacement parking attendants excited.

"Crook! Crook!" they shouted. "Crook come early, take money for parking, but they not parking workers," explained the older of the two.

"I don't get it," said Lily.

"It's a scam," said Helen. "Those guys show up before the lot opens and take money from anyone who gets here early. It happened to my aunt in New Orleans one time."

"Yes! Yes!" cried the real attendants. "Like New Orleans. Happen here, too. Happen everywhere."

Helen, encouraged by their understanding of her explanation, turned to them and asked, "But vere eez our car?" as she pantomimed the question with dramatic facial expressions and shrugs.

The two men looked at one another with total incomprehension.

"Why don't they understand me?" She groaned.

"Well, for one thing you sound like Dracula," said Lily. "Let me try."

"We left a silver Mercedes here. Where is it?" she carefully enunciated.

"Mercedes gone? Where keys?"

"The other parking worker, the crook has them," said Helen.

"Ohh," the parking attendant groaned and put his hands to his head. "Mercedes gone." He turned to his friend and explained the situation in their native tongue. They then got into a brief but heated discussion. When they'd obviously reached some agreement, the older of the two turned to Helen and Lily.

"Know nothing. Good-bye." They started to walk away.

"Hey, wait a minute," Helen called after them.

They ignored her.

"Aren't you going to help us?" called Lily, but not only didn't they comprehend, it seems they'd suddenly gone deaf.

"What are we going to do?" cried Helen.

"We've got to get Marilee out of that meeting. Come on."

Lily sprinted off in the direction of the Mayfair building with a sweating, panting Helen not far behind.

A mere ten minutes later found the kindly Mayfair doorman shaking his head as the disheveled duo rushed past him, Helen gasping, "Emergency! Emergency!"

Lily figured he interpreted this to mean a fashion emergency and that was the reason he let them pass. She didn't have time to give it much thought because seconds later she and Helen were skulking around the entrance to the Mayfair Salon where they hoped to get Marilee's attention without attracting attention to themselves. Not much chance of that since they stood out like two left clogs at the prom, thought Lily.

Lily was about to get distracted by the fabulous blooms of the white Bird of Paradise they were crouched behind when a breathy voice said, "Ladies, may I help you?"

They turned to find a tall redhead swathed in icy green lace and wearing an equally icy smirk looking down at them. From her cool demeanor one would guess that sweaty fashion disasters hiding in the foliage were nothing new to her. It was possible she thought they were couture thieves out to copy the latest Mayfair designs. If so, she was being pretty hospitable about it.

"I'm sorry to intrude," said Lily, "But we need to speak to our friend, Marilee. Her car has been stolen."

The woman stared quizzically at Lily. Did she not think this was cause enough for interrupting the Mayfair wingding?

"Her new Mercedes," added Helen.

It was then that Lily noted the woman's name tag tucked into the lacy green folds of her frock. It was Mary Largely, herself.

"Good grief," the infamous field marshal said lightly, reacting with a level of dismay reserved for a smudged pedicure. But at least it was a reaction. "I'll get her for you. Marilee is the new associate, right?"

Before they could answer, she had turned on her chic pump and dissolved into the blur of femininity in the Mayfair Salon, leaving Lily and Helen in a subtle cloud of Chanel No. 5. *So that's how it's supposed to smell*, thought Lily as she mentally compared the lovely fragrance swirling around her to the strange aroma of her mother-in-law that regularly infiltrated the McVay home. *My home,* she corrected herself, and realized that this was the first time she'd thought of her problems since arriving in Atlanta. She had new problems now, she realized as Marilee breezed toward them, a panicky little smile plastered on her face.

"Are y'all sure y'all were at the right lot? There's one on every corner, and they all look alike," said Marilee hopefully when they'd explained the situation.

"We've been all through that," said Lily. "Your car has been stolen, and we need to call the police right now."

Finally resigned to the fact that the car was gone, she sighed and said, "Well, it's just a car, after all, and I'm sure it's insured." She made a little face. "You know, I wasn't wild about that silver color anyway."

Minutes later a policeman was taking notes from the parking attendants as Marilee bravely blotted perspiration from her forehead with her lemony silk scarf. A report of the stolen car was made. Marilee called her husband who took the whole thing surprisingly well, admonishing her to "please be more careful" and assuring her that the Mercedes was indeed insured.

Marilee headed back toward her Mayfair meeting looking slightly less crisp and enthusiastic than she had earlier that morning. Lily and Helen made lunch reservations and arrangements to rent a vehicle big enough to hold all of Marilee's luggage and four women, one of the females being a life-sized statue that Lily had found on Les Jardins' Web site.

Mr. Craig, as the proprietor referred to himself, was holding "Kneeling Water Maiden" for her, and as promised, the mention of Maisy Downey's name insured a twenty-five percent discount.

When Lily and Helen finally met up with Marilee at the hotel, they hadn't had the heart to tell her that the Mayfair Second Season Apparel Warehouse was closed on Saturdays and that they would be attired in non-Mayfair apparel for the big event that night. As it turned out, they didn't have to worry.

20.

Lemons to Lemonade

Helen's eyebrows shot up into her silver bangs. "You're already quitting Clothes-R-Us? This has got to be a record. Like speed-dating only speed-employment."

Marilee chewed her lower lip for few seconds then let out a sigh of resignation.

"I can't stand Mary Largely."

"What happened?" said Lily.

"Not only did she not care that my car had been stolen, she was irritated that I had to leave her meeting to see about it. She also made an unkind remark, which I will not repeat about my friends who were lurking in the potted flora."

"So she's really as mean as a cottonmouth," declared Lily, trying to keep her face serious.

"Meaner than a whole nest of 'em. The talk around Mayfair is that her husband walked out on her, which has ramped her witchiness up to a whole new level. She's blaming the future ex-Mr. Mary Largely for everything from her nasty disposition to her fallen arches and taking it out on the new associates. So I quit!"

"Good girl," said Helen, who was feeling guilty about the speed-employment quip. Then it dawned on her that this meant the end of her involvement with the world of high fashion. "You did exactly the right thing, Marilee," she said with renewed conviction.

The next morning they piled into the rented SUV and headed for Les Jardins. The combination gift and garden shop was separated from the proprietor's finely-appointed digs by a large courtyard. Mr. Craig, the owner, shared this little jewel box of a house with his "partner in all things"—a man named Leon.

The other ultra-charming building as well as the courtyard was chocked full of unique collections. Dried stems, garden tools, gifts and furniture—a delightful hodgepodge—was scattered throughout a jungle of exotic tropical plants. In addition, there were wall fountains and statuary and antique architectural pieces that Mr. Craig and Leon had scavenged on their regular trips to Tuscany and Provence. It was fabulous.

Gazing around at one extraordinary find after another, Lily's first thought was, *Will would love this place*, and she realized that she hadn't left him behind at all. There was no point in trying to deceive herself. But had he moved on and left her behind? The fact that he hadn't returned her calls after the "Kama Sutra" episode lead her to believe so.

Closing her eyes, she was back in the "secret garden." She could feel Will behind her, his muscular chest against her back, his arms around her as she struggled to tie up the Cherokee rose. Recalling the now-familiar masculine smell of him, she felt his breath near her ear, his lips on hers when she'd impulsively kissed him.

The kiss.

It had been short, but without a doubt the sweetest, most sensual kiss she'd ever experienced. Just thinking about it made her light-headed and warm all over. There was no doubt about it. Lily missed him. Really missed him. And it occurred to her that Will and her love of gardening had become as intertwined as the honeysuckle vines in Mrs. M.'s neglected flower beds.

She frowned remembering how difficult it was to untangle those vines without damaging the fragile buds flowering beneath them. Disengaging herself from Will would be at least as tricky.

"Lily, are you listening? Mr. Craig and Marilee are really hitting it off," said Helen, and Lily's daydream dissolved into the soft, scented air of Les Jardins.

There was no doubt that Mr. Craig was gay and devoted to the absent Leon, but an instant rapport had sprung up between him and Marilee. Lily looked on in amused amazement as the new friends complimented one another's shoes and shared titillating info on various Mayfair associates, all of whom Mr. Craig was intimately acquainted with.

He insisted on giving Marilee and her friends the complete tour of his and Leon's digs (they were in the bathroom, discussing his claw-footed bath tub for twenty minutes) followed by coffee on his balcony.

As they sipped café au lait beneath enormous hanging baskets of white geraniums, Marilee poured out her litany of business misadventures to Mr. Craig. Remarkably, he was unfazed by her apparent ineptitude and thoroughly charmed by her unworried attitude.

As it turned out, his problems were the opposite of Marilee's. He'd been wildly successful and wanted to open another shop, but Leon would have no part of it. His "partner in all things" was weary of long hours in the shop. Biannual trips scouring shops and flea markets and farm yards abroad were quickly losing their romantic appeal.

"You know, Mr. Craig ..."

"Call me Craig," he said, hanging on her every word.

"You know, Craig, this place reminds me of the building where I had my last ... or maybe I should say next-to-last business—my art gallery. It even had a courtyard."

Of course Lily and Helen had seen the writing on the courtyard wall the minute Marilee mentioned the vacant building. Before the café au lait was cool, Marilee and Mr. Craig were formulating a business plan. The discovery that they were fourth cousins on Craig's daddy's side didn't hurt their burgeoning alliance. Nothing cements a new southern friendship like the unearthing of shared kin, you know.

Marilee and her irrepressible optimism (and abundant family tree) had turned mean Mary Largely and a stolen Mercedes into a new adventure. *Lemons to lemonade*, thought Lily. That was Marilee's motto. And it was all great, but it was not the reason they were there. Her lemons were still lemons.

When Marilee and Mr. Craig finally took a breath she said, "What about the statue, Mr. Craig?"

"I want you to call me Craig," he said. He looked at Helen. "You, too, Helen. Call me Craig."

Helen was controlling her impatience well, but Lily could

see it was taking everything she had.

"Tell us about the statue, Craig," she said flatly as Lily removed the old photo from her purse and handed it to Craig.

"It's her," he said. His voice cracked with emotion, and he sniffed loudly. Marilee patted his arm. "This is how she is meant to be—splashing water, sunlight dappling her alabaster limbs."

"You mean this is the exact same statue?" Lily asked.

"Oh, yes. It's her."

"Could we see her?" asked Helen.

Seconds later they were staring down at "Kneeling Water Maiden."

"As I said, I'll give you a good price since you're a friend of Maisy's. But also because she's damaged goods. The statue I mean. My pet name for her is Marie Antoinette because she was decapitated." To Lily's surprise, he took out a lavender hanky and dabbed at his eyes. "I cemented her head back together myself."

Lily couldn't believe it. Except for a hairline crack running around her slender neck and a few nicks here and there, Kneeling Water Maiden aka Marie Antoinette seemed identical to the statue that had been in the picture of Mrs. McVay's Garden. When she shared this with Mr. Craig, he smiled impishly at her and insisted they have another cup of coffee. He had a little story about Marie the headless water maiden.

Craig refreshed their cups and put a pewter tray of miniature raspberry tarts on the mosaic surface of the coffee table. Linen cocktail napkins, each embroidered with a different flower and the Les Jardins logo, finished out the scene.

As Lily suspected, Craig had bought the statue from Maisy Downey some years prior. Someone had tossed "Marie" (and her severed head) out onto the street for the trash man. Marie's remains were rescued by Maisy and were interred in the old lady's garden shed until in a fit of cleaning-out she had decided to get rid of everything she hadn't used in the last fifteen years.

Maisy's old friends at Les Jardins, Leon and Craig swapped her a wall fountain for the statue. Craig painstakingly repaired Marie Antoinette and listed her as "Kneeling Water Maiden" in his catalog. He put an exorbitant price on the statue because he didn't really want to part with her for reasons he couldn't explain to the bewildered Leon.

"Something told me to hold on to her," said Craig. "Now I know why." He looked at the picture and sniffed. "This is where she belongs."

Soon two burly guys were wedging Marie in between Marilee's luggage in the back of the SUV. The statue's head rested next to Lily who occupied the one rear seat not flattened to accommodate the kneeling water maiden.

The "girls," as Craig referred to Lily, Helen and Marilee, made a last stop in his adorable powder room and got on the road at last. With all the café au lait they had consumed, they hadn't gotten twenty miles down the interstate before they had to stop again.

21.

Mixed Messages

"You have eleven messages," said the male voice who sounded like some come-hither robot trapped in Lily's answering machine.

"Lily, this is Will. Got your message, but I've been swamped," he said. "I might have to send someone else over to help you finish up. Things are kind of crazy right now." He might have been talking to a stranger for all the emotion in his voice. "Sorry. Uh, I'll try to call you later."

He'll try to call me later? "He's breaking up with me," Lily said to the portrait of her dead mother-in-law as she slumped onto the sofa in the den/parlor.

Mrs. McVay scowled at her. As familiar voices chirped their messages in the background, Lily reminded herself that Will was not breaking up with her because they were never together. *I've been dumped by someone I wasn't even going with,* she thought. *How sad is that?*

She had prepared herself for the probability that she had misread Will's feelings toward her, but somehow she had overlooked the possibility of him being out of her life all together. She had assumed he would be her friend at least. She was devastated. Heartbroken. And these terrible feelings forced Lily to admit once and for all that she was in love with Will.

After all the years of nothingness, she was hopelessly in love. With a beautiful, thirty-four year old man who not only didn't return that love, but didn't even want to be her gardening buddy from the sound of his message. The tears pricked and stung, but she couldn't release them, couldn't release whatever it was that had her all locked up inside.

The unheard messages played on. Lily stared unseeing at Mrs. McVay. Mrs. McVay stared back.

Sinatra singing My Way got her attention. The music stopped abruptly, and a barely muffled voice said, "Mrs. McVay always hated you, Lily. Howard hates you. I hate you." The words slurred worse than ever, but the caller was getting careless. Maybe the next time she would forget to muffle her words at all. And Lily was close to remembering. She could feel it. She was so close.

But who is she! I know that voice, so why won't it come to me? she berated herself, but the more she focused the farther the answer slipped from her grasp.

Beep. "Hey, there, Lily. Dwayne Bond here. You know the big Memorial Day weekend is coming up. Thought you might want to head down to the gulf. I've got a condo at Emerald Towers. You'd have your own room. I'll keep it in low gear, I promise. Come on Friday, Saturday, whenever. Stay as long as you like. Lemme know." And he left his number.

She stopped the answering machine. The weekend was just days away. Everybody would be enjoying the holidays with families and friends. Everybody she knew would be at the beach—except Lily who would be sitting alone with the McVay memories.

Lily was friends with many of the people who had condos at Emerald Towers. There would be parties and boating and sunbathing. She was way ahead of schedule with the garden. Getting Marie Antoinette on her feet was the last big chore. Lily was tired and needed a break. She was going to the beach.

"Dwayne, it's Lily. Yes, I just got your message. Thank you for the invitation. If I accept, it's important you know I'm not interested in—well, in anything but friendship. You're sure you're okay with that? Okay, then. I'll drive down on Saturday. See you then."

Lily was feeling good about her decision as she turned the machine back on to hear the last few messages.

"Lily, this is Will." His voice sounded warm now, embarrassed even. "Uh, I really need to talk to you. I tried your cell, but it doesn't seem to be working. I'll try you later."

"Damn," muttered Lily. "Why didn't I take a phone to Atlanta? What was I thinking?"

There was a beep. "Lily, this is Will again. Could you give me a call uh, when you get a minute?" Beep. Nothing. Beep. The robot voice informed her that she was at the end of her messages.

Lily felt relief flood through her. Next came anger. Then the familiar confusion. Things weren't so bad after all. Or were they? Maybe Will simply realized how cold his first message sounded and wanted to talk to her in person, let her down gently.

This is ridiculous! What am I, thirteen years old? I am done with this torment. She went into the kitchen, opened the doors to the garden and breathed deeply. The fragrant evening air did its magic, and she began to calm down. Soothed by her little shot of nature, she picked up the phone, put a light-hearted smile on her face and punched in Will's number.

"This is Will. Leave a message."

"Will, this is Lily. Sorry I missed your call," she said breezily. "I just got back from Atlanta—with a statue. I'll be out of town again this weekend. I'll try to call you when I get back."

Lily found some brie that didn't look too bad and an unopened box of crackers. Supper. She poured herself a glass of wine and sat at her kitchen table, exhausted from her travels and the emotional roller coaster Will's messages had put her on.

She looked out at the garden, white blossoms glowing and lightening bugs twinkling in the gathering dusk. Marie Antoinette lay clutching her dry, tilted bucket in an undignified heap next to the pond and her severed lifeline, the ugly, exposed water pipe. Lily pictured her back on her pedestal, water gently splashing into the waiting pond as she finished the last of the cheese and put her plate in the sink.

There on the counter was Mrs. McVay's photo album. She found the picture of Howard and Jake Johnson and Marie Antoinette, and slipped it between the padded velvet covers of the photo album. As she did this, her fingernail snagged the time-rotted silk lining and pulled it loose. There was paper tucked inside. When Lily slid it from its hiding place, dried petals fluttered onto the table, sending a shiver through her.

At first she thought she could still smell the stale sweetness of the decayed rose, but no, it was you-know-who and her malodorous perfume-perm aura growing stronger by the second. And the air in Lily's kitchen was getting downright frosty. She unfolded the sheet of paper that had held the rose intact for so many years. *To my Rosie. I'll love you forever. J.*

"Well, I'll be," Lily said aloud. "Rosie." It had to be Mrs. McVay. Rosemary McVay. Lily had almost forgotten that was her name. As a matter of fact, she couldn't remember anyone but Howard's father calling her Rosemary. She'd certainly never heard anyone refer to her mother-in-law as Rosie. "Too familiar!" she could just hear her say. Besides, Mrs. McVay didn't believe in nicknames.

"Rosie and J. Jake, the gardener?" It couldn't be, but it had to be, she thought, getting up to open the door in an effort to rid the room of the musty chill. It was starting to sprinkle outside, and the breeze picked up a bit, blowing a delicious rain-on-plants smell across the porch and into the kitchen.

The mother-in-law smell had all but dissipated when the breeze intensified, howling past Lily. Photos, letters and the remnants of a rose that had bloomed so many years ago scattered over the McVay kitchen floor. The door slammed shut. The chilly air and musty odor vanished. Lily sat staring at the closed door. She slowly let out the breath she'd been holding and forced herself to remain calm.

Smoothing her windblown hair, she thought very seriously about whether she should be foraging through other people's lives—their secret lives. What was she doing here in McVay House, anyway? She looked at the McVay past strewn across the floor. It seemed as if Howard's mother might be wondering the same thing.

22.

Be there or be Square

Saturday afternoon found Lily in her red jeep heading over the pass bridge. A wide strip of beach more like powdered sugar than sand was dotted with sunbathers, umbrellas, catamarans and jet skis. As the car climbed, the panoramic view expanded to include infinite blue sky intersecting bluer water at the distant horizon.

To her left were the elaborate, pastel-colored beach houses of Pelican Island. Ahead was an endless ribbon of condos lacing the shore. Sun glinted on tile roofs and tipped the gentle waves of the gulf. Lily smiled at a gray pelican with its long beak and great pouch as it sailed along beside her at the peak of the towering bridge. She was feeling very good about the weekend—even if it did mean sharing it with Dwayne Bond.

Just beyond the bridge was the crème de la crème of condos, Emerald Towers. Dwayne's corner unit was on the third floor. Ideal—great view without the dizzying height of the higher floors.

"You made it!" Dwayne said, beaming at her and taking her bag before stowing it, to Lily's great relief, in a guest room.

"Everybody's waitin' on the Hooker—that's my boat. Why don't you change, and we'll take her out for a spin around Pelican Island. But first, a quick tour of the premises."

The place was spacious with a wrap-around balcony affording Dwayne a fabulous view. It was more like being on a ship that in a building. Glass doors were open and a sea breeze lifted white, gauzy curtains making them seem like clouds floating into the room. The rest of the condo was predictable, as if bought as a package from one of the high-end stores that provided such things. The decor was white and chrome with sea green accents here and there.

Pictures of vintage cars and boats adorned the walls and table tops. There were a few framed photos of Dwayne and friends with giant fish, but mostly just cars and boats. The master bedroom was a testosterone nightmare. Everything was black and chrome and animal prints. A huge mounted sailfish stared at Lily from above the king-sized bed's metal headboard. A lavishly framed print of a reclining nude graced a side wall.

Lily went into the guest room and locked the door. As she struggled to get The Suit over her thighs, she couldn't help but think of the last time she'd worn it—the day she'd gone sailing with Will. Forcing the polyester/nylon/lycra spandex over her hips, she forced the memory of Will standing on her front porch grinning at her (and sailing his boat in the afternoon sun and almost kissing her while the rain poured outside) out of her mind. She threw on a new, black cover-up, a pair of black and white striped flip-flops, covered herself in sunscreen and hurried out. The car wash king was waiting.

The Hooker (short for Happy Hooker) turned out to be a gleaming forty-two-foot Bertram with a dozen or so people already aboard. Business associates of Dwayne's, they were all from out of town, and seemed nice for the most part. Lily couldn't help thinking how Howard would have hated it.

"Not exactly PLU's (people like us)," would have been his smug assessment.

The boat's configuration necessitated the guests dividing up into small groups—some up on the bridge with Dwayne, some inside taking advantage of the air-conditioning, a few sun-bathers stretched out on the bow, and some seated in the stern. People came and went to these different areas, availing themselves of hors d'oeuvres and drinks in the cabin or beer and soft drinks from ice chests on the bridge and stern.

As the Hooker cruised through the aqua water surrounding Pelican Island, Lily soaked up the salty air and sunshine, watched dolphins at play, returned admiring waves from passing boats and got to know the other guests.

Being the dutiful date, she spent a good bit of time up on

the bridge with Dwayne and a man named Boudreaux from Louisiana who told funny Cajun jokes. His date, Bonnie, had the biggest fake boobs Lily had ever seen. Stretched over these "headlights" as Dwayne would no doubt refer to them, was a tee shirt with a Blue marlin on the front.

Beneath the fish it said, "Size does matter." On the back it read, "I've been tagged and released." Giant fake boobs aside, Bonnie turned out to be a sweet, funny woman whose main interests were fishing, gardening and her four grandchildren. It was a good thing Lily liked Bonnie and Boudreaux. They were also staying at Dwayne's condo.

Dwayne refrained from talking "car wash" business or using any sexist car euphemisms. When not trying to impress, he seemed to be a pretty decent guy. (Of course, Dwayne could afford to be humble — the Happy Hooker was doing his bragging for him.) All in all, it was a very pleasant afternoon that turned into any equally enjoyable evening up to a point.

The condo association was throwing an upscale shrimp boil by the pool. Beneath dozens of imported palms rustling in a strong sea breeze, residents and guests mingled, ate from heaping platters of shrimp, corn and sausage, drank and danced to a band complete with a female vocalist who could sing anything from country to jazz to rock to hip-hop.

Dwayne and Lily were headed out to the "dance floor" when Boudreaux the Cajun joke-teller sauntered up and murmured something into Dwayne's ear.

Dwayne's face turned a bit pale beneath his tan.

"Excuse me, darlin'," he said. "Got a small domestic goin' on needs ol' Dwayne's attention. Bonnie here'll keep you company, won't you, babe?"

"Sure, Dwayne," she said, but the two men had already hurried off.

Bonnie sucked from a straw in her frozen piña colada and said, "Poor Dwayne." She lowered her voice conspiratorially, though no one could have heard her over the band, party voices and crashing surf. "It's his in-significant other." She rolled her eyes for added emphasis. "You know, Stacy. The ex. She's driving him crazy." A loud gurgling sound came from Bonnie as she sucked the last drops from her drink. "Time for a refill," she said. She looked at Lily's empty glass. "Can I bring you anything?"

"No. I think I'll take a little walk down the beach. I won't be long."

Lily slipped out of her shoes and left them behind a palm tree. The wide beach was full of people—kids chasing sand crabs, couples out for a late stroll, condo residents on balconies and decks. But still, it was a nice respite from the partiers packed into the pool area at Emerald Towers. She headed for the shoreline where the walking was easier on the hard-packed sand.

Before returning to the Emerald Towers and Dwayne, she would go as far as the Sand Crab, she decided. The Crab, as it was affectionately known, was an ancient, sprawling bar that had been added on to with every generation of beachgoers. Half of the party at the Towers would end up there later on, lured by nostalgia—it was where most of them had enjoyed their first beer—and reliably great entertainment. There was standing room only on its sprawling decks already, but still a relatively quiet scene for a weekend night at the Crab.

Phosphorous-tinged waves splashed against Lily's ankles as she walked. There was a lovely, three-quarter moon to keep her company. A ship's lights winked far out in the gulf. She was so taken with the beauty of the evening that she didn't notice a big wave until it broke, sending salt water up her calves and halfway up her white skirt.

She squealed with surprise. "Oh, great!" she said aloud, but had to laugh. The water felt good on her hot legs, and she doubted anyone at the party would notice if she was wearing a skirt, much less whether it was wet.

"Lily? Is that you?"

A lanky figure emerged from the shadows, pushing his fingers through his hair in that unmistakable gesture. In his other hand was a beer.

"Will? Oh, my gosh, I'm so happy to see you," she blurted out before she could stop herself.

"Really?" He swayed a little and took a sip of what was obviously not his first beer of the day. "Because you didn't return my calls. Then I heard you were going away for the weekend with the car wash guy."

"The old grapevine is humming, it sounds like."

"Yeah. It is. Well, I guess I'll see you in town."

And he walked off a little crookedly down the beach.

Lily watched him until he turned toward the Sand Crab and the crowd on its lower deck. In a few seconds he would be lost from view.

"Will! Wait."

She hurried toward him, and he met her halfway.

"Listen, Will." She sighed, not sure what to say, then decided the truth was probably a good place to start. "When I got your message saying you weren't going to work with me any more, I was so … disappointed. I mean, you had every right, but you sounded so cold. Like you didn't even want to be my friend anymore. I just didn't know what to think. Then when Dwayne called I thought, the backyard by myself or a party at the beach? Besides, Dwayne's okay when he's not bragging, and I've got my own room and everything, so …"

"What?" Will was grinning at her, his white teeth shining against his tanned face in the moonlight. "You have your own room? You mean you and Dwayne aren't—"

"Is that what you thought? Heavens, no. And I made that perfectly clear to him."

Will was still smiling at her. Finally, he shook his head, ran his fingers though his hair again.

"I'm sorry. About not calling you back after that afternoon in the garden. When you kissed me." He looked at her, softly, remembering. "You did kiss me," he repeated as if reassuring himself that it had actually happened. "And I thought … Then Howard showed up like he owned the place, like he owned you."

He took a deep breath. "And I'm sorry about leaving that message saying I wasn't going to work with you. As soon as I left it, I regretted it. I called back several times, but I don't blame you for not calling me. I acted … It was stupid."

He hung his head, weaving a little, as if unsure whether to go on, then looked at her. "Lily, I'll be honest with you. That whole scene with Howard and his girlfriend got to me. Brought back some bad memories from my New York days. Now is definitely not the time, but I want to tell you all about it. I want us to sit down and talk, first thing after the weekend if you're interested."

"I am very interested," she said.

"Does that mean I'm forgiven?"

"Yes, I think it does."

"Thanks. You don't know how much better I feel."

I think I have a pretty good idea, thought Lily as Will put an arm around her shoulders.

"Come on" he said. "I'll walk you back to the Towers."

"How do you know where I'm staying?"

"Like you said, the grapevine is always humming."

As they neared the party, the female singer started singing, "Chain, chain, chain ... chain of fools." She sounded just like the great Aretha Franklin.

"I do believe they're playing your song," said Will with an evil grin.

"I believe they are," said Lily, laughing.

He took her hand. "Let's see some of those moves. Course it won't be the same since you're not wearing your little towel and little shower cap."

Lily gave him a look that said, *you ain't seen nothin' yet,* and took his hand.

For an inebriated guy dancing in the sand and semi-darkness, Will was pretty good.

"You've got some impressive moves yourself," laughed Lily.

This observation caused him to throw any inhibition (not already chased away by alcohol) to the wind.

"I'm jus gettin' started, baby," he said, slurring his words but completely full of himself at this point. "I ain't nothin' but your fool," he sang along with the music.

Lily rolled her eyes in mock ecstasy.

"My doctor says take it easy," Lily and Will sang to each other, their faces inches apart.

Lily laughed as Will attempted to spin her around in the sand, and she stumbled against him.

Several young women were walking and laughing nearby. One of them called out, "Hey, Wills, I wondered what happened to you."

It was Jaime, her friend, Kate, and another girl.

Lily gave him a look that said, *you're with her and had the nerve to give me a hard time about Dwayne?*

Will stopped dancing and shook his head. "Iss not what you think." He turned toward Jaime. *Is he going to just leave me here?* Lily wondered.

"I'm kinda busy right now," yelled Will a little louder than he needed to. To Lily he said, "She's not my date. I don't have a date. She just showed up at the Crab."

"I need to talk to you," insisted Jaime also a little louder than was necessary to be heard over the surf and music.

Lily was getting irritated, but there was something else. A déjà vu attack? No, it was like the date with Dwayne when they were at his ex-wife, Stacey's house.

Completely forgetting about Jaime, she grabbed Will's arm. "Will! It's the ex car wash queen!"

Will looked at her dumbly. "Nah, that's just Ja—"

"No, I mean that Dwayne's ex-wife, Stacey Bond, is the phone freak, the litterbug. I finally placed the voice. It's her. And she's here."

"Where?" He looked around.

"Will, I seriously need to talk to you," shrieked Jaime, who, it was obvious, had also consumed many beers.

"And I am seriously busy," said Will, not taking his eyes off of Lily. "Now, about the phone freak—you're not going back there alone."

"I'm going to find Dwayne and tell him," said Lily. "Then I'm going to get my things and drive home."

"I'm coming wiss you," said Will. "I've had a few beers," he admitted sheepishly.

A drunk bodyguard is better than no bodyguard, thought Lily. "Let's go find 007," she said, heading back to the swirling crowd around the Towers' pool.

She found her sandals, then started asking if anyone had seen Dwayne. The band was going strong. "What you want? Baby I got it," sang the Aretha clone—and so was the party. It was so loud she didn't think most of the people even heard her before shaking their heads. Will was too busy fending off females of all ages who were trying to dance with him.

Finally, Lily yelled into his ear, "Let's try the condo."

"Fine," he yelled back. "But if Bond's not there, you can leave him a note. I'm not leaving you here with that woman on the loose."

When they got to the condo, the door was open and the room full of people, some of them on the balcony dancing to the music below. None of them happened to be Dwayne.

Lily and Will went into the master bedroom. To Lily's surprise, Bonnie, who had changed into a V-neck Life's a Beach T-shirt, fresh piña colada at her side, was instructing Craig in the art of fly fishing. Craig's partner in all things, Leon, reclined on the bed beneath the mounted sailfish observing the fishing lesson.

"Just a flick of the wrist, sweetie," Bonnie was saying.

"Honey, if there's one thing I can do, it's flick my wrist," said Craig, landing the fly into an upside down cowboy hat.

When Craig saw Lily he literally dropped what he was doing and rushed over to give her kisses on both cheeks. (Something he'd picked up while antiquing in France, no doubt.) Leon waved and threw a kiss, but Lily wasn't sure that it wasn't in Will's direction.

"Oh, of course we know the king of the car washes," said Craig. "We've had a condo here since it was built. Got in on the pre-construction price, you know."

It was at that moment that the king himself sauntered in wearing a mega-watt smile. When he saw Will the smile lost a good bit of wattage for a second, then brightened back up.

"Lily, I heard you were lookin' for me."

He reached over and extended his hand to Will. "Hi, there, son. The name's Bond." Sober pause. "Dwayne Bond."

Will managed to introduce himself with a straight face.

"Dwayne, I need to talk to you," said Lily.

"Sure thing, baby." He glanced at Will. "Anything you want."

"It's about Stacey," said Lily.

Lily and Dwayne went into the only unoccupied spot presently available which was the master bath—a marvel of black marble and chrome. To Dwayne's obvious consternation,

Will followed, but the king wisely said nothing.

Lily told him about the harassing calls and how she finally recognized the voice as Stacey's. Dwayne looked doubtful until she mentioned the Dairy Queen wrappers on her lawn and the red convertible.

It turned out that Stacy was dealing with lots of "issues" — is how Dwayne put it. When divorce forced her to relinquish her title as the car wash queen, it sent her completely over the edge.

After a little hemming and hawing, Dwayne admitted his ex was addicted to pills (thus the slurred speech), was a bulimic (hence the DQ pig-outs and deceptively skinny body) and suffered from anger-management issues (oh, really?)

"But she's promised to get professional help as soon as she got back to town, and besides, she's safely passed out on the Hooker, so let's enjoy the rest of the weekend, okay? Old Dwayne'll take care of everything."

Will's buzz was wearing off, giving him a serious headache, and Dwayne's glib response to Lily's ordeal with Stacey wasn't helping. Lily couldn't help but notice how Will kept rubbing his temples and giving Dwayne the evil eye, so she said, "Dwayne, I don't think you understand what I've been going through. This is not some little prank. I'm not staying here. And if I don't have proof that Stacey's getting some real help, I'm calling the police. I'm sorry, Dwayne."

Dwayne sighed, and all the bravado seemed to whoosh out of him on that breath. He looked old and whipped.

Lily reached over and patted his arm. "I'm really sorry, Dwayne," she said. "I'll just get my things."

As Lily crossed the main room, the band was playing Thriller and sounded louder than ever. She left Will standing in the doorway mesmerized by Craig and Leon. They were out on the balcony teaching Bonnie a dance routine that seemed to be a Michael Jackson version of the Electric Slide. It was definitely time to go.

She went into the bedroom, and the door slammed shut behind her. A blonde with big hair whose pupils seemed way too large for the well-lit room shoved Lily up against the white, faux bamboo dresser.

Before she could react, the woman who had to be the ex Mrs. Dwayne Bond, had whipped a pronged tool out of her bag. As Stacey raised it to Lily's throat, Lily caught a glimpse of an insignia—a rebel flag inscribed with Darling—on the strangely familiar object. It came to her in a flash. The metal tool with its deadly prongs was actually a hair lifter. Lily hadn't seen one since the sixties when her older cousins had used them.

"I'm gonna keel you," snarled Stacey, her glazed eyes full of menace and hate.

There was only one chance to come out of this ridiculous situation alive—at least only one that Lily could think of.

"Omigod. Were you a darlin'?" she cried.

Stacey nodded smugly. "The 1978 squad. I had to drop out after that. Baton accident."

"I always wanted to be a Dixie Darling," said Lily. "But I didn't go to Southern Miss."

"Where'd you go?" asked Stacey.

She didn't dare say Alabama. Lily seemed to remember they were national champions that year. If so, they had probably beaten the stew out of Southern Miss when Stacey was twirling, so she said, "Junior College."

Stacey gave a derisive snort.

Lily put on a humbled face and took a chance.

"That's a great lifter."

"I know." She sniffed. "It was a gift from my mama when I got on the squad."

Thinking of her own sweet mama, Lily really did feel empathy for her deranged captor. "Look, Stacey, do you really want to besmirch the good name of the darlings and your mama by using that lifter to commit murder?"

She could tell by Stacey's face that she was making headway, so she forged ahead with, "Do you want to go to prison?" Then another stroke of genius. "You can't have lifters or makeup in prison, you know." She glanced at Stacey's coloring. "And you have to wear orange every day."

Stacey seemed to be mulling this over for a few seconds. Then she said, "I know that. I'm not exactly a dumb kid anymore, you know."

Well, not a kid, anyway, thought Lily.

"What've I got to lose," she hissed. "You took Dwayne away from me."

"I did not take Dwayne. I don't want Dwayne. I will never speak to him again. I promise."

"Oh, you think you're too good for Dwayne with your tall self and that hair of yours?" She moved the lifter enough to flip Lily's hair then stuck it back into her neck. Lily was sure it would break her skin at any moment. "What about Howard? You took Howard."

"What?" Lily was totally in the dark on this one.

"I was datin' Howard. He would've proposed, I just know it. But then you came along and married him. You took my boyfriend, and then you took my husband."

"I—I'm sorry. I had no idea about Howard." Lily could not digest this piece of info. "You and Howard?" she asked, incredulously. It was the wrong thing to say.

"You think I'm not good enough for Howard? You witch, you." Her eyes squeezed shut as big tears rolled down her cheeks. "I've lost everything," she wailed. Then suddenly getting control of herself, she growled, "Well, you're gonna lose everything, too, missy."

The prongs poked further into Lily's neck. Stacey's eyes narrowed as she tightened her grip on the lifter and prepared to shove it through Lily's quivering skin.

But then Stacey's head snapped back, the lifter clattered onto the polyurethane finish of the dresser, and Bonnie and Will and Dwayne and Craig and Leon rushed into the room. Bonnie was holding her fly rod. The fly was lodged in Stacey's hair.

Stacey collapsed in a heap, threatening to throw herself off of the balcony and "ruin Dwayne's damn party." The suicide threat got Dwayne's attention (and emptied the condo of guests.) He put a call into his doctor who had Stacey admitted to a "clinic" that very evening.

Dwayne put her in the hummer and headed back to town, insisting before he left that everyone make themselves at home in his absence. There was no argument from anyone. It had been an exhausting day, and none of them were fit to drive. Boudreaux disappeared into Dwayne's room. Bonnie took the guest room meant for Lily, figuring it would give Lily nightmares.

Lily hopped in the shower. Will had assured her he wasn't leaving her side until they knew for sure Stacey was under lock and key, so Lily washed and dried her hair, struggling to keep her eyes open. She yawned as she brushed her teeth and thought she may have actually nodded off for a few minutes while flossing.

When she went into the condo's living room to tell Will he could use the shower—and get his attention with her new periwinkle blue sexy-without-trying-to-look-sexy nightie—she found him passed out, barefooted (she guessed his shoes were still on the beach somewhere), mouth open, snoring away on Dwayne's white leather sectional.

Disappointed, but taking solace in the immortal words of Scarlett O'Hara, Lily smiled at her modern-day version of Rhett Butler sprawled on the couch and said softly, "After all, tomorrow is another day."

23.

Failure to Gee-haw

Tuesday morning found Herbert Adams' Azalea City Lawn Service unloading mowers and blowers at McVay House as he was now servicing Lily's backyard as well as the front. Lily had instructed Herbert to send the bills to Howard's office. Based on the lack of complaints from Herbert, Howard had been paying them.

Could it be that Howard feels guilty about Heather's engagement-flaunting behavior on my front porch or his own childish temper tantrum upon finding me in the shrubbery with the gardener—in what was obviously a silly accident, by the way? Guilt and remorse are not in Howard McVay's vocabulary, so it has to be my very sincere threat of lawyers that has Howard backing down.

Whatever the reason, it allowed Azalea City Lawn Service to do what they did best—edge, mow, blow and go. This enabled Lily to keep up with the weeding, deadheading and endless other chores that came with proprietorship of the McVay garden.

The bedding plants—trays and trays of annuals—had been procured at cost from Pearson nurseries. (Will had decided to keep the old name and hopefully the reputation that went with it). This "instant color" had been carefully placed by Lily and Will to maximize its effect and was flourishing among Mrs. McVays established perennials.

With the exception of the pond, the garden was more beautiful than Lily had ever hoped for. It was breathtaking— an overused word if ever there was one, yet when she looked around, it truly took her breath away.

"Whatcha gonna do wit dat statue layin' by the pond?" asked Herbert. "Ever find somebody to set 'er upright?"

"Not yet."

Knowing how busy Will was, Lily had tried to hire Herbert to set Marie Antoinette back on her long-vacant pedestal, but Herbert wasn't interested.

"No. We don't do dat kinda stuff," he said. "She sure is purdy though." A dreamy look floated across his weathered face. "She puts my mind to Samantha who got turned to stone in *Summer of the Sheikh*."

"Okay, Herbert, who is Samantha and who is the sheikh?"

In answer, Herbert pulled a ratty paperback out of his back pocket. Sure enough, a dashing, sheikh-looking fellow was on the cover gazing wistfully at a stone statue who Lily figured had to be the ill-fated Samantha.

Herbert gazed at the book cover for a few seconds before sliding it into the rear pocket of his overalls.

"Your buddy, Helen, gave it to me. We trade books all the time." He looked back at Marie Antoinette. "I believe this yard's gotten to be the purdiest one I work on, but dat statue's gonna make it even mo' special when you get 'er up on 'er little stand there."

Lily didn't know which amazed her more—that even Herbert could see that the pond and statue were meant to be the garden's centerpiece, or that Helen had managed to turn Herbert into a romantic.

As soon as he left, Lily headed for the back gate. Maisy had asked her over for lunch saying she wanted to hear all about the trip to Les Jardins. And Lily wanted to hear all about why Maisy didn't just tell her about the statue's location.

Despite the lovely weather, luncheon was to be served in the Downey dining room in the front of the house, Maisy informed Lily, ushering her across the patio and through the French doors.

Maisy's home was typical of its period with a wide central hall and double parlors, one of which was now the Downeys' master bedroom and bath. The upstairs with its four bedrooms stayed closed off until "the kiddies" came for a visit.

"I haven't been up there in ages," said Maisy, flipping her

platinum bob and shrugging her bony shoulders. "Lord only knows what condition it's in."

What a nut, thought Lily fondly as she followed Maisy (who was attired in a hot pink velour warm-up suit with matching running shoes and earrings) down the hall. The old lady seemed like a tiny doll hobbling down the long room with its twelve-foot ceilings.

She noticed what Maisy referred to as an "old folks" smell, but it was really the mixed aromas of a thousand home-cooked meals, beloved family pets and furniture handed down for generations—a nostalgic smell that reminded Lily of long-ago visits to her grandparents' house. It was nothing like the acrid odor that permeated McVay house from time to time.

As they wandered down the hall, Lily peered into one room after another. Each seemed to have been decorated in a totally different style. There was the kitchen that looked as if it had been plucked out of a Provencal farm house and set down into the Downeys' Victorian townhouse.

The bedroom was full of heavy antiques and toile fabrics with cornices and swags and Austrian shades on the floor-to-ceiling windows. There was a small library done up in chrome and leather with a zebra skin rug on the floor. A large abstract painting hung over its mantle.

"I never could settle on one style, you know?" she said, reading Lily's thoughts.

Lily laughed. "I like it, Maisy. It's so … you."

"It's not boring, anyway," she said, leading the way into the dining room, which held an enormous round pine table and chairs beneath a handsome brass chandelier. There was a china cabinet filled with sparkling crystal and hand-painted china and a fabulous mahogany Sheraton sideboard.

Family portraits and candelabra adorned pale green walls. An antique Persian Heriz rug in shades of soft blue, brick and green covered the gleaming pine floor. These hues were reflected in a bouquet of greenish hydrangeas and peachy roses in the center of the table. It was by far the prettiest room in the house.

Dubbie joined them for a crisp salad topped with pears, pecans and crumbled goat cheese. This accompanied bowls of chilled tomato soup and saltine crackers—Dubbie's favorite.

Lily reintroduced herself twice to Dubbie before he gobbled up the last saltine, wiped his old chin and announced it was time for a nap.

When he'd shuffled off toward his bedroom, the conversation finally turned to Lily's recent visit to Les Jardins.

"Why didn't you just tell me where the statue was? I could have paid someone to haul it back down here," Lily said.

"Wasn't it more fun that way? Discovering it yourself? Like a treasure hunt?"

Lily had to admit it was.

"Besides," Maisy continued, "I felt like you needed to get to know Craig. And that worked out, didn't it? For Marilee?"

Again Lily had to admit it certainly had and that everything the old lady said was true. It had been fun. And it was important she'd done it herself.

"Besides, Craig got himself so attached to that statue." Maisy shook her head. "Weird, but still ... I knew if he met you he would feel better about selling her."

"There's something else, Maisy. I couldn't decide whether or not I should tell anyone, but I have a feeling you know it anyway."

The tiny old lady leaned forward, eyes sparkling in anticipation.

"Somethin' to do with old McVay?"

Lily told her about the photo of Jake and Howard, about the change that had taken place in Howard, and finally about the apparent love letter from Jake to Rosie.

"But there are still so many questions," said Lily. "Did Howard's father know about Mrs. McVay and the gardener? Was it possible Howard knew about his mother's fling? Could Jake have even been Howard's father?" Lily described the unmistakable look of paternal pride in Jake's eyes.

Maisy sipped her iced tea and leaned back in her chair, thoughtful, as if deciding where to begin.

"Well, to start with, the McVays never should've married in the first place. Failure to gee-haw. That's what I call it. You can feel it when you're around people like that. They just don't mesh." She looked at her lap and said, "Like you and Howard." She waved her twisted fingers in the air as if trying to deflect

Lily's objections. "But I won't get into all that again. I know how it irritates you. Okay, back to the questions. First of all, old man McVay was so preoccupied with himself, he wouldn't've noticed if his bride and Jake were performin' the horizontal rumba on the dining room table. No, I don't think he knew. Second, Howard junior's too much of a chip off the old block of ice to be anybody else's kid. And third. And this is the crux of the story right here."

"Howard knew about his mother and Jake," said Lily.

"You're gettin' ahead of yourself now. Let me start from the beginnin'. Old man McVay was bad to run around, and on top of that, he was never around the house much. Believe it or not your mother-in-law was a good lookin' woman at one time. And Jake the gardener was a good lookin' man. Bad combination with them workin' together in the garden all the time." She smiled at Lily, her old eyes all crinkled up and twinkling. "You know what I mean, I'm sure."

When Lily made no comment, she continued. "Like I mentioned before, I used to have a pretty clear view of things over there from my upstairs balcony—used to have my bedroom up there, you know. I could hear the two of them laughing sometimes, not like employer and employee.

"Then one evening I saw them silhouetted against the light. Jake was kissin' her. Really kissin' her. I couldn't believe it, but I swear I didn't breathe a word to anybody. Not even Dubbie. Would've upset him. Well, it wasn't too long after the kiss that I heard a big to-do going on over there. Howard junior was screamin' like I don't know what and things were crashin' and splashin'.

"Next thing you know, Howard comes through the back gate like a bat out of Hades, crying so hard he couldn't talk. But he got enough out that I knew he'd found out about Jake and his mama. Said he hated them both and could he move in with us. Next thing you know, your mother-in-law is dragging him back home, tellin' me he's hysterical and not to pay any attention to him.

"Early the next mornin', that statue was layin' in pieces by the curb for the trash man. I made Dubbie and my boys haul it over here to my shed. I never heard another word about any of it, except when some of the garden club ladies told me how the pond had been filled in and planted with shrubs.

"They couldn't understand it. Nobody could. The McVay garden was the prettiest one in town, maybe in the state. The pond with its statue was everybody's favorite thing about it, too." Maisy shook her head, sending her pink earrings swaying. "The next thing I knew, Howard was off at a boardin' school. That didn't help his outlook on life, I'll tell you."

"Poor Howard," was all Lily could say.

"Yes. Poor Howard," agreed Maisy. "You can see why he had a fit over findin' you and Will together."

"How did you know about that?"

"I may be old as the hills, but I still hear pretty good. Happened to be out in my roses when all that was going on." She chuckled. "Kama Sutra, huh?"

Lily ignored this. "Lord, I never thought about that," she said. "About Howard reliving the incident with his mother, I mean. That's what he meant about getting rid of the fountain once."

"That would be my guess. He shoved it over in a fit of fury at his mother. She covered up the pond because—who knows why? Trying to erase the memory, maybe. Like that could make it go away. But I don't think she ever dealt with it at all. I bet she and Howard never spoke about it again. That's just how those people are. 'A lady never notices an odor,' I heard her say once. I don't think things were ever the same between Jake and her after that either. I never heard 'em laughin' again. And now you're diggin' it all up, so to speak. Think about it, Lily. Romance between a Mrs. McVay and her gardener is bloomin' in that yard again. If that's not enough to get old McVay stirred up, I don't know what is."

"Oh, my Lord," said Lily as it all became crystal clear. "What have I done?"

"Good grief, Lily, it's not your fault. You know what they say. 'The truth shall set you free.' Well, I think the truth will set a lot of folks free. But you've got to see it through. If you don't, you'll be livin' with old McVay forever."

Maisy rose stiffly from her chair. "Excuse me a minute," she said with a tiny mischievous smile.

She returned with a plate of lemon squares. "Now I insist on hearin' about the stolen car," she said.

By the time Lily had finished the story, Maisy was laughing so hard, tears were streaming down her face. "Have they found the car?" she gasped.

"Oh, yes, and Marilee is so disappointed."

"Disappointed? Why?"

"Well, she had a new one all picked out. And when she got hers back, the glove compartment was full of strange condoms."

"What do you mean, strange condoms?"

"You know. Exotic colors and names like French tickler. Helen told her she could at least be happy that the thief was having safe sex in her car. Marilee was not amused."

"Oh, poor Marilee," laughed Maisy.

"That's not the worst. She found the remains of a Dixie dog loaded with chili and onions, wedged between the driver's seat and the console. She says she can never eat another hot dog, which is one of her favorite vices."

"She'll be smellin' Dixie dog for as long as she owns that car," laughed Maisy.

"She took it to the car wash king, who promised to give it his personal attention, which turned out to be a double dose of piña colada scented car freshener."

"Bad to worse," said Maisy, managing the last of her lemon square between chuckles.

They agreed (while still giggling) that they shouldn't be having so much fun at a friend's expense, but decided with Marilee's ability to land on her well-shod feet, some chili dog and piña colada loving person would probably come along and offer her more than the car was worth, and she would get the new one she had her eye on.

Lily had barely finished her tale when Elton John's Bennie and the Jets sounded from Maisy's general direction. It turned out to be the ring on the old lady's cell phone.

She pulled it from her pocket and said, "Hey, there. Almost done? Thanks, sweetie. See you soon." Maisy turned her attention to Lily. "What do you say we walk over to your house in a little while? I want to take a look at that statue."

"Sure, although she's kind of pitiful lying in a heap on the ground. I sure hope I can find someone to help me resurrect her."

"What about Will?" Maisy asked with a definite twinkle in her old eyes.

Lily told her about Will's phone messages and the misadventure at Emerald Towers.

"That's one mystery solved. I don't think I'll be hearing from Stacey or Dwayne again." Lily sighed. "I think everything's okay as far as Will is concerned. You know, I really like him, Maisy."

"I know you do, sweetie," she said. "And you don't have to be psychic to know he feels the same about you."

Lily sighed. "We can't ever seem to get on the same page at the same time. For all I know, he's changed his mind about things. I haven't talked to him since Sunday morning when I dropped him in the parking lot of the Sand Crab to get his truck."

"Conflicted," said Maisy.

"What?"

"He's been a bit conflicted is my guess. About a lot of things. But I have a feeling he'll have more time now." She winked at Lily.

"Why is that?"

"Well, he's not hangin' out with that little Jaime anymore, for one thing. She was cute in her own way, but too young. Of course, that wasn't the main problem anyway."

Lily's head was spinning with all of this new information. "Maisy, what are you talking about? What was the main problem with Will and Jaime?"

Maisy looked at her in exasperation. Finally she rolled her eyes and said, "Failure to gee-haw!"

24.

Return to the Pedestal

Lily heard it before she saw it. The splashing water. Not like before when it had gurgled obscenely out of its exposed pipe, but as she had imagined it the first time she saw a picture of the pond and statue intact.

Then there she was, "Marie Antoinette" upright with her head on straight. Water poured gently from her tilted bucket with a delightful sound. The sunlight dappled through the magnolia branches on her lovely, white skin and hair, and danced on the moving water.

Lily rushed over to get a better look, and that's when she saw Will, sitting there on her porch steps. Waiting. His arms were on his knees, long fingers folded together. He looked hot and tired, and very pleased with himself.

"Will, did you do this?"

"Yeah. What do you think?" he asked, unfolding his long frame and coming toward her.

"She's perfect. Just perfect."

She looked up into his kind eyes and knew how much it meant to him that he had pleased her. *And so are you*, Will. *You are perfect, too*, she thought.

Will reached into his back pocket and pulled out a handkerchief. It wasn't until he gently wiped Lily's cheeks that she realized she was crying. She was crying for the first time in over a year. And the year's accumulation of pent-up grief and sadness was flowing out of her on those tears. God, it felt good.

"Hey, what's all this? I thought you said she was perfect,"

he said, dabbing at Lily's face. It was about as effectual as the little boy's finger in the dike because once the floodgate of Lily's emotions opened, everything poured out.

When she was able to speak, she said, "We did it, Will. The garden is finished and it's so … so right, just as we imagined it."

"You did it, Lily. You had the vision, the plan." He grinned at her. "I'm just the yardman."

She knew he was teasing, fishing for a compliment, but she wanted him to know how much she appreciated him.

"Will, there aren't enough words to tell you how much more you are to me than a yardman. All of your help, the moral support," she hesitated just a moment before going on. "Just being with you has done for me what we have done for this garden."

Will looked embarrassed and started to speak, but Lily stopped him.

"After all you've done, the last thing I want to do is to make you uncomfortable. And don't worry. I'm not expecting anything from you other than friendship." She looked directly into his eyes. "I just needed to tell you how I feel."

Lily was surprised to see that he now looked not only embarrassed but puzzled as well. Finally, he smiled at her. And as Maisy would say, the way he looked at her put the blue in her sky.

"Lily, you really don't get it. It's you who saved me."

"How on earth did I do that?" Lily was sincerely baffled.

"I don't know exactly. Just by being you, I guess. You've shown me what a … well, what a coward I've been. You taught me things—that failure doesn't give anyone a license to wallow in self-pity or worse, self-criticism, and that's what I've been doing ever since I left New York. You're a clear thinker, Lily, a problem solver. You've helped me figure out what to do with my house, encouraged me in my nursery business and you never pried, never demanded anything. You're amazing. And the best part is you don't even know it."

He kissed her gently on her mouth. "I think it's time we had that talk." He smiled at her. "And a real date."

He stood back a step, cleared his throat and said rather

formally, "Lily, would you have dinner with me tonight?" He didn't wait for her reply. The smile on her face was answer enough. "And get dressed up," he added. "We're going somewhere special."

He kissed her again, as quickly as he had before, then again, his lips lingering on hers. When he pulled away, she felt his breath on her face and knew he wanted to keep kissing her.

"I'll pick you up at seven, okay?"

"I can't wait," she said.

25.

The Real Date

Lily wore an outfit of yellow linen. The flared skirt showed off her legs, and the matching blouse with its cap sleeves and ruffles flattered her figure. A pair of great looking but totally unsensible shoes that Marilee had talked her into buying completed the outfit. ("Just take a few Advils before you go out. You won't even know your feet hurt till the next day," she'd advised.)

"You look beautiful," said Will. "Really beautiful."

Lily decided her future sore feet were a small price to pay for the look on Will's face.

"You're looking very handsome yourself," she said.

In the months that she'd known Will, this was the first time she had seen him in a coat and tie. It was well worth the wait.

Will managed to get reservations at the newest of the new restaurants downtown. The food was fabulous, but Lily wouldn't have noticed if it had been one of Marilee's beloved Dixie dogs, she was having such a good time. She and Will chatted and laughed their way through bisque loaded with chunks of tender lobster, warm mushroom salad, pecan-encrusted trout and a good bottle of chardonnay.

During the evening several people who knew Lily or Will stopped by the table to say hello. It seemed to Lily that the ones in her age group spent more time looking from Lily to her much younger, extremely handsome date as if trying to discern the nature of their relationship.

Most of the town's serious gardeners (which were most of the town's inhabitants, it seemed) knew Will or had heard of his horticultural talents, and knew he was helping Lily with the famous McVay garden. They were also plugged into the always-humming town grapevine and were well-acquainted with the sad story of Lily's marriage including the scandalous Howard-Heather chapter.

Lily figured they were quickly drawing their conclusions as they made polite conversation with the age-disparate pair. *It's only human nature*, Lily thought. After all, wouldn't she be doing the same thing if the tables were turned? *At one time I would've*, she decided, *but not now. I've learned a lot in the last year.*

Will's friends, a married couple who had been in his law school class and recently moved to town, seemed far less nosy. It appeared that they simply wanted to say hello. No eyebrows were raised, no inquisitive smiles appeared when Will introduced Lily.

There's a lot to be said for this generation of yours, Will, Lily thought as she chatted with the couple. The wife expressed an interest in gardening and getting to know her neighbors better, so Lily impulsively extended an invitation to the soiree. Having heard about the McVay garden and curious to see Will's work, they eagerly accepted.

Lily and Will finished the splendid meal with a delicate lemon mousse. When they were finally through, and Will had paid the check, he grinned at Lily. "Your place or mine?" he said.

Lily didn't hesitate. "Yours," she said.

The last thing she needed was the specter of her dead mother-in-law chaperoning her romantic evening with Will.

26.

Will Bares All

Lily followed Will back into the kitchen where he blended up an after-dinner concoction that tasted vaguely like a Brandy Alexander. They sat on the sofa and sipped their drinks. Lily couldn't remember when she'd felt such contentment. Of, course, it was short-lived.

"Alright, Lily, it's true confession time," said Will, trying to keep the conversation light, though his voice sounded strained.

He looked at Lily as if waiting for a reply, but she wasn't about to either encourage or discourage him. Instead, she sat as impassively as she could and waited for him to continue.

He took a deep breath and plunged ahead. "I think I told you I got involved with some seriously bad people in New York." Another deep breath. "Well, one of them was this woman. To my naïve eyes, she was the epitome of the big city sophisticate. I was into the whole scene, trying to shed my country boy persona and all that."

He took a long sip of his drink and shook his head. "It started out as lunch meetings, discussing legal stuff. Lunch progressed to drinks after work which progressed to … to an affair. The problem was she happened to be married to one of our firm's biggest clients. She claimed he was abusive, and I saw myself as her legal knight in shining armor or something."

"Wow," Lily said quietly.

"It gets worse. Her tales of spousal abuse were partially true, but believe me, that woman could give as good as she could get. Anyway, when I came to my senses and tried to break it off, she threatened to go to the partners with proof of our affair if I didn't provide her with some privileged financial information of her husband's. By this time he had figured out she was cheating on him, although he didn't know with whom, and had started divorce proceedings."

"Good grief," said Lily.

"When I found out he'd hired a private detective referred to him by my own firm, I went to a partner—he was my mentor and we'd become good friends. I told him everything. That was the hardest part. Letting him down. He had helped me so much, and I had just thrown it all in his face. And after I'd screwed everything up, he saved my license. He even tried to get me another job, but by then I'd had it. I was nothing but a little fish in a big pond—and one trying to swim with the sharks at that."

He ran his fingers through his hair and shook his head. "Not to belabor the metaphor, but I was in way over my head. What I needed was a whole new start. A whole new life, really. I'd inherited my uncle's property. A small-town nursery business was about as far from being a big city lawyer as you could get. Like they say, it was a no-brainer."

"Wow," she said again. "That's some story."

She really didn't know what to say. She'd heard the rumors via the Helen grapevine, but hearing the truth in Will's own words was different. It was a shock. She suddenly felt as if she didn't know him at all. How could he have been like that? Gotten involved with someone like that?

He seemed to guess her thoughts, and said, "People change, Lily. I was in New York for almost five years, and didn't even see what I was becoming. Then when everything caved in on me, it took about five minutes for me to see myself clearly. I'm not that guy anymore, Lily. That's why I had to start over, why I came back here." He leaned forward with his arms on his knees, fingers lacing and unlacing. "New York seems like a lifetime ago, like it all happened to someone else. But I've been here almost a year now." He looked at her. "A lot can happen in a year."

Lily thought back over the year after her divorce and how far she'd come. Will was right. How many people, including

Lily herself, would have believed she could climb out of the depressing mess she'd found herself in? But she had climbed out. She had changed, so why should she doubt Will? Will, of all people, who had been so good to her.

She put her hand lightly on his. "Thanks for telling me, Will. I know it wasn't easy."

He shook his head. "No, it wasn't. I have a lot of respect for you, Lily. I want you to feel the same way about me. You're the last person I want to think badly of me, but I had to tell you."

"The only Will I know is the man who has helped me get my life back," Lily said. "And I have nothing but respect for him." She smiled at Will. "I don't know anything about that guy in New York."

He grinned at her. "So I'm not fired?"

"You are definitely not fired," she said and kissed him lightly. She loosened his tie and removed it while he shrugged out of his coat. He took her hand, and she followed him into the bedroom where he whispered into her hair and kissed her neck, her face, her mouth.

He unbuttoned her blouse as she slipped out of her skirt exposing the peach lace of her new bra and panties. "Wow," he whispered, grinning at her. "I almost hate to take them off," he said, unsnapping the tiny clasp between her breasts. The bra fell to the floor as Will kissed her breasts lightly, then looked at her. "You're beautiful, Lily." And then he said that simple, little phrase that fills us with such gratitude and joy, three words that are capable of changing one's life in an instant.

"I love you, Lily," he said.

"And I love you, Will," she answered.

Lily and Will fell into his bed and into a night that Lily realized she had been waiting for all of her life.

She went home the next morning, but just long enough to change out of her wrinkled linen outfit. She spent the day and the next night with Will.

In addition to making love, they swam in the river, worked in the nursery, made plans for the soiree, listened to music, discussed the soon-to-be up-and-running zinnia business, and cooked for each other. They talked of their childhoods, planned a sailing trip, and as they sat on the pier watching the sun set,

Lily told Will all about the other loves of her life, her twin daughters, Elizabeth and Virginia.

The subject of Lily's children turned the discussion to the inevitable. Where was their relationship going? Where could it go? Lily asked him. All of the negative thoughts that had been dancing around Lily's brain came pouring out.

Will needed someone even younger than himself if he was planning on having a family some day. Wasn't this a waste of valuable time on his part? Lily didn't really have anything to lose. She'd had her children and experienced everything from toddlers to teenagers to college graduations. Was it fair for her to monopolize Will's time when he should be looking for Ms. Right? And he would find her. Maybe not this year or the next, but it was inevitable. There was over fifteen years between them. Too many years. By the time he was her age, she would be … well, fifteen years older.

This is what she said to Will as they sat on the dock, her doing all the talking while he fished. When she had finished her litany of fears and reservations concerning their relationship, she leaned against the sun-warmed boards of the bench and waited. He reeled in his baited hook, carefully laid the rod on the dock, and turned back to her.

"I fell for you the first time I saw you standing there in Maisy's backyard. By the time you kissed me in the hydrangeas, it was all over. I was in love. Really in love, Lily. For the first time in my life."

Lily felt her eyes filling up again. Ever since the day Will fixed Marie Antoinette, Lily had become incredibly proficient at crying. Tears came at the drop of a kind word or sweet thought. Will was getting used to it and smiled indulgently at her moist eyes.

"In spite of that or because of it, I've thought about everything you said and more."

"More?" She thought she'd covered everything.

"Remember that day you kissed me, and Howard accused us of practicing the Kama Sutra?"

She laughed. "I'll never forget it."

"That kiss … It was something. I remember thinking, God, I can't believe my luck! She feels the same way I do. But when

Howard showed up, it felt like a flashback to New York. Irate husbands and all that."

"Ex-husband."

"Exactly. Which is what I later reminded myself of. But at the time, all I could think of was that this was the guy who raised your daughters, who I've never met by the way, and who are closer to my age than you are. When Howard was standing over me in his mother's yard, yelling at you with Heather giving me the once-over, it seemed like an impossible situation. And Lily, I'm not criticizing—it's your business, but you're still so tied in with the McVays. Howard, your house, the thing with your mother-in-law. Like you said, it's a lot to think about."

He looked down at his bare feet for a few seconds before continuing. "That's why I didn't return your call that day, why I left the message saying I couldn't work with you any more. But I missed you, Lily. I missed you more than I've ever missed anyone. I don't know what the answer is." He was quiet for a few seconds as if deliberating his next words. "You know, it's strange. I never thought one way or another about having children until I met you. You're exactly the kind of person I would like to have kids with.

"The other strange thing is that I feel younger and more, well … more alive when I'm around you than I've ever felt. Other than your age I have more in common with you than any woman I've ever known. I love you, Lily. You're the one. I'm not going to walk away from you because of our ages."

At hearing this, Lily's eyes brimmed over. She dabbed at them with her sleeve.

Will smiled at her. "What do you say we just try to be a regular couple? Just do the stuff couples do. Like we have these last few days."

Lily sniffed. This idea had possibilities. "You mean just ignore the age difference?"

"Why not? It will come up with Elizabeth and Virginia, of course, but it's really nobody else's business. Let's take it a day at a time, see how it goes, okay?"

"Okay. You have convinced me." She grinned at him. "I really don't have a choice, anyway."

"Why is that?"

"Because I'm in love with you, too." She went over to him and kissed him. "So it was the kiss in the hydrangeas that did it?" she asked.

He put his arms around her. "Really it's a toss up between the kiss in the hydrangeas and your amazing Aretha Franklin impersonation."

27.

Howard's Turn

"Howard, it's Lily. Can you come by this afternoon after work? I need to talk to you about some things. And Howard, don't take this the wrong way, but could you not bring Heather this time?"

Howard, who had been strangely but blessedly absent since the Kama Sutra incident (as Lily now called Howard's ridiculous outburst after catching Will and her in the bushes) was now being surprisingly agreeable. He would drop by around five if that was convenient, he said.

At exactly five o'clock, the doorbell rang, and Lily showed Howard into the parlor. She did not want him seeing the garden before she'd had a chance to talk to him. The resurrection of Marie Antoinette would no doubt send him into another tantrum. Lily didn't want Howard or the statue losing their heads again if she could avoid it.

"What's that?" asked Howard stiffly as he gestured toward the McVay photo album that Lily had placed prominently on the coffee table.

"That is what I want to talk to you about."

She took the picture of Howard and Jake Johnson and Marie Antoinette and placed it on top of the album. Howard picked it up slowly by its corner as if it were something very hot, though the room was becoming noticeably icy. Lily was aware of a slight, all-too-familiar odor of stale Chanel and fresh setting solution, subtle at first but growing stronger as she watched Howard's face and braced herself for his reaction.

He looked coldly up at the portrait of his mother. Mrs. McVay looked back even more coldly, it seemed to Lily. Finally Howard slumped back into his chair, pinched the bridge of his nose between his thumb and forefinger—a rather theatrical gesture of feigned physical or mental fatigue that Lily had witnessed too many times.

"What do you know about this, Lily?"

The truth will set us all free, she reminded herself and proceeded to tell him everything she knew in the kindest way possible. She also shared everything she felt—about Howard's mother and her beloved garden—in the most honest and heartfelt way she could.

"Howard, your mother was human. Like all of us. We all have to live with our choices as best we can. I was never close to her, but I'm a mother, and I know she loved you." The air was getting seriously frosty and malodorous by now, but Howard refused to acknowledge it, so Lily resisted the urge to rub her arms or hold her nose.

She pressed on. "Howard, I have this idea that a mother—the good ones anyway, can't get any rest as long as there's any kind of unforgiveness between them and their children. It's time to let your mother rest.

For God's sake, let her rest before I freeze to death right here in this parlor, she thought, as Howard sat staring at his mother's likeness. She followed his gaze to the stiff, over-permed woman with the tight lips and impenetrable, dark-eyed stare who had once loved and laughed in her beautiful garden. When she turned back to Howard she was amazed to see tears in his eyes.

"You're right. Of course, you're right Lily." He shook his head. "God, what I put that woman through. Then I did the same thing. I swear I think ..."

"What?"

But he shook his head.

"For once, Howard, won't you please tell me what you really feel."

"Sometimes I think my affairs—I know you knew about them—were a way of making it up to her. Like, see Mother, I don't condemn you. How could I? I'm doing it myself. Insane, right? But Mother and I could never have spoken about such a thing. Not the McVay way of doing things." He wiped at his eyes, and Lily almost felt sorry for him, but she was tired of it all, ready to move on from the McVay weirdness.

"She was a good mother in so many ways, Lily. A dreadful snob, as you know, but loving and fun when I was growing up. Especially when Jake was around."

He looked at the picture again, fondly, this time. "I hardly ever saw my father, and Jake pretty much took his place. Jake and I dug that pond, laid the bricks around it and set the statue in the middle there. That's the day this picture was taken—when the pond was finished. We were all so happy. Then I saw them one day by the fountain, the fountain mother loved so. That I had helped build for her. She and Jake were kissing. They betrayed me, but worse than that, they had tricked me into betraying my father. That's how I saw it. I guess you know what happened to the statue."

"Maisy told me. I'm sorry, Howard."

And she was. Sorry that they hadn't had this talk years ago, even sadder that Howard and his mother, who had truly loved each other, hadn't been able to communicate. It wasn't the McVay way of doing things.

"I know Mother was hard on you, Lily. I never understood it, but I think it was jealousy. She was desperate for love and forgiveness from her only child, and I withheld it. God, what a mess. I'd give anything to be able to tell her how sorry I am."

I wonder how many times those words have been spoken, thought Lily.

They both looked at the portrait, and Lily could have sworn her mother-in-law's face had softened a bit. Something in the eyes.

"I think she knows, Howard. I really do. Take it from a mother. There's a bond between mothers and their children that never goes away." She stood up and handed him the photograph album. "Now I've got a surprise for you."

She took him into the garden where Marie Antoinette was serenely pouring water from her bucket. "It's for your mother, Howard. And you."

They walked from one end of the property to the other, Howard alternately reminiscing about his boyhood in the town's loveliest garden and admiring everything Lily had done. Lily told him about Will, how he'd been instrumental in the garden's transformation, and ultimately, in her own transformation. She could see that it upset him, but he smiled weakly and said he was happy for her. What choice did he have, really? But she appreciated it and told him so.

When she saw him out, he said, "I'm so sorry about … everything."

"I know, Howard. But it's past now, time for us all to move on."

He thanked her and kissed her cheek. "Well, then. I'll see you at the soiree," he said and headed down the front steps to his car.

On the way back down the hall, Lily stopped at the doorway to the parlor/den. The foul frostiness had dissipated on its own without Lily having to open the windows or doors. She stared at Mrs. McVay whose eyes now seemed downright soft.

Maybe I am crazy, but I swear you look different, she thought.

28.

Finishing Touches

Lily and Marilee completed their orders from the restaurant's "nutritious/delicious" menu while complimenting Helen on her ever-decreasing waistline.

"Oh, but I've been gorging on gossip," said Helen with a sly smile. "The village grapevine is just a'cracklin' with the story of Stacey Bond. Tell me, Lily. Did she really threaten you?"

"With a hair lifter, no less," said Lily.

"You mean one of those things with the prongs?" asked Marilee.

"Exactly." And Lily proceeded to give them a blow by blow account of the wild night at Emerald Towers.

"My God," squealed Marilee. "Death by lifter." She shuttered visibly at the thought. "And at the hands of a Dixie Darling!"

"So it was Stacey trashing your yard during her drive-bys to see if Dwayne's car was at your house," said Helen.

"Yes. I knew I'd heard that voice somewhere. It was at Stacey's house the night I had that first date with Dwayne." Lily frowned. "There are still some things I don't understand, though. Like how did Stacey get my cell phone number? And how did she know that Mrs. McVay loved Sinatra?"

"Oh, oh," said Helen.

"What?" said Lily and Marilee at once.

"I feel awful about this," moaned Helen.

"What? What do you feel awful about?" cried Lily.

"Stacey's sister, Tracey …"

"Stacey and Tracey?" asked Marilee. Helen shot her a look. "Never mind, tell us what you feel awful about."

"Until two days ago, Tracey worked in the park maintenance

office, which is temporarily across the hall. I caught her using my computer, which everyone knows is strictly forbidden. She was probably reading my mail. Your emails to me were on there, Lily. And I had noticed her standing outside my door when I was on the phone. She could have easily heard me talking to you about Mrs. McVay and her Sinatra records.

"Anyway, I warned her about using my computer. The next day I caught her going through my purse—probably getting your cell number off of my phone. I reported her to her boss and she was fired. It never occurred to me that she could be involved with the harassment, Lily. I remember thinking it was odd, though. She didn't seem to be the petty theft type. Stacey must have talked Tracey into snooping for her."

"And got her own sister fired," said Marilee. "That woman is some piece of work."

"That has to be it," said Lily.

"Lily, I am so sorry. First I fix you up on that date and then I leave my computer on with your personal messages to me on it. This is all my fault. I could have gotten you killed."

"And by a lifter," said Marilee, shaking her head in disbelief.

"Don't blame yourself, Helen," said Lily. "I should never have gone to the Gulf with Dwayne. Of course, then Stacey might never have gotten the help she needs, and I wouldn't have met Will on the beach … Anyway, all's well that ends well, as they say."

The conversation soon turned to less exciting but pleasanter developments. Lily outlined her plan to sell the zinnias now thriving in Will's nursery. This would begin happening as soon as the soiree was over. Next she related the heart-to-heart chat and resulting truce with Howard, and reluctantly broached the idea that there had been a change in Mrs. McVay's portrait and possibly in her hostile spirit as well.

Marilee's reaction was predictably skeptical, Helen's predictably practical.

"You're no longer intimidated by Mrs. McVay, so the portrait looks different," said Marilee.

"Get Maisy over there," said Helen. "She's the expert on that kind of thing."

"Now that that's settled, tell us about Will—I mean the romantic parts," said Marilee.

"We want all but the most intimate details," added Helen, literally on the edge of her chair.

By the time they'd finished their low-cal desserts, Lily had provided her friends with the requested details—which had Marilee dabbing at her mascara and Helen sighing repeatedly.

"Romance literature comes to life. I love it," she said.

"I guess if this were a TV movie, I would break it off with Will so he could find Ms. Right. You know, someone his age with a biological clock that still ticks. Do you know that when Will is my age, I'll be in my mid-sixties?" She shook her head. "I know Will loves me, but I'm not kidding myself. Even if this relationship lasts out the year, the chances are he'll eventually want some young, firm person who can stay up past midnight."

"You're doing it again," said Helen. "Dwelling on the negative to keep yourself from being blindsided—like Howard did to you. Besides, Will had a very young, very firm person who wanted to stay out all night. Jaime. He wants *you*."

"That's right," said Marilee. "Besides, you'll be a great-looking mid-sixty-year-old."

"And as for children, not everyone wants them. Sandy and I have had a wonderful life enjoying our nieces and nephews."

"She's right," said Marilee. "And so is Will. When you find someone you love and love being with, you have to work around the obstacles. Live in the moment for a change, Lily. You've earned it."

Lily laughed. "That's what Elizabeth and Virginia said."

"You told the twins about Will? I mean that you're dating him and everything?"

"They're fine with it now that we've talked it out. They're mainly relieved I'm not sad anymore. The age difference is a concern, of course, but they know I realize what I'm getting into. Anyway, I'm determined to heed all of this good advice—like letting go of the past, enjoying the present and getting excited about my future instead of dreading it."

"I really like this new Lily," said Marilee.

"Me, too," said Helen. "Congratulations honey."

"Thanks," said Lily. "Now, enough about me. Marilee, tell

me about you and Mr. Craig and the new business."

Marilee, squirming with excitement, poured out the details. She and Craig were almost done with minor renovations, which had transformed Marilee's former art gallery into Boboli. The famous Boboli Garden in Florence was a favorite of both of theirs. It was a smaller version of Craig's and Leon's place in Atlanta. The previously neglected courtyard was perfect for a small selection of plants, which she was hoping Will could supply. A large cooler for storing cut flowers had been installed. She made Lily promise to save her lots of zinnias.

"You know," said Lily, "a year ago I never could have dreamed we would be where we are today. Marilee with the perfect business partner. Helen in such good health. And me with such a promising future. We have a lot to be thankful for."

Helen raised her glass of herbal iced tea. "To new beginnings and happy endings," she said.

29.

The Soiree

The morning of the soiree was warm, sunny and blessedly low in humidity, promising a perfect evening for an outdoor summer party. Lily swept a few remaining leaves from the back steps and thanked the Lord for the good weather. She stopped long enough to admire a pile of white blossoms spilling from the old clay frog that she'd given Mrs. McVay so many years ago. The old toad beamed his perennial, algae-covered smile at her, taking her thoughts back to the day Will had found him in the garden shed.

"Every garden needs a good-luck charm. He'll be yours," he had said. *Seems to be working*, she thought.

As the day wore on, McVay House became a bee hive of activity. Workers swarmed over the garden, setting up tables and chairs, lining the walkways with hurricane lamps and scrambling up ladders to hang cream-colored paper lanterns that looked like a dozen full moons rising in the trees.

Candles were nestled into casual arrangements of hydrangeas and Maisy's tea roses, which were centered on tablecloths of pale pink and ecru stripes. More candles floated among the water hyacinths in the fish pond by the wall.

A musician took over the far corner of the porch, tending to his guitar and amplifiers. Bartenders hummed as they clanked whiskey bottles and glasses and iced down wine and beer. In the rear of the yard, near the garden gate, Maisy, already in her bizarre gypsy get-up, instructed two young men in the erection of her little fortune-telling tent. Elizabeth and Virginia arranged flowers in the house while trying to avoid collisions with the catering staff who stuffed the refrigerator with tray after tray of seafood hors d'oeuvres and tiny desserts.

With an hour to spare, Lily had showered, pulled her hair into a knot at the back of her head and dressed in creamy linen and pearls. She had just finished a tour of the house, adjusting flowers, fluffing pillows and double-checking the supply of hand towels and guest soap in the bathrooms when Helen and Marilee arrived.

"You two look fabulous," said Lily.

"Mayfair," said Helen, twirling around to show off silky pants and a matching sweater the color of robins' eggs. "Marilee had to send it back and get a smaller size."

"Mine's Mayfair, too," said Marilee who was decked out in a pale yellow and white chiffon sundress. "I got it from Mary Largely, believe it or not. She's reinvented herself again—back with her husband and to hear her tell it, changed her wicked ways. I don't believe it for a minute, of course. But she and the hubby are starting over in a new townhouse and want Craig and me to 'transform the patio.' It was the least I could do to buy something from her. I made Helen go with me. Doesn't she look great?"

"You really do, Helen. That color is wonderful on you. But speaking of hubbies, where are your dates?"

"On their way," said Marilee. "We came early in case you needed some last-minute help."

"I think everything's done, but now you'll have a chance to visit with the twins before everyone else gets here. They're out on the porch, and they're dying to see you both."

Elizabeth and Virginia and Marilee and Helen were all talking at once, kissing cheeks and giving hugs when Lily heard someone at the front door and excused herself to answer it. It was Will. In a white dinner jacket. Holding twin bouquets of zinnias. When he saw her, his tanned face broke into that grin that took her breath away. *How can I be so lucky that this man loves me*, she thought.

"These are your first zinnias," he said, kissing her cheek. "For Elizabeth and Virginia."

"They're beautiful. So healthy-looking."

He stuck out a thumb. "Nothin' but green," he said.

Lily laughed. "You are just too good to be true," she said, grabbing his elbow. "Come on. The girls are out on the porch. They can't wait to meet you."

"Elizabeth. Virginia. I'd like you to meet Will."

The women abruptly ended their four-way conversation.

It might have been the sight of Will looking like every girl's dream date with his black hair curling just above the collar of the white dinner jacket, grinning sheepishly above fists full of flowers.

Maybe it was the sight of the dream date with their mother who had never looked lovelier, healthier, or more at ease with herself. It could have been that Will with his dark good looks and the ever-elegant Lily looked like a gorgeous, if slightly mismatched couple. Whatever the reason, the girls stared with identical shocked expressions on their faces.

Finally Virginia said, "This is Will?" Regaining her composure a bit, she added, "Uh, it's nice to meet you."

"Yes," said Elizabeth. "So nice to meet you."

"Thanks," said Will. He held out the flowers, which were tied up with raffia. "These are for you. From Lily's garden." He smiled proudly at Lily.

"How thoughtful," said Virginia. "Oh, and what's this?" A small vellum card was attached to the raffia ribbon. She turned the card over and read it aloud. "Lily's Garden."

"My business cards," said Lily. "What do you think of the name? Too simple?"

"I think it's perfect. Mom, we're so proud of you. And Will, we can never thank you enough. Mom says she couldn't have done it without you."

Will started to object, but Elizabeth interrupted him. "She has also told us about all the work you've done on the old Pearson place. When do Virginia and I get the grand tour?"

"Anytime," said Will. "Lily can bring y'all out tomorrow afternoon if you like."

"Great," said Elizabeth. "I can't wait. And thanks for the flowers, Will. They're beautiful." She turned to her sister. "Virginia, why don't you and I find a prominent spot in the house for those zinnias. Mom's got to advertise her new business."

"Good idea," said Will. "And while you're doing that, I'll get us a drink. We have a lot to celebrate."

"The gods are smiling on you, Lily," said Helen when Will had gone to fetch drinks. "It looks like everybody's going to get along just fine."

"I don't think they were prepared for how good looking their mama's new beau is," giggled Marilee. "Lord, he cleans up nice."

"He does, doesn't he?" agreed Lily. "Most of the time he's in work clothes."

"He fills a pair of jeans out pretty nicely, too," said Marilee.

Helen responded with a big eye roll and whispered, "Get a grip on yourself, Marilee. Here he comes."

Will set the tray of drinks on the table just as the twins returned.

"We put the flowers in pewter jugs in the hall," said Virginia. "They look beautiful, and everyone will see them when they come in."

"Along with the tags, which we turned to the front," said Elizabeth. "You can't miss 'em."

"The garden club ladies will frown on such flagrant self-promotion," said Lily.

"They'll get over it," said Helen.

"Okay, Mom," Elizabeth said. "It's time for the big announcement."

"What now?" said Helen. "You people are exhausting."

"I have definitely decided to put McVay House on the market. I've given Howard first right of refusal, and believe it or not, if he can work out the financing, he wants the place—including his mother's portrait and all that Victorian furniture up in the attic. It's really as it should be. It's how his mother would have wanted it."

"Except for Heather as mistress of her garden," said Marilee.

"Well, there's not much I can do about that," said Lily, "Although I don't think it will be much of a problem. Heather is much happier in the mall than on her hands and knees in the dirt."

"I knew that girl had to have some redeeming quality," said Marilee. "By the way, where are those scary wind chimes she brought over here?"

"I just had to draw the line on those things," said Lily. "All that clanging would have ruined the party. It wouldn't have been fair to Howard's mother."

"Good for you," said Marilee. "But speaking of Mrs. McVay, let's have a look at the haunted portrait."

They all marched into the parlor/den and stared silently at Mrs. McVay. They tilted their heads, moved to different positions in the room, and thoughtfully sipped their drinks.

Finally Will walked back to Lily who was standing in the doorway waiting for everyone's cries of astonishment. He put his arm around her shoulders. "Sorry, Lil, but I can't see that she's mellowed a whole lot since the last time I saw her."

"I don't see it either," said Marilee. "You're just looking at the world through rose-colored glasses these days. Everything looks better to you."

"Marilee's right," said Helen. "You're not intimidated by her anymore, so she doesn't look the same to you. Like Marilee said the other day. It's you who has changed."

Lily looked from Elizabeth to Virginia.

"Sorry, Mom," said Virginia. "It's the same old Grandmother McVay."

"Yep," said Elizabeth. "Looks the same to me."

That settles it. I am crazy. But I'm also very happy, so I refuse to worry about it.

"Where in the hell is everybody?" Maisy's voice and jangling gypsy bracelets sounded from down the hall. She came and stood by Lily in the doorway. Her wig was askew, showing the thin, platinum blonde hair beneath. "What are y'all lookin' at?"

As everyone moved out of the tiny octogenarian's way, she was able to see the portrait over the fireplace.

"Well, I'll be," she said. "Looks completely different now, doesn't she, Lily? I don't think you have to worry about old McVay doggin' you anymore."

Everyone looked at Maisy in stunned silence.

"Hello everyone," said Howard who had appeared with Heather from the front end of the hall. "Let ourselves in, Lily. Hope you don't mind." He shook Will's hand stiffly. "Uh, Will, isn't it? Nice to see you again. You remember my fiancée,

Heather, don't you?" It was obvious that Heather remembered Will. When she grabbed his hand, she was close enough to drool on his lapels.

Howard cleared his throat loudly, thereby breaking through Heather's trance. "Uh, look, Heather, we've caught everyone admiring mother's portrait." He cocked his head and appraised the painting. "It looks different somehow. Softer. More like I remember her. Must be the lighting."

"She looks the same to me," said Heather. "She doesn't come with the house, does she?"

They all exchanged assorted eye rolls and smirks, but no one said anything except Maisy. And she just snorted.

Lily and Will took one last stroll through the garden before it was filled with people. "It's really something with all the lanterns and candlelight," said Will.

"I know. It looks like a fairyland." Lily stopped and gazed around her. "It's beautiful, isn't it? Can you believe we did this?"

"Nothing but hard work and a woman with a mission," said Will.

When they got to the area Marilee had dubbed the "magic garden," Will put his arms around Lily and kissed her.

"Lily, are you sure you want to give all this to Howard? You've worked so hard on it. And you won't be bothered by old lady McVay's presence or whatever it is any more. I mean, you're not doing this because of what I said, are you?"

"You mean about me being so tied in with the McVays?"

"Yeah. It has to be your decision."

"Will, I can't wait to turn this place over to Howard. Not because of you, but because what you said is true. The McVays and this house and even this beautiful garden are suffocating me. I don't want to be Lily McVay anymore. I just want to be Lily. Whoever she is. And I can't wait to start finding out."

"Any plans as to where you'll be going? I know a nice little spot down by the river."

"You're asking me to move in with you?"

"I love you, Lily. Yeah. I'm asking you to move in with me."

Lily wondered if she would ever get used to hearing him say that he loved her. She hoped not. "And I love you, Will. I love every minute that I'm with you, but I'm an old-fashioned girl."

"No co-habitation without a ring, huh?"

"Right. But that's not meant to be any kind of an ultimatum. I have to be on my own for a while longer. I want to find my own place, something newer and smaller." She looked around her. "Something with a manageable garden. In the mean time I think we should take some advice given to me by a very cute gardener I know. Let's take it a day at a time and just try being a couple, enjoy doing the things that couples do. See how that works out."

"Anything you want, Lily."

I have everything I want, thought Lily, as guitar music suddenly filled the air. Will looked at his watch.

"Okay Lily," he said. "I think it's show time."

It was a very diverse crowd. Yet as the romantic chords of the guitar floated on the evening air, they mingled comfortably, the conversation always falling back to their common interest — gardening.

The garden club ladies who pretty much ran the town were all there. They inspected everything and congratulated Lily and Will on the "perfect recreation of Rosemary's beloved garden." Surprisingly, they then rushed to get their fortunes read by Maisy.

Most of Howard's colleagues came. Their wives were noticeably icy to Heather and especially warm to Lily and Will, due less to the amazing transformation of the McVay garden than to Heather's home-wrecking reputation.

Heather managed to ignore this, and after a fruitless search for her wind chimes, spent most the evening inside checking out her prospective new digs.

Dubbie Downey managed to attend and stay awake for an entire hour. When he left it was somewhat of a relief since he kept referring to Will as Howard.

Marilee's and Helen's husbands came together. They had known and admired Will's uncle and both loved to fish and sail, so they were on the way to becoming real friends before the party was half over.

Craig and Leon charmed the bloomers off the garden club ladies who were beside themselves over the opening of Craig and Marilee's new shop, Boboli. Leon took Craig's picture with Marie Antoinette who was as lovely in dappled moonlight as she was in dappled sunlight. The photograph was to be suitably framed and would occupy a prominent spot in Boboli, Leon assured Lily.

Though the group was definitely a mixed one, their assessment of the garden was unanimous. *Perfection*. Lily heard the word over and over during the evening.

Howard received the prestigious garden club award for his mother and made a very nice speech about Mrs. McVay's contributions to the town during her lifetime. He surprised Lily by graciously crediting her and Will for the restoration of his mother's beloved garden.

Of course, whenever Lily and Will were together, she noticed people watching them and making discreet comments to whoever was standing nearby. The majority of guests were Lily's age or older, but these would be Will's bread and butter as his business grew, so he didn't mind when person after curious person pressed Lily for an introduction to her "young man" as Mrs. McVay's old friends persisted in calling him.

Lily was happy to discover that Will was not quite the loner she had thought him to be. He had invited several friends, in addition to the lawyer and his wife, Lauren, whom they had met while having dinner on their first "real date."

Lily found that she had a natural rapport with Lauren, who restated her interest in gardening and suggested that she and Lily have lunch in the near future. Lily looked over to see Will watching them.

He returned her smile with a wink, obviously happy that she and Lauren were getting to know one another. There were some of his single guy friends who looked vaguely uncomfortable—until they were introduced to Virginia and Elizabeth, who kept them entertained for the rest of the evening.

Before Lily knew it, the guests began leaving. Elizabeth and Virginia were off to a bar downtown with the friends of Will's they had met.

Howard was paying the guitar player, and the bartenders and caterers were racing around like a film in reverse, clearing up and clearing out in record time.

The candles were extinguished and the lanterns turned off. As Leon and Craig said their final good-byes, Maisy kissed Lily and Will, literally folded up her tent and disappeared through the back gate.

30.

Good Night

Lily McVay sat on the wooden steps of Howard's mother's back porch and thought of her dead mother-in-law.

It seemed like another lifetime that she had sat on these steps staring out at the weeds. Then she reminded herself, it *was* another lifetime.

Mrs. McVay had found happiness and then tragedy in this lovely place where the two women had managed to communicate in some primeval way through their mutual love of gardening. Ultimately it was due to this particular garden, due to their common affection and dedication to this beautiful spot that had brought them together and, as Maisy had predicted, set them both free.

Will sat down beside her on the steps as he had the first day she'd met him. He handed her a glass of wine.

"Alone at last," he said, smiling at her.

Lily noticed he'd taken his shoes and socks off. She looked down at his bare foot next to her silk sandal.

"Hope you don't mind," he said. "I couldn't take those dress shoes any longer."

"No, I don't mind," said Lily, slipping her own shoes off.

Will leaned over and kissed her neck just below her ear, and she felt herself melt against him. Lily couldn't remember when she'd felt this happy — or this tired.

Marie Antoinette poured water from her bottomless bucket, catching a moment in time. Her paleness, like the white flowers scattered here and there caught the moonlight and stood out from the shadows. The gaudy blooms of the magnolia and the gardenia heavy with blossoms managed to hold the light and shine through the darkness. Lily could even see the petunias cascading from the pot by the shed and the tiny clusters of jasmine blooming on the arbor.

Will gave her a little nudge. "What are you thinking about?"

"Oh, just something I learned in junior high."

"What's that?"

Lily smiled up at Will and said, "Success is definitely the best revenge."

• • •

Margaret P. Cunningham

Margaret P. Cunningham's short stories have won several national contests and appeared in magazines and anthologies including five *Chicken Soup for the Soul* books. She grew up on her father's nursery in Mobile, Alabama, where she lives with her husband, Tom. She enjoys writing, reading, gardening and "beaching it" with her friends and family.

Caught together in a South Carolina plantation house by a hurricane, college student Amanda Whitmore and forty-year-old Jordan Eversole fight the winds and their growing love for one another, caught by a storm that seems destined to push them together ... no matter the cost.

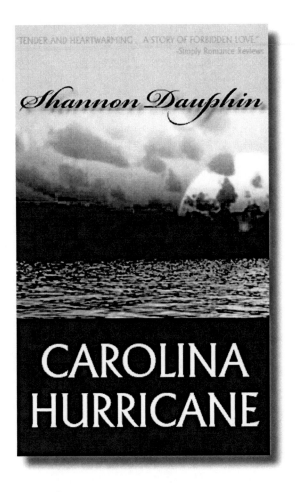

"TENDER AND HEARTWARMING ... A STORY OF FORBIDDEN LOVE"
-Simply Romance Reviews

Shannon Dauphin

CAROLINA HURRICANE

www.BlackLyonPublishing.com

Printed in the United States
201999BV00001B/28-87/P

9 781934 912027